MW01089405

OTHERS AVAILABLE BY DK HOLMBERG

The Cloud Warrior Saga

Chased by Fire
Bound by Fire
Changed by Fire
Fortress of Fire
Forged in Fire
Serpent of Fire
Servant of Fire

The Dark Ability

The Dark Ability
The Heartstone Blade
The Tower of Venass

The Painter Mage

Shifted Agony
Arcane Mark
Painter for Hire
Stolen Compass

The Lost Garden

Keeper of the Forest
The Desolate Bond
Keeper of Light

FORGED IN FIRE

THE CLOUD WARRIOR SAGA
BOOK 5

ASH Publishing
dkholmberg.com

Forged in Fire

Published by ASH Publishing

ISBN-13: 978-1518830228
ISBN-10: 1518830226

ASH Publishing
dkholmberg.com

Forged in Fire

THE CLOUD WARRIOR SAGA

BOOK 5

CHAPTER 1

Draasin Sight

TANNEN MINDEN SAT ATOP his bonded draasin, Asboel, as they swooped over the southern part of the kingdoms. Warm air buffeted around him, swirling through the long, heated spikes protruding from the draasin's black-scaled back, slapped by massive wings stretched far out from him. Mist sprayed as the air hit the heat of the draasin's body, and Tan wiped a hand across his face to clear his vision.

In the distance stretched Incendin.

The land looked barren from this high up, staring down from above with nothing but thousands of feet between him and the ground, but he knew Incendin to be anything but barren. The desert contained dangerous and poisonous plants, all raging with the same hatred that Tan had felt every time he'd been in Incendin. Each time, he'd nearly died.

"Does he see anything?" Amia asked, gripping his waist.

Tan had to tip his head to hear over the whistling of the wind. He could have asked Honl, the ashi wind elemental, to limit their exposure, but there was something freeing about soaring above the air, riding atop the draasin, that was even better than traveling on a warrior's shaping. This way, he hunted *with* Asboel. It was important for the draasin, and for their bond.

He reached through the connection he shared with Asboel. The more he learned of the connection, the easier it became to simply see through Asboel's eyes. Communication had never been challenging between them, but adding the ability to use what his bond pair saw gave him a great advantage, especially given how crisp Asboel's eyesight was.

Using the draasin sight, he saw the ground as patches of reds and oranges, each shades of heat much like what Tan had seen when he'd been nearly transformed into one of the lisincend. Plants took on a different shade of red, more like a bright blur against the more muted background. The more he used the draasin sight, the better he understood what he was seeing. Other than the plants and the cracked and broken ground beneath them, nothing moved.

"Nothing."

Amia sighed behind him and he felt her relax. "Par-shon hasn't attacked yet."

"I don't think so," Tan agreed.

The draasin banked and turned back toward the kingdoms, avoiding flying over Incendin itself. Asboel still had harsh memories of Incendin and regardless of what might be necessary in the coming months, Tan didn't think Asboel would ever get over what the lisincend had done to him.

Had it been the same with the draasin when shapers hunted them? Tan had found little referencing that time in the archives, but what he *had* found implied that the draasin were to be hunted when discovered. The most recent text he'd found described various ways to use shapings to trap the draasin, usually with some combination of earth and water to counter the fire and wind that helped keep the fire elemental aloft. In that one book, there were detailed descriptions of what the shapers had done to the draasin, ways in which they had captured and killed them. He had yet to fully decipher others, but the illustrations on the page worried him.

How much of the current problems were the fault of those earliest shapers? The draasin now didn't want to hunt people. From what Tan had seen, they would rather stay as far from people as possible; only, sometimes it wasn't possible. Worse, Tan had drawn the draasin into his battles, but without them, Tan wouldn't have survived nearly as long as he had. Asboel was more than one of the great fire elementals. He was a friend.

"What is it?" Amia asked. "You seem troubled."

He gripped one of the long spikes coming from Asboel's back and twisted to look at her. Her golden hair caught some of the wind, playing around her face. The wide band of gold around her neck, the replacement for the silver one she had abandoned that marked her people, caught the light from the sun overhead. Piercing blue eyes stared into his. He had thought her beautiful from the moment he first saw her rolling toward his village, wearied and trying to hide the fear her people felt as they ran from the Incendin hounds, but the time they spent together had created a bond between them deeper than the one shaped between Tan and Asboel.

"Worried would be more like it," he said. "We've been back for nearly a month. In that time, we've heard nothing from Par-shon, though we know their bonded shapers are aware of ours. And they know the draasin exist. I know they will return."

And each day they didn't, the remaining kingdoms' shapers began to think that Par-shon *wouldn't* return. They were thankful for what Tan had done in fending off the attack, but there was a growing sentiment that another attack wasn't going to come now that they had seen how strong the kingdoms' shapers were. Tan knew better.

"Why do you think they haven't?" she asked.

Tan could only think of one reason their shapers had not returned. He doubted that fear kept them away. There might be some caution from the Utu Tonah, the heavily bonded leader of Par-shon, but that likely wasn't the entire reason.

"Bonds, I think. They need more."

They had to replace those they'd lost. That meant finding and forcing more bonds. *Stealing* more bonds. So far, he had managed to keep the draasin safe beneath the city, hiding them from the Par-shon shapers. He still didn't know how Asboel got in and out of the city—his bond hadn't revealed that and Asboel wasn't keen to share it—but at least the hatchlings were safe and given the time they needed to grow larger and stronger. The bonds were the reason for the concern he felt.

Amia squeezed him around the waist. "The udilm will keep her safe."

Amia knew how Tan worried about Elle, now returned to Doma, hopefully bonded to the udilm, but what if Par-shon stole that bond from her? What would happen to her?

"Will they? They couldn't keep Vel safe, and he had bonded to one of them. What happens if Elle is taken, the connection stripped? When I last saw her, she still hadn't learned to shape. Without that, she's at the mercy of the elementals."

Asboel twisted so that one eye could see him.

You know the udilm can be fickle, Tan said to Asboel.

They are ancient, but they have always been strong.

Tan hoped that was enough. He'd barely had time to know Elle. Now that he knew she was family, he wished for more time to get to know her. He had so little family remaining. His mother, but that relationship had been strained ever since he'd left Nor to go with Roine. It had continued to decline as Tan continued his relationship with Amia against his mother's advice. She thought that Amia had shaped him, worried that she forced him, like the archivists had forced the shapers to do things they would not otherwise do. Even now, as things improved, she still treated Amia with more caution than she deserved.

"Zephra has gone to Doma. She will find Elle," Amia said.

At least his mother wasn't alone this time. She had taken to traveling with Vel. The water shaper gave Tan a little more confidence that Zephra would find her. Tan might not have managed to heal Vel—he wasn't certain whether that was yet possible—but he had regained his shaping ability quickly. Tan only hoped he learned some restraint, especially when dealing with Par-shon.

Maelen, Asboel said, using the name he'd long ago given Tan. It meant something along the lines of ferocious warrior, though Tan still wasn't quite sure whether it was compliment or not. *Look below.*

Tan focused on looking through Asboel's eyes. What would the draasin have seen? He'd been with Asboel when he'd hunted before, felt the thrill through the bond as the draasin swept down from the sky and grabbed a mouthful of wild animal, but he wasn't sure he wanted to subject Amia to one of Asboel's hunts, though he doubted she would be offended. Amia had known Asboel as long as Tan had. She was part of the reason the draasin had been freed. Without her forging the shaping that kept them from hunting man, Roine might not have been willing to free them.

What he saw surprised him.

Far below, a long caravan of wagons rumbled across the flatlands. Tan thought they were over Ter, though Asboel flew quickly, so it was difficult to tell. It could even be the outer edges of Galen, though he didn't see the mountains that marked that part of the kingdoms.

The shape of the wagons was familiar. With Asboel's enhanced sight, he could even make out the patchwork paint along the tops and sides of the wagons, the tiny bells that announced the passing of the caravan, and the wagon driver sitting atop and steering the caravan forward. They were Aeta, much like Amia had once been.

"You don't have to tell me," Amia said, drawing his attention away from what he saw through Asboel's eyes. "I sensed them."

"How long have you known?" Tan asked.

She didn't answer at first. After everything she had been through because of her people, he didn't blame her. He only wanted to be there for her, to be able to help her as they tried to find a way to provide safety for the Aeta. They were normally wandering people, but with the likelihood of war—a war the kingdoms had thought would come from Incendin rather than elsewhere—missives had been sent by Roine, inviting the Aeta to the kingdoms. The First Mother still wanted Amia to lead them, but after what had happened, that was a lost cause.

"They are gathering," she finally said. Her voice carried over the wind, aided by a quiet request Tan made to the wind elemental.

"Not the Gathering," he said.

"No. That is only called by the First Mother. It has been held in Doma for so long that I don't think anyone knows where else to meet."

Tan strained through the connection with Asboel to see if he could tell where the caravan headed, but saw nothing that would explain it to him. "Do you," he started, craning his neck to watch her expression. All he sensed from her was the hesitation she felt. "Do you want to go down there?"

Amia shook her head. He hadn't really expected her to want to see the Aeta. She had a hard enough time dealing with the First Mother; seeing other Aeta might still be more than she could handle.

"Then we should return. Roine is expecting us back. He thinks we simply travel by shaping." Roine might understand the need to ride with Asboel, but there was a level of distrust in the old warrior nonetheless. Asboel had helped Tan often enough that Roine should feel nothing but gratitude for the draasin's continued assistance, but it would take time to build that relationship. Even within the kingdoms, fire was feared.

Tan leaned forward and patted Asboel's flank. The draasin's tail twitched and he twisted so that he could look back at Tan. *Hunt well, Asboel.*

Asboel snorted and flames burst from his nostrils. *Always, Maelen.*

Tan formed a shaping of wind and fire, adding earth for strength, and used water to stabilize it. To this, he added a shaping of spirit, the connection that he'd finally managed to master, and pulled the entire shaping toward himself.

They traveled on a bolt of lightning that lifted him from Asboel's back. It happened in a flash, quicker than thought. Now that Tan had traveled this way enough times, he had become comfortable with it, no longer fearing that it wouldn't work for him. There was a sense of calm around them as they traveled, nothing like the roar of wind while flying with Asboel and Honl, or the steady spray of mist that accompanied sitting atop the draasin. This was quiet, a sense of power, a feeling that he was a part of the world and meant to control the elemental powers that he now used.

They came out of the lightning bolt in a smooth streak of shaped light, landing in the center of what had once been the university. Walls had grown taller over the last few weeks, stone steadily replaced by the shapers, though not in the way that it had once been. This was different: wider and stouter, but with a certain elegance to the way the wings of the university would flare around the open clearing around the shaper's circle.

As they landed, chaos quickly overwhelmed him.

Fire erupted nearby.

Tan wrapped himself around Amia, letting the flames roll over him. Connected as he was to the element and the elemental, fire burned inside him, much like the draasin. Nothing short of the lisincend could harm him, and even that he wasn't sure would actually harm him anymore. Elemental power might be able to, but Tan could work with both the draasin and saa. In time, he would seek out inferin and saldam. The more elementals he could connect to, the better the likelihood that he could protect those he cared about.

Could this be Par-shon?

Tan strained, searching for an elemental attack, but there was none. Not Par-shon, then.

What if this was the lisincend? Tan hadn't seen sign of them while with Asboel, but Incendin had been silent since the Par-shon attack as well. From what he'd seen, silence from Incendin was rare. And dangerous.

Fire parted around him. The heat and the way the flames spurted told him that it was shaped but not twisted.

He pushed out with a shaping of his own, at the same time calling on saa to draw away the fire and sending it toward the ground, where it would collide harmlessly against the might of golud in the earth.

"Tan?" Amia asked.

Her voice was muffled under his arm and he released her, ready to grab her again if needed. He didn't see the fire shaper that had attacked. "Careful," he said. "I don't know what this—"

He was cut off as the ground heaved, lifting him off his feet.

Tan called quickly to Honl and jumped to the air on a wind shaping, pulling Amia with him. He searched about him, looking for whoever might be attacking, searching for some *reason* that they had been attacked.

Had the archivists returned? They might be able to sneak into Ethea and gain control of any shapers present, but most of the shapers in the city had been taught how to protect themselves. Still, it was possible. Tan hadn't had time to search for the surviving archivists, but he knew they were out there, probably still working on behalf of Althem.

The courtyard was otherwise empty. Whoever attacked must be within the rebuilt section. "Can you sense anyone?" he asked.

Amia was more skilled with spirit sensing than he was. He could shape spirit but hadn't learned any fine control, nothing that would allow him to know who or why someone would attack. Most of the time when he shaped spirit, he added it to other shapings. It seemed to augment each, and he suspected it drew the elementals.

Near the street leading toward the university, he saw the frail woman he'd rescued from Par-shon. They'd learned her name, Cora, but little else about her. She stared at him, her eyes wild. Healers continued to work with her, but she hadn't recovered nearly as quickly as Vel.

"Help Cora," Tan said to Amia.

She raced across the yard while Tan focused on where the shapers might attack next. So far, there had been earth and fire. Maybe there were only two shapers.

Unless he was wrong. What if Par-shon had managed to send one of their bonded shapers to Ethea? Attacking the city would be difficult, especially now that they knew Par-shon existed. Theondar expected the first attack—if it ever came—to be along the border, but could they have found a way to slip past the kingdoms' shapers stationed on the border?

A wind shaping struck him, trying to pull him from the air.

Honl, he said.

The wind elemental held him in place, shielding him from the shaping.

Tan frowned, noting the direction of the wind and how it seemed to come away from the university. Now that he recognized that, he realized that both the fire shaping and the earth shaping had come from the same direction.

From where Cora stood.

"Amia!" he shouted.

Another shaping built. Tan sensed each shaping come as pressure in his ears. This built sharply, quickly, and targeted Amia.

He couldn't wait. With a shaping of spirit, he struck Cora.

It was as light a touch as he could manage, meant to do nothing more than knock her unconscious. She fell to the ground in a heap.

The wind shaping she'd been working eased. The earth stopped rumbling. The flames sizzling across the stone died quickly.

Tan shot toward Amia and lifted her, spinning to check if she was injured.

"I'm fine, Tan." She looked down at Cora. "What was that?"

He stared at the older woman. She had gray and thinning hair, now neatly trimmed. She wore simple clothes, a chestnut wool sweater over a light brown dress and looked nothing like a shaper, but of course, she had been in the separation chamber, her bond stolen from her by Parshon, and was one of the lucky—or unlucky—to have survived. Tan had not managed to get her to say anything to him since he'd rescued her.

"That," he began, "is a warrior shaper."

CHAPTER 2

A Warrior

TAN STARED AT CORA, unable to shake the surprise he felt at her attack. Not simply the fact that she'd attacked them, but that she had managed to do so using each of the elements. Other than Roine, Tan thought himself the only warrior shaper alive.

Tan's shaping left her lying on the street near the entrance to the university. No one else walked along the street, though that wasn't altogether uncommon. With all the work the shapers were doing to repair it, most steered clear, unwilling to get too close. Since the attack on the city and the way the shapers had been controlled by the archivists, a general unease had developed about shapers, even those of the kingdoms. The unease spread throughout the city, leaving something of a quiet anxiety hanging over everyone living in Ethea, though with each day, that anxiety eased.

"*She's* the shaper? Are you certain?" Amia asked.

There were no windows in the rebuilt walls for someone to have looked through while they shaped their attack and he sensed no one else. Then he scanned Cora, looking for signs of the runes that would mark her as one of the bonded shapers, but didn't see anything.

"There's no one else. It had to be her."

A warrior shaper. Had she been from the kingdoms once? Roine should have known her, though. Even Tan's mother should have known her, and she'd never made mention of a warrior named Cora.

"There should have been one of our shapers with her," he said.

Amia closed her eyes and shaped quickly, then pointed down the street.

They found Cora's escort not far away. Wallyn was a skilled water shaper who reminded Tan in some ways of the Par-shon bonded water shaper Garza. Wallyn had a similar build, all wide in the belly with loose jowls that shook as he laughed, which was often. He preferred loose-fitting clothes, wearing what looked like a lady's dress that flowed over him and was tied loosely around the waist with a length of thick rope. He was balding, left with only patches of hair on each side of his head.

Amia touched his neck. "He'll be fine. I don't even know how injured he is," she said.

As she spoke, Wallyn shook his head. "Not injured, girl, just ashamed. An old woman managed to surprise me. There was a time when no one managed to surprise Wallyn. I can sense when they shape, but you've got to expect that of them first. I've gone soft, not thinking her capable of it."

Tan stretched out a hand and helped Wallyn to his feet. The water shaper pursed his lips in concentration and grunted, barely helping and forcing Tan to draw on a shaping of earth to give him increased strength. "I didn't think she's said much since she's returned," Tan said once he had Wallyn back on his feet.

Wallyn shook his head, the thick folds of skin under his neck shaking as he did. "Nay, she had not. That's why I was foolish enough to think her safe. Now where is she? Did she run off?"

Tan pointed to Cora.

"Is she dead?" Wallyn asked. The bland way he asked made it clear he wouldn't have minded.

"No, knocked out with a shaping of spirit."

Wallyn pursed his lips as he eyed Amia. "Spirit? Haven't we seen enough shapings of spirit around here?"

"*I* was the one to shape spirit," Tan said, dragging Wallyn's attention away from Amia. "And we've seen entirely the wrong types of spirit shapings. There are beneficial uses to spirit."

"Hmm. It seems to me that the kingdoms have survived for hundreds of years without warriors who can shape spirit. It does make you wonder whether it is even necessary. Perhaps the Great Mother thought to draw it away from our shapers. She would know the dangers of spirit."

Tan decided against getting into an argument with Wallyn. There were too many like him who feared spirit, feared the way it could be used, even though Tan had begun to suspect that many shapers could use a form of it. In time, Roine could be taught to weave the elements together in such a way that he could shape spirit. In some ways, it was different than a true shaping of spirit, but it was through the shaping of spirit in that way that Tan had learned to reach true spirit.

Cora started to stir, so Tan crouched next to her. She flickered her eyes open, staring at him for a moment, and then began thrashing.

Tan looked up at Wallyn. "Can you help with this?"

The massive water shaper grunted and lowered his sizable heft to the ground, taking the time to splay his dress out around him so that it wouldn't get dirtied. His shaping built from deep within and washed out from him slowly, first in a trickle, then building to a steadier wave that spread over the woman. She continued shaking uncontrollably.

Tan had seen something like it before, only he hadn't expected to see it here, or from Cora. As far as he had known, she was already separated from her bonded elemental. That had been the reason she was confined in Par-shon.

Wallyn's shaping eased and he pushed himself up, lifting the edges of his dress as he did. He wiped his hands together. "There is nothing I can do. I have not seen anything like this before."

Tan shot him an annoyed look and touched Cora on the wrist. He might not have the same skill with healing as the water shaper, but there were things that he *could* do.

He focused first on his breathing and then stretched out toward the nymid that worked through the bedrock of the city. The great water elemental infused the stone, mingling with golud deep beneath the city where the dampness and moisture still clung, down where Tan had chosen to hide the draasin.

Nymid. Help me heal this woman.

The calling took strength, but Tan had grown much stronger since first reaching for the elemental all those months before. Without thinking about it, he mixed the request with a shaping of water and spirit, strengthening it.

There was a soft fluttering against his senses as the nymid came to the surface. *He Who is Tan. She is damaged. There is no healing.*

Why?

She was, the nymid seemed to search for a word that Tan would understand, *connected to that which is no more.*

Yes. She was bonded. Her elemental was severed from her.

The ground grew damp as the nymid surfaced, leaving a thin green sheen on the rock. It bubbled up and washed over Cora, leaving her skin with a faint hint of green as well. The convulsing eased but did not stop altogether.

Was this my fault? Tan asked. *Did the shaping of spirit cause this?*

Not cause, He Who is Tan. She remembers. Her body rejects. There is no healing from water.

Tan rocked back on his heels, trying to come up with some way to help Cora. Water might not be able to heal, but when he'd attempted to save his mother, he had wondered what role spirit might play. Tan focused on the connection to the nymid, used what he sensed from the elemental to help him understand Cora's injuries. There, faintly, was the severed connection. It was weak and pulsing, different than it had been with Zephra. With her, he had felt the jagged edge where the wind elemental should have been. With Cora, what remained was blunted. He could not reattach it, only seal it off to prevent it from harming her further.

Using spirit, he placed a shaping over her mind, wrapping the blunted end of the bond in spirit and pulling it back, sealing it once more within her mind. Tan couldn't tell what the bond had been to and couldn't repair what had been lost, but it didn't matter for what he intended to do.

At least the convulsing eased. She no longer twitched, or even kicked; instead, she simply lay on the ground, the thin green film atop her a reminder that the nymid had helped.

"What did you do?" Wallyn asked. "There was water, but too much for a warrior."

Tan glared at him, annoyance at how easily Wallyn had given up surging through him. "Do you speak to the nymid?"

Wallyn frowned. "Why, no. The nymid are nothing more than a lesser—"

Tan raised a hand to cut him off. "For someone who speaks to none of the elementals, you really think you should be making claims of one's relative strength compared to another?"

Wallyn huffed, glaring at Cora. "She will live now?"

"I don't know. I've done what I can. The nymid helped."

"Good. Then you may stay with her." With that, Wallyn turned and started back down the street, moving with more grace than a man his size ought to manage.

"You should really be gentler with them," Amia suggested. "They have suffered through so many changes already."

"We've all been through change," Tan said, touching Cora's head and smoothing the hair back from her face. "Why should Wallyn be any different?"

"He wasn't the one who tried to separate you from them," Amia said softly.

Tan tensed. Of course Amia would know what he was feeling. It wasn't only that Wallyn had reminded him of Garza by his size, but his mannerisms had evoked memories as well. Water shapers should be interested in healing, but Garza had thrown him in the testing room, had taken him to the place of separation without so much as an apology. When Wallyn hadn't shown interest—real interest—in helping Cora, it brought those memories back.

Tan lifted Cora. She was light and frail from years spent as a Par-shon prisoner, kept alive for reasons only the Great Mother could fathom, that had stripped her of any muscle. When Tan had first found her, he hadn't even been sure she still lived. Vel had been the only one able to speak, and without his help, they might not have escaped Par-shon.

The third shaper they'd rescued was in nearly the same shape as Cora. Since returning to Ethea, the healers had shaven his beard off because it had been far too matted to untangle and his hair shorn short, but his eyes retained that lost look. At least with Cora, they had learned her name. With the other man, they didn't even have that. He remained silent, able to do nothing more than eat and breathe.

"Where should we take her?" Tan asked.

Amia touched the woman's face, shaping her softly. "She'll need more help than we can give her, but we need time to get her that help." She looked up at him, her blue eyes catching the light of the fading sun. "There is something off with her spirit. It's complex, more than I can do anything to help. Maybe in time..."

Tan sighed. "They won't give her the time she needs if she attacks again." If she did, others would consider her too dangerous. He didn't know what would happen to her then. Probably not the same thing as what had happened with the lisincend, but he wouldn't put it past the other shapers to banish her from the kingdoms.

"She has been through so much. There aren't many who understand what it was like."

"My mother understands," Tan said. She'd lost her bond once and nearly had it stolen from her a second time. "We need to be better than them. Better than those who would steal a bond that should be freely given. We will need to free the elemental from the bonds forced on them."

Cora opened her eyes and stared blankly at him. Tan waited, ready for another attack should it come, but she didn't do anything else.

"We will have to do much more than simply free them from the bonds."

Tan turned to see Roine hovering on a shaping of wind. He held it easily, nearly as skilled with wind as Zephra, but then, he'd been a wind shaper before learning he was a Cloud Warrior.

How had Roine found them so quickly? "Wallyn sent you?" he asked.

Roine shrugged. "He summoned," he said, holding out the summoning coin. "In all the years I have known him, he has never shaped a request like that." Roine dropped to the ground and glanced over his shoulder. "He said she was hurt."

Tan suspected Wallyn had said more than that, but Roine had known Tan the longest of anyone in Ethea, other than Amia. Roine had been with him through almost everything. He helped grab Cora and they made their way through the yard and stopped outside the shaper's circle.

"We returned. She attacked."

Roine waited, as if expecting more. "What kind of attack?"

"Fire first, then earth and wind."

Roine turned to study Cora. "There were no warriors by her name," he said. "Not of the kingdoms."

That last was probably the most important, Tan realized. If Cora *wasn't* from the kingdoms, they needed to learn where Par-shon had found her. The kingdoms would need allies in the coming months, ideally shapers who understood what was at risk were Par-shon to advance beyond the sea, to stretch their reach into Ethea and beyond.

"She needs time and healing that we can't provide," Tan said.

"Wallyn is skilled, Tannen. You need to give him the chance to—"

"She needs a different type of shaping than what Wallyn can provide. This is damage to more than her body. This is spirit," Tan said. He looked over at Amia, who shook her head softly, already knowing what he suggested.

"We can't trust her," she said.

"It's not a question of trusting her. There is much she can teach."

Roine looked from Tan to Amia, nodding as he began to understand what Tan intended. "The First Mother has offered her aid before."

"And she *shaped* an entire people, forcing them to serve Incendin!"

Amia didn't say it, but for all they knew, Cora had been one of those Doma shapers that the First Mother had shaped, using the ability given to her by the Great Mother to serve the darkness in Incendin.

Tan slipped his arm around Amia and pulled her toward him. "You saw what we faced in Par-shon. We will need to learn all that we can if we are to survive." And even that might not be enough, not against the Utu Tonah. "You don't have to like her to learn from her."

"I don't know if I can do it, Tan. What you suggest, after what she's done—"

"Cora is not the only one who will need you," he said.

Using what he saw from Asboel, he sent the image of the Aeta caravan through the shaped connection they shared, reminding her of the scattered Aeta, now without a leader. Amia tensed but then sighed.

"That was only one caravan. How many families remain? How many search for someone to bring the People back together?"

"I'm not that person," Amia said. "Once I thought I could be, but she took that from me. She took that from the People."

Tan hugged her, not knowing what else to say. Amia had been broken more than any of them. Most of the time, she managed to stay strong, but she did it by burying the pain she felt deep within her. Only Tan still felt it, aware that it was there, but hidden. If she were to survive what was to come, she would need to work through that pain. The first step, he knew, was coming to grips with what the First Mother had done. There might never be forgiveness—Tan didn't think she deserved forgiveness—but there could be healing.

"I will help," he offered. "Together. We can learn together."

She didn't answer.

Tan didn't need her to in order to know what she thought. "Can you let me work with Cora, not the other shapers?" he asked Roine.

Roine tipped his head. "Tannen—"

"No. I saw the way Wallyn treated her. There was no real interest in healing her. Oh, he tried, but he gave up too easily. He doesn't understand what she went through. No one can really understand unless they shared that experience of having the bond torn from you."

Tan had only known that pain for a brief period of time, barely enough to gain a true appreciation, nothing like what Cora or Vel had gone through at the hands of the Par-shon shapers. But he knew how he had felt when he sensed Asboel being ripped from him. He knew how he would feel were Amia's bond taken from him. It was different, but no less a connection.

"You don't understand," Roine said with a smile. "What I was trying to say is that you don't have to ask. You're a warrior now, Tannen. You've proven it time and again to me, but now the others see it, too. So trust me when I say that you don't have to ask. You have every right to be involved."

Tan glanced down at Cora. He might be a warrior, and he might have a shaping ability that had been lost for centuries, the ability to reach spirit, to shape spirit, and bind that with the other elements, but he still felt so unprepared. With everything that had happened to him, he felt as ignorant as he had felt the first time he realized that Roine could shape and what that meant. But he was determined to learn. He *needed* to learn, to understand everything the Great Mother had given him.

"There's a caravan of Aeta coming toward the city," Tan said. "Can we welcome them?"

Roine looked over at Amia, but she kept her eyes down. Tan sensed the unease she felt at the impending questions. In time, he hoped that would subside. She deserved to have a connection to her people. And he hadn't shared with Roine, but they might need the Aeta. If there were spirit shapers among them, such ability might be needed in the times ahead. Not to shape others' minds, but spirit had been important in removing the forced bonds from the elementals.

"They will be welcomed," Roine answered. "You went searching again?"

"With the draasin," he said.

Roine flickered his eyes toward the sky, as if expecting to see it circling. "There is still too much fear around here regarding the draasin. You have been wise to keep them from the city." He paused and looked down. "They are safe?"

Tan hated that he had to keep what he was doing from Roine. Likely, he would understand. He might even agree with Tan's actions. "They are safe."

There was a nagging question in the back of his mind, the concern he felt around the draasin, especially knowing the Utu Tonah's desire to bond to one of them: How long could he keep them safe?

CHAPTER 3

A Mother's Healing

TAN STOOD NEXT TO CORA'S BED. Her long hair spilled over her shoulders and a thin woolen blanket covered her. She hadn't moved since they had brought her to this room, in a house much like the one he shared with Amia. And just like at his house, a small hearth held dancing flames that saa slithered through. As Tan watched, he could *almost* see the fire elemental.

There was a small window open to the street below, and a warm breeze flittered through, reminding him of his bonded wind elemental. Since bonding to Honl, one of the warm wind elementals, ara had mostly left him alone. But there was more responsiveness to ara now when he reached for it, something he suspected came from the fact that Tan had managed to heal Zephra and save Aric, her wind elemental, from a forced bond.

The First Mother stood near the end of the bed, one wrinkled hand on either side of Cora's head. She held her with more gentleness than Tan had expected after everything she had done. The First Mother's shaping pulled from deep within her, drawing out from her and stretching into Cora.

The shaping was subtle and steady, probing not only Cora's mind, but her heart and stomach. The last two were unexpected.

"Can you see what I'm doing?" she asked without looking up. Her voice was strong and sharp, so much like the woman she had once been.

"Yes," Tan said.

The First Mother glanced over at him before staring at Amia. "And you?"

Amia didn't answer at first, and when she did, she spoke softly. "I see what you're doing."

"Good. If you are to repeat this, you will need to know the shaping."

As they watched, Tan realized the shaping she placed over Cora repeated, coming in waves. Each time, it changed slightly, but each change made sense, as if the change added to what the First Mother had already done.

"You won't repeat this?" he asked.

"How am I to know whether you will allow me out again, Tannen?" she asked. Her shaping paused. "You come to me with a request for healing, but the People suffer, and will suffer more without a steady hand to guide them."

"Theondar has offered protection," Tan said.

She covered her mouth and coughed once. "How is the protection he offers so different than what I offered? Everything is not as simple as you would like. I made choices necessary to keep the People safe, the choices a First Mother must make."

When Tan didn't give in to the argument, the First Mother turned her attention back to Cora. "This is one of the more complex shapings the Mothers learn. There are others, but this one serves most of the time." She didn't look over at Amia, but the words were meant for her. "There is no change done by the shaper with this. It is meant to heal trauma, which this young woman certainly experienced."

Cora was young? With her gray hair, he had figured her older than his mother. "The shaping heals the trauma?"

"The shaping allows the mind to heal. They work together, body and mind, which is why the shaping cannot focus simply on the mind. You can see that it does not?"

"I can see," Tan said.

Amia remained silent.

The First Mother grunted. "Once the shaping is in place, then you can begin the more difficult work. Like this."

Tan had thought the shaping she used was difficult enough, but then she changed it, the steady pressure of spirit coming from the First Mother now pressing with more intensity and focused completely on Cora's mind. The shaping seemed to flicker, twisting as it probed through her, the movements more complicated than Tan thought he would be able to create.

"What are you doing with that?" Amia asked suddenly.

The shaping slowed, enough to make it clearer how the First Mother manipulated spirit. Tan could see what she did, though he would need much more practice before he could manage such complexity.

"This," the First Mother explained, pointing to where the spirit shaping slithered into Cora's mind, "must be done with care, but once it's there, you can press like this."

She did something that Tan couldn't really see, moving her fingers in such a way that the shaping shifted and twisted. It had a delicacy that reminded him of Zephra's ability to handle the wind. The control was so much more refined and exquisite than the blunt shapings of spirit that he used for strength and to bolster other shapings.

"Try, Daughter," the First Mother said.

Amia said nothing, but she assumed control of the shaping, quickly taking the spirit shaping and wrapping it delicately around Cora, using much of the same skill that the First Mother had shown. She was not as deft, but the control was there, and Tan could tell that in time, she would be able to use the shaping with much the same skill. That was the reason the First Mother had been so disappointed that Amia had abandoned the People.

The shaping went on like that for nearly an hour. The First Mother would demonstrate one and Amia would replicate it. Each time, the shaping became ever more complex, to the point where Tan could no longer follow the distinction between each.

While connected to spirit, he could sense Cora slowly coming around. Whatever the First Mother and Amia were doing seemed to be working. Tan was certain that it had nothing to do with him. He had taken to holding the steady spirit shaping the First Mother used when the healing began. Even that taxed him, straining his ability to concentrate.

Then the First Mother nodded. "That is enough for now." She glanced at Tan as she stepped away from the bed and pulled a chair away from the small oak table nestled into the corner by the window, dropping to it. Exhaustion painted onto her face, but there was something else there as well. Relief? "When I first met you, I did not think you would manage spirit. Then when you forced spirit together with sheer strength, I did not think you would ever manage spirit with much skill. You have grown, Tannen."

He wasn't certain what to make of the compliment. "I think I've always been able to shape spirit. That's why Amia I and are connected."

The First Mother smiled wearily. "You think spirit the only reason for your connection?"

"Not the only reason, but a part," Tan said.

The summoning coin vibrated softly in his pocket. He resisted the urge to check who it was. Probably Roine trying to make certain they were safe.

The First Mother frowned and leaned back in the chair. Her eyes looked as tired as the rest of her, but she watched how Amia remained near Cora, shaping occasionally, not exhausted after everything that they had done. A hint of pride shone in her eyes.

"Will she recover?" Tan asked. He had sensed a hint of what could happen with Cora, but it was not enough for him to know with certainty.

"Only the Great Mother knows the answer."

"How was it that she was fine before?" he asked. "When she came with me from Par-shon, she wasn't like this."

"She was never fine," Amia said softly.

Tan went over to her and placed his arm around her shoulders, pulling her against him. With his other hand, he pulled the summoning coin from his pocket and glanced at the rune. Wind. That meant his mother.

"When we left Par-shon, I could sense it. She might have walked and eaten, but that was all. She was something like a shell, nothing more. With healing, her body recovered enough that her mind began to rebel. That was when she attacked us." Amia met his eyes. "Your shaping took away that last protection on her mind. I can feel what she had done. It's almost like she placed a shaping of spirit to keep her from remembering."

"Are you saying Cora can shape spirit?" Tan asked.

Amia shook her head. "I don't know what I'm saying. Spirit is a part of it, but it's hard to tell. You did what you could to keep her alive.

I can see that. But it confuses what is left."

Tan shifted his attention to Cora. She breathed slowly but steadily. Her eyes remained closed and she had not moved in the entire time that they had been working. "I… I thought I was helping," he said.

"You *did* help. Without your shaping, I think she would have died."

"And without my shaping, she wouldn't have lost what protection remained over her."

"You did what you needed to," Amia said.

Tan sighed. There might have been a different way, but he had thought using spirit would have been the least likely to risk harm. Instead, his shaping had only caused her more.

"I will stay with her," Amia said. "It is slow, but there is hope for her."

Tan didn't push, but if Cora could shape spirit as well as the other elements, they would need to know how. She might have bound the other elements together and used those to forge the connection to spirit. Even that had value.

"I wish I knew what elemental she had bound," he said. "Maybe that would help you to understand how to heal her."

The First Mother came over to the bed, standing where Amia had been when the shaping began. "It may be too difficult to determine without her help. Whatever bond was there has been gone for a long time."

Tan took a deep breath and stepped away. The effort of shaping Cora had weakened him too, but strength came back more quickly these days than it had when he first learned how to shape. Now he was able to draw on the strength of the elementals, use them to restore his reserves. It didn't even seem to matter *what* he shaped.

Tan glanced at the rune coin again. Amia nodded at it. "Go. See what she wants from you."

"You don't want to come?" he asked.

"I would like to see if there's anything more I can do for her." She focused on the First Mother, her expression growing harder. "That is, if you are able."

The First Mother placed her hands flat on the bed and took a deep breath. "I think it will be helpful for her to have additional healing," she agreed.

Tan pulled Amia to him and gave her a tight hug. "Be safe."

"You'll know if I am not."

The connection would tell him. He was thankful for that fact.

As he left, he heard the First Mother's voice become sharper, and more like it once had been. "Now, Daughter, this next shaping will be even more complex."

Tan found Zephra waiting for him in the home he shared with Amia. She sat in one of the plush chairs angled in front of the hearth. A book spread across her lap as she stared down at it, scanning the page.

She looked up as he entered. "Where did you find this?" she asked, holding the book out in front of her.

It had a thin leather cover marked with a rune for fire, and was one of the oldest books he'd come across that had such rune markings. The other covers had been blank.

The book speculated about the various ways the draasin could be harnessed, though most of the beginning had to do with the actual hunting of draasin. In order to understand what Asboel had known before he had been frozen in the lake at the place of convergence, he had to learn what the ancient shapers had known of the draasin.

"The archives," he said.

Zephra glanced at the book and back to him. "I have searched the archives. There weren't texts like this."

Tan sat in the chair next to her. He took it from her hands and set it on the armrest. The book had once been meant only for shapers like him, but he wanted to understand the views of the ancient shapers before he let his mother or any others begin to go through it. The author's feelings about the draasin were too much like what he'd seen from the kingdoms shapers.

"These are where most can't reach," Tan said.

"They should be brought out for others to study. The teachings of the ancient shapers should be shared, not confined like that. Think of how much we've lost because we can't replicate the shapings they so easily managed."

Once, he'd felt the same way. He had wanted nothing more than to understand how those shapers of old had managed some of the things they had. The way their wielded their abilities seemed impossible. He had yearned for that level of mastery and skill.

It had taken no more than this one book to change his attitudes. He had grabbed it, thinking he might understand something new about the draasin. Instead, he had learned the various ways shapers trapped the draasin, the techniques to hold them, the creations to confine them. As he had suspected, part of the tunnels beneath the city had been carved out with the intent to trap them. He still didn't understand why. Asboel didn't think the draasin had ever bonded before, but could it have been forced?

"There are some teachings that should be forgotten," Tan said.

"Are you so certain that we can't learn from the past?"

He paused for a moment, gathering his thoughts. How to put it to her in a way that she would listen to him? With her grey hair wound tightly behind her head, held in place by slender rods and the thin lines that stretched from her eyes – brighter than he'd seen in some time – she looked every bit the master shaper she was.

"I think we must learn from what happened before," Tan agreed. "But some lessons are dangerous."

She rested a hand gently on his leg. "What do you fear, Tannen?"

"The same as you, Mother. I fear losing my bond, of having my connection to the draasin severed from me. Now that I've bonded wind, I fear losing him as well." The connection to Honl didn't go as deep as it did with Asboel, but that would likely come in time. Tan and Asboel had shared too much in too short a time to not have depth to their bond. It was much like what he shared with Amia. "I fear what Par-shon intends, knowing the lengths they went to try and trap the draasin before. Now that they know what I can do, now that they know what the kingdoms can do, what more will they try?"

"You think you will lose your connections?"

"I know how Par-shon severs bonds. And you've seen how they can do it without the room of separation."

Zephra sighed and thought for a moment. "You're wrong about one thing, Tannen," she said softly. "The ancients didn't force bonds on the elementals."

Tan wasn't so sure. There had to be a reason to hold the draasin confined as they were in the pens beneath the city, using golud and the nymid to trap them. What other reason than to force the bond, to gain the additional power that came with connecting to the elemental? And if the ancient shapers had done that, what made them so different from Par-shon?

"This book," Tan said, "describes the steps needed to trap the draasin. It describes how each shaper can use their talents to stop the draasin, and kill if needed. The entire book is like that. You really think that is the kind of knowledge that should still exist?"

His mother stared at him for a moment before answering. "You have a unique perspective on the draasin, Tannen, one that I think would have been unique even then. The draasin that you know, the connection that you share, gives you understanding of them, but try to imagine what it must be like for those of us without such a connection. To us, they are massive and terrifying creatures capable of destroying with ease. To the shapers of that time, they would have been something else. Now, there are only a few draasin. Back then…"

"The danger from the draasin is no different than udilm claiming people for the sea," he said. "They are elemental powers."

"And we mean very little to them," Zephra said.

Tan shook his head. "You are bound to one of the elementals. You of all people know that is not true."

Zephra sighed. "My connection lets me know that *I* am important to ara, but I have never had the sense that others are as important to Aric as I am."

Tan picked up the book and set it on his lap. Whatever else the ancient shapers had been, they had not understood the elementals nearly as well as he thought they would have. The bond was not meant for control. It was meant for understanding. How much had he learned from Asboel simply by sharing the bond?

For starters, he'd mastered the ability to sense and use fire with exquisite control. That was an amazing gift, but even more important was his understanding of the draasin, a way of knowing power greater than him, of connecting that much closer to the Great Mother. And maybe *that*, more than anything else, was what the draasin got out of the bond: the chance to share with another what it meant to control fire with as much strength as they did.

"I think of all the things the draasin has done since I first bonded," Tan said. "There were many things done to help me, but I can't expect the draasin to know the importance of the other connections, of the people around me. That is what I bring to the bond, just as the draasin brings his understanding of the elemental power to the bond. It forges understanding, Mother, and understanding must go two ways."

She took a moment to consider. "I am afraid for you," she said softly. Somehow, as she shifted more deeply into her chair, her face found a shadow and her expression changed, to reflect that fear.

"I know what we face, what the bonded shapers of Par-shon will do. What the Utu Tonah is capable of doing." Only, he didn't know that, not completely. The Utu Tonah was too powerful for him to know well. "If I don't do anything—if we don't do what we can to keep the kingdoms safe—then who will?"

She sat back and sighed. "You have come a long way since Nor, Tannen. Your father would be proud of the man you have become."

"I wish he would have been around. We could use someone with his talents."

His mother reached toward him and took his hand, squeezing it. "He made sure that you can carry on his talents. That was his greatest ability. And I am thankful to him for that." She closed her eyes, a sad smile coming to her face. "You are much like him, you know. He would always argue with me. Not in anger, but using reason and passion for those around him to convince me to do what he thought was right. That was how he convinced me to answer the last summons."

She opened her eyes and caught his. "Did you know that I didn't want him to go? I begged him, telling him that we were needed along the border. I no longer shaped as I once did and feared that with him leaving, the barrier would weaken, but Grethan felt that it was his duty to go, to help those who could not help themselves. I see much the same in you."

"I don't want to risk myself any more than Father did," Tan said. The revelation made him feel closer to his father – and to the Great Mother, as well. Maybe they were watching over him together. "But I know what will happen if we do nothing."

"As do I," Zephra said softly.

They sat for a moment in silence. Tan felt the soft pull of the wind on his arms, alternating from the cool of ara to the warmth of ashi, almost as if Aric and Honl battled for control of the room. The fire crackled softly, the gentle sense of saa working within the flames. Tan was reminded of the need to learn more about saldam and inferin, but for now, his connection to Asboel and his ability to draw upon saa would be enough.

"What of Elle?" he asked, breaking the silence.

His mother tilted her head as if listening to someone speaking in her ear. "I have not been able to reach Doma safely," she said.

"I thought that's where you've been the last week."

"No. Incendin."

"Incendin isn't the real threat," Tan said. "They've been battling Par-shon for longer than we know. Maybe as long as the lisincend have existed. It's because of Incendin that we haven't seen the threat of Par-shon before now."

"Yet Incendin has still felt compelled to attack the kingdoms." She raised a hand to cut him off before he could speak again. "Incendin is the reason your father is gone, Tannen. They are the reason many shapers have lost those they care about. Without the barrier, we're weakened and we don't yet have the strength needed to raise it again. We need time and we need to watch Incendin, to be ready for what they might do next."

"So there is no word out of Doma?" he asked.

"None that I can reach." She smiled at him, the same smile she had used when he was a child to soothe him. As much as she might recognize that he was now a warrior shaper, there seemed a part of her unable to view him as anything other than her child. "But Doma has been fine for generations. Elle will be fine."

Tan thought about Vel, about how the water shaper had been taken from Doma, his bond forced from him in Par-shon, and wasn't so sure. "I should go—"

His mother raised a hand. "Theondar wants you to focus on Incendin, Tannen. The kingdoms need that from you. We need the warrior."

"But Elle…" he started but didn't know how to finish.

"Even you have agreed that Elle is safe with the udilm. She has returned to Doma."

Tan couldn't help but wonder if that was true. Had he not learned what Par-shon was capable of doing to those bonded to the elementals, he would have felt that Elle was fine, but how could she be safe if her bond could be stripped from her? What if she wasn't one of the lucky ones, people like Vel and Cora, to survive? What if Par-shon already had taken her bond?

His mother patted his arm. "When it is safer, I will reach Doma and find her. She is safe, Tannen. Don't worry."

The soothing words did nothing to stop his worry.

CHAPTER 4

Elemental Bonds

THE SHAPERS LANTERN IN THE LOWER level of the archives provided a steady white light, parting the shadows and leaving the dark gray stone walls appearing almost black. Tan sat in the heavy wooden chair that he'd brought down, staring at the walls rather than the book he'd chosen. At least the walls didn't reveal tales of when the elementals were captured and used. *Harnessed*, as the ancients called it.

He had thought the practice confined to certain elementals, but from what he could tell, all of the elementals had been harnessed. This book, the one with a rune for water on it, spoke of harnessing the lesser elementals, referencing their use as justifiable. Of the so-called greater elementals, only the draasin had been captured with an attempt to harness them, though less to use them than for the need to control them.

Was that how the ancient scholars managed to create such skilled shapings? Had they forced the elementals to guide them, much like Par-shon forced the bonds today? From what Tan could tell, there wasn't all that much difference between the practices, other than the fact that Par-shon made no comments about doing it for the benefit of the people.

Tan set the book aside and stood, glancing at the row of shelves. Other volumes were there, stacked along the shelf, but he didn't want to go through them and find more evidence of the way the ancient scholars used the elementals. He had thought those shapers able to speak to the elementals, but what if that had not been it at all? What if they had simply forced the elementals to work with them?

He turned away from the archives and closed the door with a shaping. He considered a visit to Cora, but he would only slow down the healing. The last time he'd stepped in to try and help, the shaping had been much more complex than he could even fathom, leaving him simply staring while they worked, unable to even help hold the initial shaping. Tan could tell that in the short time she'd been working one on one with the First Mother, Amia had grown more skilled. More confident. There was a sense of purpose he felt through the bond, as well, that hadn't been there before, more than simply the desire to help. He would not take that from her, not as she was finally starting to regain that part of herself.

Instead, he turned away from the shelves and used a shaping to open the door to the tunnels beneath the city.

He trailed his hand along the damp stone. Down here, in the bones of the city, nymid mingled with golud. Tan didn't understand why the elementals had remained after everything that had been done to them by those ancient shapers, unless they were still bound to the city in some way. But this was a place of convergence. It made little sense that they would be forced to remain here. That meant there were still so many things he didn't understand.

Honl, Tan called to the soft wind blowing through the tunnel.

The wind elemental swirled around him, sending the light of his flame flickering. Tan let saa take control of the fire and stabilize it so that he didn't have to hold the shaping and could focus on Honl.

Tan. You are troubled.

I am trying to understand the bond between elementals.

What is to understand? The bond is there. We share. It is as the Great Mother intends.

Tan wished it were so simple for him. The Great Mother might intend for the bonds to exist, but did she also intend for people to choose to abuse them? What purpose would that serve? How would that help the elementals?

Was ashi here when the draasin last flew freely?

Wind has always blown, Tan. Without wind, there is no breath, no life.

And ashi?

He already knew that the nymid had once been considered one of the lesser elementals, but Tan had disproven that. Would the same have been true of ashi? Ara was felt to be the greater elemental of wind, but ashi was equally strong, blowing with much the same force, especially once Tan coaxed it. Ara was more fickle but less fearful than ashi. And then there was ilaz, the strange wind elemental found in Par-shon. Here too, though he had never spoken to ilaz, and a part of him feared it.

Ashi was young, then. We are not so bold as ara.

And the others? What of the other wind elementals, wyln and ilaz?

The others have always followed ara.

Tan wondered why that should be, though it was much the same with the draasin and fire. The other elementals followed the draasin—at least, they did when not forcibly bound and required to attack. When saa had attacked, Asboel had grown angry. The draasin might not be able to be hurt by a fire shaping, but something during the attack with Par-shon had injured him. Could the fire elementals hurt the draasin, or had it been the other shapers?

Why can't the young elementals bond?

Tan thought he understood now that was the reason that the nymid had taken so long to reach out to shapers. They were a younger elemental, perhaps—as ashi said—not as bold as the elder elementals. It might be that it took time for them to choose to bond, or time to gain the necessary experience to bond.

They must learn wind before they can teach it.

That's why you bond? To teach?

Ashi fluttered around him and settled near Tan's face. The flame caught the wind elemental and made his translucency somewhat brighter, giving a sense of definition as they continued down the tunnel. The path leading up and into the dungeons of the palace veered off here, but Tan continued on. Up ahead were the doors he was drawn toward.

Not only to teach, but to learn. When young, there is only the wind to learn. It takes time to master, but mastery comes. Then it is time to go beyond.

Tan wondered if the same could be said about shapers. Would they reach mastery enough to be able to go beyond and learn? Would Tan ever feel such mastery that he would risk leaving everything he knew to bond to some unknown?

He reached the massive arched doors hidden deep beneath the city. A single rune marked the center of the door, and Tan pushed a shaping of fire mixed with spirit into the rune. At least this shaping restricted who could open the door, though it kept the draasin in as much as it held others out. The door opened slowly, and Tan paused.

If it takes mastery to learn, can the young draasin bond?

Honl took a moment, making Tan wonder if the wind elemental even knew the answer.

The draasin are different. Fire was not always so different.

Tan's sense of Honl faded. The elemental would still be there but wouldn't impose upon the draasin hiding in the massive rooms beneath the city. Ashi worked with the draasin, but there was a sense of respect with a hint of fear mixed in as well.

Tan pushed the flame forward, resuming control of the shaping from saa. He didn't want to force the fire elemental to impose any more than he wanted to force Honl.

The inside of the room had changed since Tan first discovered it. Then it had been bare, nothing but walls worked with golud-infused stone, the nymid lingering along the borders, seeping through the moisture crawling up from the depths beneath the city. Now, golud had receded, offering the draasin the solace of silence. With it, the nymid had gone as well. Both could still be found in the surrounding stone, just not in what the draasin now used as a den.

Asboel filled most of the room. He shook his head, and turned to face Tan with eyes that nearly glowed. His great, leathery wings folded around him, making him look like some enormous barbed serpent.

A large pile of pale, white bones were stacked in the corner of the room. A few rocks, one larger than anything Tan thought he could shape, formed a sort of arch, a way of replicating the den the draasin had lost when they were forced away from Nara. A pool of fresh water came up from the ground in another corner, no signs of nymid green within.

Maelen.

How are the hatchlings? Tan asked, standing at the door. He saw no sign of them, nor of Sashari, the other adult draasin. He wondered if

Enya ever followed Asboel into the depths of the city, or if she preferred her solitude.

She hunts alone, Asboel said.

Their connection was different than it once had been, reforged with a shaping of spirit and mixed with fire after the Par-shon shapers attempted to steal it, and now Asboel seemed to know his thoughts without Tan intending to share.

You know what I've been reading, Tan said. If Asboel knew his thoughts on Enya, then it was just as likely that he could understand everything.

Not all. The connection is not that powerful. There must be intent. Asboel crawled forward. The ceiling of the room was high overhead, but still not high enough for him to stand freely. It was a den, and one that served as well as it could. His spiked neck scraped at the stone above. Without golud infusing the walls, Tan suspected the draasin would destroy the place. *What you have shared burns within you.*

Tan grimaced at the choice of words. *I thought those who came before me possessed knowledge that I do not.*

They did.

Tan hesitated. *But they chose to harness the elementals. The draasin.*

Asboel lowered his head and rested it on long, sharp forelegs. His barbed tail wrapped around him. *Knowledge has never equaled wisdom, Maelen. Gaining knowledge is easy. Wisdom takes time and experience. Unlike those who came before, you are well on the way to understanding.*

Tan thought that a compliment. *I had hoped I could learn from them, but all I have seen are things I would choose to avoid.*

Then you already are wiser than your ancestors. There were many things done that should never have been. Mistakes were made, and all suffered for it.

He sensed Asboel unwilling to share more than he had, and Tan wasn't sure he fully understood, but maybe Asboel was right that he would learn in time.

What of the hatchlings? I trust they are well?

Asboel twisted toward the back of the room. Tan couldn't see anything, so he borrowed sight from Asboel. There, hiding behind the rock, was a massive hole in the wall. Behind that, he saw shades of red and orange. The hatchlings.

How did you make that?

I asked of golud. The draasin might be few, but we are still respected.

Tan laughed. *You convinced the earth elemental to expand your rooms?*

They had little choice. The rock would have melted otherwise. There was a note of amusement in the draasin's voice.

Tan didn't doubt that Asboel could melt the rock, but he didn't get the sense that he would have done anything that would have endangered another of the elementals. That had been the reason for his rage when the Par-shon shapers attacked. Bonded as they were, controlled by Par-shon, elementals were forced to attack other elementals. Doing so was unnatural.

He sensed Asboel doing something, calling to the hatchlings, and they crawled out from beneath the rock. They looked much like Asboel, though smaller. They had long snouts, and spikes rose from their backs. Thin, papery wings folded behind them. Tails that seemed too long for their bodies gave a sense of how large they would one day become.

The hatchling closest to him snuffed, and steam rose from his nostrils. He had bluish scales and orange eyes that caught the flame Tan held suspended in the air. The other snorted, staying close to Asboel. Her scales were deep red, nearly maroon.

Their spikes weren't as stout as those on Asboel, and appeared sharp tipped. The nearest dipped his head toward the pile of bones and pulled one out and began chewing on it with a soft grunt.

Tan felt something from them. It was different than with Asboel, but it was there, like a faded sense at the back of his mind. He wondered if he could summon that sense to the forefront of his mind, augment it with spirit, and be able to speak with them, much as he did with Asboel. Doing so might mean bonding them.

Have you considered my suggestion? Tan asked.

Asboel snorted. *Suggestion? What you ask is not for me to choose.*

Our bond has proven valuable to both of us, Tan reminded him.

Only because I have bound to Maelen. Others of your kind are not so willing to listen.

I fear what will happen if there is no bond. If the draasin are captured, one will be forced on them. With a bond, at least there is help.

Asboel lowered his head. The nearest hatchling climbed atop him and breathed a finger of yellowish flame at his ear. Asboel twisted and nipped at him, shrugging the hatchling off. *Bonds are not as simple as you seem to think, Maelen. There are reasons the draasin have not bonded before.*

I thought there had been some who had bonded.

Once, and foolishly.

What happened?

They thought to control the bond. Few understand. You do, or you would not have survived.

Asboel said it simply, and Tan didn't have any sense of boasting from him. There had been a real possibility that he might not survive the bond, especially given how powerfully Asboel spoke within his mind. Had Tan not managed to push him back, he might have been overpowered.

Our bond formed only because I found you, Tan reminded him.

You listened. You were strong enough to turn away, even then, little warrior.

Tan smiled at the memory. It was easy to think of it in a positive way now. Now he'd learned some control, almost like learning shaping.

There is one who Sashari should meet. Let her decide.

Asboel snorted again. Both of the hatchlings latched onto his pointed ears and yanked. Asboel shook his head, and they went flying back. *She will consider.*

That was all that Tan could ask. He couldn't shake the feeling that they needed to bond the adult draasin, if not for any other reason than to keep them safe. But he would not force it. Tan would not be like the Utu Tonah or the ancient shapers. Bonds must be chosen. It didn't protect the hatchlings, but it was a start.

Have they claimed their names? Tan asked. Naming for a draasin took time, he'd learned. Asboel found it amusing that humans were named at birth. Draasin had to acquire their name, much like Tan had acquired the name Maelen.

They have barely begun to hunt. Names will come.

Tan struggled with getting Asboel to feel the same sense of urgency that he felt about the Par-shon shapers. To Asboel, Par-shon was another place to hunt, however dangerous. Once the Utu Tonah claimed a draasin, he would become nearly unstoppable. He might not be able to be stopped as it was.

Perhaps I will give them a name, as you gave me mine, Tan suggested.

The nearest of the young draasin, the one with the bluish scales, spun in place, his tail smacking against the stone. He glanced at Tan and fire streamed from his nostrils, parting harmlessly around Tan. He laughed. The other young draasin remained by Asboel, hesitant around Tan.

You are strong, Maelen, but you are not yet that strong.

Tan frowned at the comment. *Naming takes strength?*

Asboel clucked, a sound much like laughter. *You still have much to learn, Maelen.*

Tan rested his hand on Asboel and took a steady breath. *I'm afraid that I don't have the time needed to learn what's necessary. I want to keep you safe. To keep everyone safe.*

You think that is what the Mother asks of you?

Tan met Asboel's eyes. There was a deeper question to what he asked. *I'm still trying to understand what the Great Mother asks of me.*

Asboel nudged the hatchlings to the side, giving him room to study Tan. *You might find wisdom yet, Maelen. But you cannot keep everyone safe. That is not your task.*

What is my task? Tan asked.

You will know when the Mother seeks to reveal her intention. But that is not why you're here, is it, Maelen?

Tan sighed. *I will have to face Par-shon again, and probably soon. For that, I will need your help.*

You know I will hunt with you, Maelen.

Everyone should have a choice. Even the elementals.

Asboel snuffed, and steam hissed out from his nostrils. *As I said, you might find wisdom yet.*

Chapter 5

An Enemy Returns

When his summoning rune called to him, Tan answered, meeting Roine in the courtyard of the university. At this time of day, the walls of the university—walls shaped higher with each passing day—rose around him, creating gentle shadows across the courtyard. The air held dust from broken stone and a hint of must. A soft breeze blew through and sent fallen leaves spinning in wide circles.

The king regent wore a thick green jacket with slashes of color sewn into the sleeves, and tight breeches that matched. A heavy ring on his first finger was new. Tan studied it before realizing that it had once been the king's. It was good that Roine was finally settling into his role.

"What is it?" he asked.

Roine craned his head, trying to see behind Tan. "Only you? I expected Amia to be with you."

Tan shook his head. Since Tan had left Asboel last night, Amia had been intermittently sleeping and shaping. He didn't need to be with her to sense how hard she worked.

It troubled him that such a powerful shaping was necessary to try and heal Cora. Amia claimed that his spirit shaping was not to blame, but how much damage had he caused and how much of it was from Par-shon?

"She's working with the First Mother," he said.

When Roine reached absently to the warrior's sword sheathed at his side, Tan realized how much he missed the matching sword he'd lost in Par-shon. Once, he had been an archer, but it had been months since he carried a bow, months since he had thought one necessary. The sword fit him better now, especially with the runes along the blade that would augment his shaping.

"Then it will be the two of us."

"Where are we going?"

Roine's mouth pulled in a tight line. "Business of the throne, I suppose."

"Are you sure I should be going?"

Roine eyed Tan. A flat expression crossed his face, pulling at the corners of his eyes. The soft nod said that he'd come to a decision. "When we met, you knew me as Roine, Athan to King Althem. I had been Athan for over a decade before Althem died. All of this," he said, sweeping his hand around him, "is new to me. I might sit the throne, but it's temporary. Even so, it's time that I have an Athan as well." He watched Tan as he spoke.

"Roine, I—"

"You're the most qualified. There will be others who can speak with my voice, but for now, it will be only you." Roine arched his brow. "Do you accept?"

Tan considered how to answer. He was already tied to the kingdoms by the sense of duty that drove him, but he'd never had any formal responsibility, not like the university shapers who owed the king a term of service. Tan had missed acquiring such service when the university was destroyed, but even then, he had served regardless, knowing that it was the only thing he *could* do. Now Roine was asking him to take on a mantle of responsibility in a more formal way. Would it restrict him if he felt the need to do something different than what Roine wanted?

Had it ever restricted Roine?

"You're keeping me waiting?" Roine asked with a laugh.

"I… I don't know that I'm the right person. I don't know if others will listen to me—"

"I wish I would have said the same when Althem asked me. Maybe things would have been different. But you're one of the few whose judgment I can trust completely. We might not always agree on *how* to do what needs done, but I've never doubted your motivation, Tannen. I need you for this." He grunted. "And the others will come around. They do not know you as I do. You have come to your abilities in a… non-traditional route."

"In some ways, I'd say it's more traditional."

Tan met Roine's eyes, saw the request burning within them. Could he accept? If he did, what would it mean for him? How tied to the kingdoms would he become?

Roine waited, his face unreadable. Finally, Tan nodded.

"Good," Roine said with a relieved sigh. He handed Tan a thick band of dark gray, different than the silver band that he'd worn to mark himself as Athan. "Thought I would make my own. There's nothing really special about it, only the rune of office."

Tan studied the ring, noting that the rune comprised parts of each element. "That's it?"

Roine shrugged. "I'm not so formal as Althem. I had a ceremony and a celebration, but I didn't think you'd want anything like that." Roine smiled. "Besides, I don't have the title before my name to make the rest necessary. If I ever manage to find his heir, I can get back to what I prefer anyway. We've found a few who are promising, but it will take time," Roine said.

"And what is it that you prefer?" Tan asked.

"The same as you," Roine said with a laugh, then he glanced to the sky. "Shall we?"

"Where are we going?"

"To the Aeta. They requested an audience with the king. Since I'm all there is, I guess I have to go."

Tan hesitated and sent word to Amia through the bond. He sensed her resting, not shaping. She stirred and came awake.

"Wait," he said.

Roine's shaping had been building and it released with a soft *pop*. "What is it?"

"With the Aeta, Amia should be with us."

"You said she was working with the First Mother."

Tan nodded. "She has been. She was sleeping."

"You could tell that?"

How much of his bond to Amia had he shared with Roine? To him, they were connected, a couple, but Roine didn't know that Tan could speak to her in a way that he'd never spoken to another person before. Well, other than Elle, but that had taken incredible focus and required her to be near him.

"We're bonded, Roine."

Tan watched his reaction. Roine didn't say anything, but nodded slowly. "Bonded. Well, that makes more sense than what I'd been thinking. Spirit to spirit?"

"How do you—"

Roine laughed. "You're not the only one who's spent time in the archives, Tan. Before I was Athan, I spent enough time that the archivists threatened to forcibly remove me. Only the fact that I'm a warrior permitted me increased access. Now I wonder if Althem had some role in it, too."

Roine frowned and scrubbed a hand across his face. His eyes were drawn and clouded, with his mouth pinched in a pained expression. "So much of what happened with Althem is hard to describe. How much of what I did was because of me, and how much was I shaped? I have memories of my interest in searching the archives for knowledge from the ancients, but was that interest always mine, or had it been added?" He shook his head. "I now know that he wanted the artifact all along. Maybe I was used, maybe that interest was placed so that I could begin the search on my own." His smile was tight and did not reach his eyes. "Or maybe it has always been me. You cannot begin to understand how it is when you question everything you've ever done. Now that he's gone, I feel freed, but sometimes I get this strange sense of anxiety, as if everything I've ever chosen was not mine."

"The fact that you worry about it tells me that you're fine."

"And the fact that I can have you as Athan provides me with peace of mind," Roine said. "With everything you've seen, you are the only person who can tell me if I'm not thinking straight." He met Tan's eyes and held them. "I trust you, Tannen. More than I can explain."

They both turned as Amia entered the courtyard. Her long golden hair was pulled into a braid. The band around her neck matched her hair. She studied both Tan and Roine and her hands gripped the fabric of her dress. "You're going to them."

"We are. The Aeta requested to meet with the king," Roine said.

"I'm no longer one of the Aeta."

Roine sighed softly. "I understand. And you don't have to come if you don't want to. My Athan seemed to think you would, though."

"Athan?" There was another question as Amia met Tan's eyes, but she held it back from him. "What does that mean for him?"

"Not much, I'm afraid. A marker of office. He can speak with my voice, for whatever that's worth."

"You know what that is worth. And you know where that will lead him," she said to Roine. "You want this?" she asked Tan.

Tan didn't yet know *what* he wanted. A chance for peace so that he could simply be with Amia. The opportunity to understand his gifts. But serving in this role made a certain sort of sense. He was a warrior now, more skilled than he'd been even a month ago. With his connection to the elementals, he understood the land better than most. And with what he'd seen in Par-shon, he understood the risk better than anyone other than Roine and his mother.

"It's a responsibility I think I need to accept."

He felt her uncertainty, but she said nothing as she took his hand. "Do you know what this will mean for you?" she asked softly. Next to them, Roine started his shaping, pulling it toward him and disappearing in a flash of white lightning.

"For me? Nothing has changed. I'm the same person. I feel the same way I did before. Par-shon needs to be stopped. We need to understand the elementals. The kingdoms need to be kept safe."

Amia nodded. "All of that is true." She kissed his cheek as he began the shaping that would carry them toward the Aeta. She seemed to bite back whatever else she was thinking, holding it away from the bond. Then she laughed softly. "There's something else you probably didn't consider."

Tan frowned at her. "What's that?"

"Your mother. Now you outrank her."

Tan laughed as he pulled the shaping toward them, lifting them into the air on a streak of lightning. With this shaping, he had to have a sense of direction, to know where he was going. He guided them to the place where he'd last seen the Aeta, coming down to the ground in a rumbling bolt of power.

They were alone. There was no sign of Roine.

Tan should have known that the Aeta wouldn't have been in the same place. Days had passed since then and the wagons would have rolled onward. How had Roine known where to go, then? Probably another trick of shaping that Tan still didn't know.

The summoning coin in his pocket vibrated and Tan focused on it and followed it with another shaping.

When they landed, Roine was watching him, a smile on his face. He stood on a small rise, a cluster of elm trees to his left and the sun high overhead. In Ethea, it had been overcast, the clouds covering the sun, but here in what Tan presumed to be Ter, the sun was high and not quite warm.

The Aeta caravan camped at the bottom of a gentle hill, stopped in a tight circle as if to trade, though none of the windows were open like they were when they traded. The paint of these wagons was faded, different than most of the Aeta he'd seen before, almost as if scrubbed free. A line of people stood in front of the wagons, looking up the hill. If there was a spirit shaper with them, they might have known they were coming.

"I overshot," Tan said.

"You'll need to learn to travel less directly."

"Less direct?"

"Because you can shape spirit, your shaping is a little different than mine. Whatever you do takes you directly where you intend. My shaping is a little less precise and it takes a moment or two longer, but has its uses. Like this," Roine said, indicating the wagons in front of them.

"How did you know they were here?" Amia asked.

Roine nodded toward the Aeta. "They sent word."

She turned, looking to the north and Ethea. "The Aeta sent word? To Ethea?"

"They shaped it," he said.

Her eyes tightened.

Tan studied the Aeta, wondering which one would be the shaper. "We once thought shaping rare among the Aeta," Tan said.

"It is," Amia said. "At least, I thought it was."

"Then how is it that we've come across it as often as we have?"

"I… I don't know. Maybe the First Mother hid the frequency from others. Maybe there is only weak shaping strength in some. When she taught me to shape, she made it seem like my ability is rare."

"Your ability *is* rare. I've seen you working with the First Mother. The way that you shape is about more than strength. You've got a delicacy to it that I cannot even fathom. I've watched you and don't think that I could even come close to what I see you doing so easily."

"It's for Cora," Amia said softly. "And for you. You've said that what she knows might be important. I still need to learn where she's from."

Roine's eyes widened as she spoke.

"That's hidden from us despite everything that we've done. But I can tell she had strength once. She has known shaping, and she knew the elementals. I only wish I could figure out which one. That's why I keep pushing."

Tan suspected it was about more than just helping Cora. Amia was learning how to use her ability from the only person alive who might be able to teach her. And if telling herself that she did it for Cora was the only way that she would do it, then Tan thought it worthwhile.

"Well, I don't know who summoned, only that there was a request to meet with the Aeta," Roine said.

"How did you know it was from the Aeta?" Tan asked.

Roine hesitated, his eyes straining toward the Aeta waiting below. They stood watching, not moving. "Trust that I know. Come. We should not keep them waiting," Roine said.

He started down the slope on a shaping of air. Tan thought it odd that he didn't answer the question, but then again, Roine was now essentially the king. He didn't *have* to answer.

Tan leaned into Amia. "Are you ready for this?"

She brushed away a stray strand of hair. "I came for you, not for them."

Tan bit back a comment. She likely knew what he was going to say anyway.

He readied a shaping of wind and drew upon Honl, lifting himself and Amia onto a cloud of wind, and used that to follow Roine. They caught him and made their way down the slope next to him, side by side.

Roine slowed as they approached the Aeta and Tan followed, lowering himself and Amia to the ground. Roine stepped forward and bowed slightly at the neck as he approached the gathered Aeta.

They stood in a line. There were two women among them, so either could be the Mother. A large man with a bulging belly stood to one end. He had tattoos along each arm, twisting and winding until they faded behind his shirt. A large hoop hung from his ear.

Two other men stood on the far end of the line. One was slender and slight, with dull gray eyes. The other was of average build and seemed to focus anywhere but on them.

Tan stayed back a few steps as they approached, holding a shaping ready in case it was needed. Fire. He always defaulted to fire.

"I am Theondar Roardan," Roine said as he approached. "I serve as king regent. There was a summons."

Tan tensed as he waited for the response. The Aeta had been offered safety in the kingdoms, but summoning the king was something different. This was asking for help, unless Roine had read it wrong.

One of the Aeta stepped forward. She was small and older, though not old, with wide hips and a dress that hung limp around her frame. Her brown hair looked dull and had no gray streaking through it.

She leaned forward, pressing her hand across her stomach. "I am Meltha, the Mother of this caravan," she started. Her voice was thready and barely carried across the distance. "Thank you for coming, but there was no summons. We are simply here for trade."

She cannot shape. Amia's voice surged through their connection.

Tan studied Meltha, wondering how Roine would have been summoned if Meltha couldn't shape. How would any of the Aeta send a summons and manage to reach Roine in Ethea?

He could think of only one way. There was an archivist among them.

Tan shaped spirit, letting it wash out from him, no longer caring who might recognize that he was shaping spirit. If there was an archivist among the Aeta, he would know.

None of the people standing in a line in front of them could shape. He stretched out with a combination of earth sensing and spirit, reaching toward the wagons. With earth sensing, he could sense all of the people within the caravan; with spirit, he could tell where there might be an absence.

He sensed it in the middle wagon at the back of the caravan. There were two people in the wagon, though spirit sensing only picked up one.

He's in the wagon, Tan told Amia.

"The kingdoms has offered protection to the Aeta. You no longer have to wander. We have seen the suffering of the People and would like it ended," Roine said.

The Mother bowed her head. "Your offer is appreciated, but the People have wandered for centuries. There is no need for our travels to end."

A shaping built from within the wagon. It targeted Roine but split and reached toward both Tan and Amia as well. Tan suspected that Roine had protected his mind from shaping but worried what would happen were the archivist as powerful as the First Mother.

Roine nodded. "Then we welcome your trade. As you no doubt know, the barrier has fallen. The ancient protection between the kingdoms and Incendin is no more. But we offer safety while you are in our lands."

"We do not fear Incendin any more than we fear any other country."

Roine paused and spread his hands. "No? Then perhaps I was mistaken in thinking that Incendin uses Aeta shapers to create lisincend."

Tan jerked his head around to gape at Roine. Had he really said that?

The Mother paused and then looked to those standing on either side of her.

"You'll excuse my bluntness, but considering that I was summoned, I would expect a certain amount of honesty from the Aeta."

"You must be mistaken, Theondar. The Aeta have no shapers. We are simple traders—"

"The First Mother is a guest in Ethea. Would you like me to say more?" The façade of friendliness had disappeared completely from Roine's face, replaced by a hard expression, one that met the eyes of each person standing in line. "Now. You will send him out."

The Mother met Roine's eyes. "My lord," she started.

Roine cut her off. "Your wagons contain one of the archivists, a man who I know can shape spirit. If he thought he would be able to shape me, then he is mistaken. And if he thought he would be able to shape those with me, then he is a fool."

Roine's voice was hard and dangerous. Tan stood quietly, uncertain what to make of the standoff. He had thought that he would need to warn Roine of the danger, but he should have known better. Roine was a warrior, skilled and hardened by his experiences. He had learned to protect his mind from shaping. As a spirit shaper, Tan was naturally protected.

"He's coming," Tan said as he sensed movement from the wagon.

"Yes," Roine said.

"That was for Amia," Tan said.

Roine gripped the hilt of his sword briefly. "Of course. You will watch for signs that he tries to shape me?"

"He has already tried," Amia said. She touched the gold band at her neck as she stared at the Mother.

"And failed, but if there's another attempt, you will warn me?"

The man who made his way to around the wagons had dark hair and a youthful face. Tan hadn't seen him before, though he hadn't been in Ethea long when the archives had fallen. He was dressed simply, a dark robe bound with a loop of silk. His eyes widened when he saw Tan and Amia. Tan might not recognize him, but he recognized Tan.

The archivist paused and whispered to the Mother before approaching Roine. A spirit shaping trailed with him, touching on the Aeta, this time leaving Roine alone. He made a point of not looking at Tan or Amia as he approached.

Asboel. Tan sent the request out with a sudden urgency, reaching for his connection to the draasin. He didn't know where Asboel hunted, though he flew somewhere in Galen.

Maelen. You do not normally summon when you are with your woman.

Tan sent an image of the archivist to Asboel. *Have we seen this one before?*

Asboel hesitated before answering. *There is more to this one?*

He can shape spirit, like the one who shaped Enya.

He could practically hear Asboel snarl. *I have not seen him.*

Tan pulled away from the connection, not wanting Asboel to linger on the archivist. After what the archivists had done, the draasin remained angry with both the archivists and Incendin. It was about more than what they had done to Enya, but also what the archivists had done to Amia and all of the kingdoms' shapers.

"Theondar. Most thought you were dead," the archivist said, not making any attempt to hide the contempt in his voice.

Theondar faced the archivist, staring at him with a glare heavy with the weight of his shaping. "Althem knew I lived. Seeing as how he was your master, that is all that mattered."

The archivist blinked, another shaping building from him. "The king was never my master. I served the archivists—"

"Who served as Althem required," Roine said before Tan had a chance to warn him. "You must think highly of your shaping skill to attempt to shape me with these two next to me." Roine forced a wide smile. "It was clear when you saw them that you recognized them. Were you involved in what happened to her?" he asked. "Or to the draasin? Were you involved there? If you were, pray you are more skilled at running than you are at shaping. The draasin have a long memory."

The archivist's face blanched. "I was not a part of what happened."

"Then you knew Althem was gone when you summoned?" Roine took a step forward, sliding on a shaping of wind so that he hovered slightly above the archivist. "From my vantage, it appears you summoned only because you sought help from your old master."

"We came for safety," the archivist said.

Roine frowned.

"You offered the safety of your lands to the People, did you not?"

"You will not attempt a shaping of my people," Roine warned.

"You think that my intent?"

"I don't know anything about your intent," Roine said. "Nor why you bothered to summon if not to reach Althem."

The archivist made a sour face at the mention of Althem and motioned to Amia. "I came for her."

"She is no longer of the Aeta," Roine said.

"Not her. *Her*. The First Mother. She calls to all who shape spirit as if it were a Gathering. That is why we come."

Tan resisted the urge to glance over at Amia. The Gathering had long since passed. If the archivist came for the First Mother, it meant she had sent a new summons.

Did you know of this? he asked Amia.

She has always been a delicate shaper. She would not have wanted me to know.

"The First Mother no longer leads the Aeta," Roine said. "For her crimes, she is now the prisoner of Ethea."

The archivist stared at Amia for a long moment. "Yes. And the summons states that a replacement will be found. As you are no longer of the Aeta, I presume that is not you."

Tan already knew Amia's thoughts. The First Mother might once have intended the replacement to be Amia, but that had changed. Could she intend for one of the archivists to replace her?

Roine stared at the archivist, the hard expression still fixed on his face. "You have failed to convince me of the reason you summoned," he said.

"I have told all I can. You will tell her that we have answered the call?" he asked.

Roine didn't respond.

The archivist his hands and waited a moment before starting back toward the caravan.

Amia watched him. Tan had expected anger or sadness, but the emotion he sensed from her was neither. She watched the archivist with uncertainty.

CHAPTER 6

Ways of Healing

THE CHANGE FROM BRIGHT SUN to the grey skies over Ethea was jarring but suited Tan's mood as they landed in the circle at the university. Tan bounced off the stone, moving away from the circle before Roine arrived. Troubled thoughts trailed him, concern about why the archivists had returned and why the First Mother had summoned them. What did she hope to accomplish while confined in Ethea? What games was she playing at with Amia?

Roine returned a moment after them, landing in the shaper circle on a bolt of lightning. There was a pained expression on his face and he gripped his sword tightly.

"What will you do?" Tan asked.

"I've already offered my protection. That will not be rescinded."

"Even knowing what she does?"

“Sometimes we need to do things that we wish we didn’t have to. This is one of those times.” Roine turned to Amia. “You will tell her that I know of her summons when you next work with her.”

“She will not force me to lead the Aeta,” Amia said, gripping the flowing white dress she wore. “And neither will you.”

“I have no intention of forcing anyone to do anything,” Roine said. “You should know me well enough by now to know that much.”

“I’m sorry, Roine. Working with her has put me on edge,” Amia said, sighing.

“Do what you can,” Roine said. “See what you can do with Cora. Use the First Mother if you must, or work alone if you’re strong enough, but find out what you can about Cora. If she’s a warrior, then we must understand where she’s from.”

She hesitated. What Roine asked meant that she would need to spend even more time with the First Mother. With the summons to the archivists, Tan understood her concern. “I’ll try.”

“And you,” he said, turning to Tan. “You will come to me in the morning. I have a task for you as well.”

He disappeared on a shaping of wind.

Amia watched Roine. “You might wish you had not committed to serving as his Athan.”

“I’m going to end up doing the same, service or not,” Tan said.

“That’s not entirely true. I know how you feel about Incendin.”

Tan tensed. He had purposefully been careful about his thoughts on Incendin. Amia would be the most likely to understand, but the history between her and Incendin was deep, deeper than what Tan shred with them. He dared not share it with Asboel. The draasin might understand, but he wanted revenge for what Incendin had done. There was a large part of Tan that did, too. Then there was Tan’s mother and Roine. Both had faced Incendin for years.

Only, Incendin served a purpose. Perhaps it always had. He might not agree with how Incendin did what it did, but there was no question that the threat of the lisincend, of the Fire Fortress itself, had kept the kingdoms safe from Par-shon.

"I feel the same as you about Incendin," Tan said.

She smiled and leaned forward on her toes to kiss him on the cheek. "Not the same, but you do well to pretend. I can understand what you intend, but still not like it."

"We don't have to like them to use them. Even if it's only long enough to figure out how we can fight back."

Tan didn't have a sense of how he would use Incendin, not yet, but there had been nothing but silence from Par-shon since the attack. They had time, strange as it seemed, almost as if they stood in the calm before the coming storm. If he could find some way to turn Par-shon's attention solely onto Incendin, the kingdoms might be able to remain safe. Then, if his mother was right, they could rebuild the barrier. It had served to keep the kingdoms safe once. Perhaps it could again.

"They killed my family, Tan. They killed your father. Whatever you think they might have the potential to do doesn't make up for what they *have* done."

"I know you're right," he said, choosing to avoid conflict with Amia.

"I should check on Cora like Roine asked. Perhaps she knows something that can help, if only I can be strong enough to help her."

"You're strong enough," he said.

"I'm not sure," Amia started. "There's something missing with the healing. Even the First Mother hasn't managed to find the secret." She hesitated and Tan squeezed her hand. "I think we have to prepare for the possibility that she doesn't recover."

They parted ways in the street, though with the bond they shared, they were never truly apart. Tan couldn't imagine a similar bond with anyone else. He had access to the deepest parts of Amia, he could close his eyes and trace the bond and simply *be* with her, the same as she could be with him. There were no secrets for them. The connection was wonderful and amazing, but also terrifying. When he'd been in Par-shon, he'd feared the possibility of losing Asboel, but losing Amia would have been thousands of times worse. And there was only so much he could do to keep her safe.

As he made his way to the archives, he wondered if he would ever be able to keep her safe. Each time he thought they were safe, some new threat emerged. If not Incendin, then Par-shon. What would happen to her next?

Tan found the inside of the archives darkened, but there were shapers lanterns. He had only to shape a trickle through them and they bloomed into bright white light. He hurried toward the lower level, intending to check on the draasin, but he paused. Seeing Roine with his sword had reminded him that it was time to claim a new one for himself.

Tan entered the room where a row of hooks along the wall held warrior swords. He looked at them, considering each one. The archives had nearly a dozen for him to choose from. More would be found in the palace, though they were forged differently than these and didn't have the same runes along the blade. None of them had reminded him of the sword he'd lost.

The first two he considered felt wrong. There was a strange heft to the blades, as if they were either made for a stronger or weaker shaper. The next was too long. Tan had grown accustomed to Lacertin's sword. The length of it had felt perfect to him, so he wanted something similar. A few others had a wide curve of the blade and would be too cumbersome. Midway along the wall, Tan noticed one that reminded him of his old sword.

Tan unsheathed it and considered the runes etched into the steel. He recognized most of them, though there were a few that he didn't. One looked something like the spirit rune he'd seen in Par-shon. The blade he'd carried had no rune for spirit. Tan had always added that to his shapings on his own.

He swung the sword carefully, then with more vigor. It felt comfortable in his hand, but then again, warrior swords were not really meant to be used like traditional swords.

He tested a shaping, pressing through the sword with a weak shaping of fire. Then wind. Water and earth were next. Last, he tried spirit. Each worked as he hoped, the sword augmenting his shaping.

As he did, his eyes were drawn to the case holding the artifact. He'd placed it in a simple case, making certain that it was protected, but hadn't dared use it since returning it to this part of the archives. The last time he had, he'd felt tempted to attempt shapings that he should not.

Clutching the sword, he dragged himself away. Amia had wanted more strength to shape Cora, but the artifact was not the answer. Hopefully, the sword would be enough.

The First Mother greeted Tan at the door to the small room holding Cora. "She should not be disturbed," she said.

"I won't disturb her," he said.

The First Mother grunted and started past him, moving to the back room. She was confined here, not allowed anywhere else in the city, and would not be allowed outside the city to reach the gathering Aeta. Tan grabbed her arm and stopped her.

"You're calling a Gathering."

The First Mother looked up at him. "Theondar agreed to provide safety."

"That's not all this is about."

Her eyes narrowed. "Are you so certain it is not, Tannen? You can shape me so well?"

Tan shook his head. "You know I cannot. Don't think you can manipulate Amia—"

She shot him a look. "You think that I manipulate the Daughter? Surely your skill with spirit is strong enough now that you can see I do not. I seek only to provide guidance."

"You want her to return to the People."

The First Mother leaned on the wall and sighed. For the first time, Tan realized how weary she seemed. "I have always wanted what is best for the People."

Tan released her arm and she started away. "Did you know about Par-shon?" he asked.

It was a question that had troubled him. If the First Mother had shaped the Doma shapers, if she had compelled them, would she have known the reason Incendin wanted them? But more than that, connected as she was to spirit, shouldn't she have recognized how the elementals suffered?

"I knew that Incendin suffered. Much of it caused by their actions, but not all. And I sensed how they would do anything to protect their people. It's a sentiment I shared with them."

She continued down the hall and turned into the room at the end.

When Tan entered the room, he found Amia standing over the bed, hands on either side of Cora as she performed another spirit shaping. Cora lay motionless, no different than the last time Tan had seen her, only her cheeks were a little paler. The only difference was her hair. If anything, there was more color to it than before.

The window was open and a cool breeze blew in, carrying with it the sounds from the street below. That it was cool told Tan that ara infused the wind rather than Honl and ashi. He wondered why that would be.

Amia had been shaping constantly since their return from the Aeta, focusing on Cora with a renewed intensity. Even during his time in the archives, he had sensed that from her.

Amia sighed and stepped away from the bed. "I need more strength," she finally said. "Working with the First Mother has helped, but I'm not strong enough. There's something there, but it's so deeply buried. I feel that if we can only reach it, I can draw her out, bring back the shaper she once was."

"There might be a way to augment the strength of your shaping," Tan said, thinking of the way the First Mother seeming increasingly frail with each day spent shaping. Amia must be feeling a similar toll.

She arched a brow at him. "I will not use the artifact. That's more temptation than any person should have."

"Not the artifact," he started. Amia's thoughts reflected those that he'd had while in the archives. The artifact *could* help, but it was too powerful for any shaper to attempt to use safely. "But there's something else we could use that can augment shaping."

Her eyes lowered to the sword at his waist. "You want me to use the sword?"

"I'm not sure that you can," he said. "But *I* can. You can reach through our bond and use the strength of the sword, use my spirit reserves if needed. Maybe you'll be able to finally heal her."

Amia stared at the sword for a long moment before finally turning to Cora. "What you suggest will be dangerous. For both of us."

From her willing tone, Tan suspected that Amia needed the success of healing Cora more than she realized. "We can try. If anything begins to go wrong, we can sever the connection."

He felt her agree without her needing to say anything.

Tan unsheathed the sword. What they would do might work with the sword sheathed, but there was a reassurance to being able to see the runes along the surface as they shaped. He placed the tip into the stone of the floor and stood over it. He drew a spirit shaping through the blade, feeling how the weapon added to his own strength.

Then he pressed through the connection he and Amia shared. She gasped softly but quickly took control. She guided the shaping, adding her touch to spirit, twisting and weaving it so that it layered over Cora. As she worked, Tan began to recognize some of what she did, almost as if holding this much spirit gave him insight. It was healing, but it was more than that. There was a questing to what she shaped, a search for understanding.

He felt the shaping as it moved through Cora. There was resistance at first and then he detected a void, a sense of nothingness that should not exist. Wrapped around the void, he sensed a shaping of spirit, layered many times, built by Amia and the First Mother.

Tan recognized the emptiness, and saw how to heal Cora, suddenly understanding that Amia and the First Mother would not be able to do it alone. Drawing through the sword, he pulled on each of the elements, mixing them together and adding this to spirit. He sent this shaping through the connection, through Amia.

"No, Tan—"

The shaping settled in Cora, filling the void. There was a flash and she moaned. Her breathing stopped and, for a moment, it seemed her heart stopped. The emptiness filled, expanding with the addition of the elements. Amia lost control of the shaping—she could handle spirit, but the others were more than she could manage—and Tan took over, recognizing what needed to be done.

He pressed the shaping directly now. The void began to disappear, filled with elemental power, until only the shaping around the remnants remained. Drawing on spirit, he peeled the layers placed by Amia and the First Mother away. Spirit flooded through her, expanding outward, pulled by the draw upon the sword.

Tan lost control and spirit flooded from him. Awareness filled him, reminding him of the day he had stepped in the pool of liquid spirit.

What had he been thinking? He didn't know enough to control this shaping. Amia might not even know enough to control this shaping.

Spirit continued to expand away from him, drawn by the sword. It exploded outward, flooding through Tan, through the sword, everywhere, until it faded.

Cora gasped.

Tan released the shaping. As he did, there was a familiar and distant sense, one he hadn't heard in months. Tan wasn't even sure he heard it correctly, but then it came again, echoing with his name, a sense of terror mixed in.

Elle?

He was certain it was her. As he thought he heard a response, he collapsed.

CHAPTER 7

Warrior's Return

TAN AWOKE ON THE HARD FLOOR. His back throbbed, and pain that hadn't been there before pulsed in his mind. Flashes of light swam around him, almost like elementals. A strange woman leaned over him, looking down at him through deep brown eyes. It took him a moment to recognize Cora.

"You're alive," she said.

Tan grunted and rolled over, pushing to his knees. Amia lay next to him, her breathing slow and steady, his connection to her telling him that she was simply asleep rather than injured more seriously.

"I could say the same about you. What happened?"

Cora still sat on the bed and Tan surveyed the rest of the small room. The fire had faded to little more than nothing. With a soft shaping—one that came from her—flames suddenly leapt and danced, and saa was drawn to it. "Where am I?" she asked.

"Ethea. The kingdoms."

"Ethea?" She said the name with a strange inflection, and her mouth pinched. "How? The last I remember, I was in Par-shon. There was pain… death… I…"

Tan breathed out slowly. His head hammered and throbbed. He felt more tired than he had in ages. What had happened to them as they shaped through the sword?

Then he remembered the voice he'd heard right before passing out. Elle's voice. Of that, he was certain. It had come from a distance, but there was pain and urgency in the way she called to him.

He glanced at the sword lying near the end of the bed. When he was recovered, he would have to try shaping spirit again to see if he could reach Elle. If she needed help, he had to be there for her.

"You were in Par-shon," Tan said, getting to his feet and checking on Amia. She stirred as he touched her and her eyes blinked open. A glaze over them told him that she wasn't completely recovered. He drew upon the elementals for strength—it was one of the gifts of his bond—but she had no elemental to pull on. He ran his hand across her hair, soothing her as he looked up at Cora. "And now you're not."

"How is it that I am no longer there?" Cora asked. "How is it that I'm in the kingdoms? How is that any of this has happened?"

"Because I brought you out of there." He faced the flames, feeling the draw of saa. He let the sense of the elemental fill him, the power rejuvenating. Some of the fatigue he felt faded. Soon he would be strong enough to shape safely again. He bent and picked up the sword, sheathing it quickly.

"You're a warrior, then," she said.

There was a firmness to her voice, a confidence that was so different from the woman he'd rescued. She was not afraid of the fact that he was a warrior. If anything, she seemed irritated that she had required the help of someone from the kingdoms.

"As are you," he said.

Cora blinked and looked away. "Once, perhaps, but that person is no longer."

"Who is that person?" he asked. "You're not of the kingdoms, but where are you from?"

"You think the kingdoms the only place where shaping exists?" she asked. She stared at the fire dancing in the hearth.

Saa twisted and flickered, moving in ways Tan didn't shape. Cora did. She pulled on the fire, the flames sliding and swirling, and he recognized a familiarity with fire that was different than anyone he'd ever seen. There was only one way she would reach the level of skill needed for what he saw.

"You're from Incendin?" he asked.

She lifted her chin almost in defiance as she looked away from the fire. Tan recognized a stark confidence that told him he'd guessed right.

"It has been many years since I claimed the Sunlands as my home." she said.

"How long were you in Par-shon?"

With the question, her shoulders sagged slightly. She touched her hair, smoothing it down. "I… I do not know. We have fought Par-shon far longer than we've fought with the kingdoms. The danger there forced some to shapings that are unsafe, even for those drawn to fire."

"You were never interested in becoming one of the lisincend?" he asked, pressing a shaping through the summoning coin in his pocket, as well as through the ring he now wore. Roine would need to know what happened.

"You speak as if you understand the reason for the transformation, but there are many reasons to embrace fire."

"Embrace fire? That's what you would call it? How many are lost during the transformation? There are those in the kingdoms who suspect it's close to half. Is it worth the price? Is it worth allowing fire to consume, to control them?"

Her head tilted slightly as she pronounced, very clearly, "Yes."

Cora slipped off the bed, and leaned in front of the hearth, pausing to stare at the flames that danced within. Her hair appeared healthier, the gray completely gone. Tan had thought her older, possibly at least his mother's age, but this woman could not have been more than ten years his senior.

When he had learned that she was from Incendin, he hadn't meant to start a debate about the merits of the lisincend. Tan might be the only one who understood what it meant to touch that power and return, but there was no question in his mind that Incendin had a reason for turning its shapers into the lisincend. The threat of Par-shon had driven them to it. What would happen when the kingdoms got their first taste of the power of the Utu Tonah? What would their shapers do?

He'd already seen what the ancient shapers had done. Tan didn't want to repeat the past.

He knelt next to Cora and placed his hand on the flat of her shoulder. She felt warm, more so than the flames in the fire could account for. The Incendin shaper did not turn to him.

"What did you lose?" he asked softly.

"Does it matter to you? I have gone from one prison to another, haven't I?" She met his eyes. "If you've brought me to the kingdoms, I am no freer here than I ever was in Par-shon."

Tan started to tell her that she wasn't a prisoner here, but that might not be true. Could they let an Incendin warrior shaper free?

"When I was in Par-shon, I met another man, one from Doma." He watched her as he spoke. Would she remember what had happened in Par-shon or had the trauma been too much? "A water shaper, one who had once been bonded to the udilm. He is safe now, too."

"I remember..." she started, and then shook her head, "nothing. There are snatches of shapes and colors. Mostly pain."

"There was another man," he went on. "In worse shape than you, though I have hope that we will be able to heal him in time, too."

Honesty would be needed. And Cora deserved to know. He might not have been able to get through to the lisincend he had once tried to heal, but he would get through to Cora.

"When I found you, it was in a place the Utu Tonah used for separation. They wanted to sever the bonds formed between shaper and elemental. I have not shaped long, and I have been bonded for only a little longer than I've known shaping, but that was possibly the worst pain I have ever known."

Cora watched him for a long moment before speaking. "You know the bond?"

"I speak to the elementals."

"Which?"

"All of them."

The ring on his finger tightened at the same instant a heavy pounding on the door made them both jump. Roine had come.

Tan opened the door, surprised to see Roine hadn't come alone. Cianna stood behind him, red hair wild and a tight maroon shirt flowing over her curves. She offered him a wide smile. Even more surprisingly, the First Mother leaned against the wall behind them both. When Roine moved to his right, the First Mother craned her neck, as if to see inside the room. She nodded and tottered away without speaking.

"Tan. You summoned," Roine said.

He stepped to the side to let Roine see Cora. She straightened, pulling away from the fire, and faced him. Her face revealed nothing.

Roine stepped into the room. "I am Theondar Roardan, king regent."

Cora glanced past him to Cianna. She seemed to hesitate as she saw the bright red hair. "And I am Corasha Saladan."

Cianna sucked in a breath. Tan felt her shaping as she readied it.

"You have heard of me?" she asked Cianna.

Roine gauged Cianna's reaction before answering. "I have not. But that my fire shaper has tells me you are from Incendin. Did you know?" he asked Tan, not removing his focus from Cora.

"Only since she's been healed."

"What happened to Amia?" he asked, glancing to where Amia still slumped unmoving on the ground.

"The shaping got away from us," Tan explained. "As we healed Cora, there was a void." He explained a little of what had happened, leaving out what he'd sensed of Elle for now.

"And you thought to seal it?" Roine asked.

"She didn't deserve what happened to her in Par-shon. You know how they nearly took my bond. What would have happened had the Utu Tonah gained control of one of the draasin?"

Cora gripped his arm and jerked him around.

Cianna was there in a heartbeat, standing next to Tan, a shaping building quickly. Roine simply watched. Tan waved Cianna off. Perhaps he should, but he didn't fear Cora, not as he did the other shapers of Incendin, and not as he did the lisincend. He knew what she had been through. What she needed now was understanding, not violence. They could use Incendin. They would have to if they were ever to survive an attack from Par-shon.

Cora stared at him with hot intensity. "You said draasin."

"I did," he said.

"They have been lost for centuries."

At least now he knew she had been in Par-shon long enough to have missed him freeing the draasin. "They were lost," Tan agreed.

"No longer?" she asked. Tan tipped his head in assent. "And you have bound one?"

"When I told you that I understood what you experienced in Par-shon, I told the truth. The Utu Tonah tried severing my connection to the draasin. He tried taking that bond for himself."

Her face contorted, her lips forming odd shapes something like multiple words that wanted to be voiced simultaneously. "How is it you escaped?"

"The same way you were healed. The Utu Tonah cannot bond spirit."

Cora stared at Amia. "She saved you?"

"*I* shape spirit, Cora," he said, pulling her attention to himself.

She spent a moment in thought, studying both Roine and Tan but ignoring Cianna. "I have been held in Par-shon long enough for the Order of Warrior to return?" she asked, laughing bitterly. "And now you hold me here, hostage in another land of my enemies."

Tan attempted a shaping of spirit to soothe her. Now that he'd recovered from the shaping that he and Amia had done, the elemental power refreshing him, he drew upon it easily. Cora rebuffed him, pushing back with a shaping of her own.

She knew how to block spirit. Knowing what the First Mother had done with the Doma shapers, it made sense that she would know. Perhaps he should have tried soothing her before revealing that he shaped spirit, but likely she had already placed protections around her mind when she awoke and saw Amia.

"We're not your enemies," he said. "We share a common threat."

She frowned at him. "Common? Has Par-shon attacked your borders for the better part of a century? Has Par-shon taken all who bond to the elemental power? Has Par-shon stripped you of all your protections, leaving you with no choice but to embrace shapings that lead your most talented shapers to perish rather than remain able to serve their people, with those who do remain changed into something else, driven in ways you can never understand? Is that the enemy you face?"

Roine's silence became somehow commanding. Tan bit back his answer and waited for the King Regent to speak. "You describe many of the kingdoms' experiences with Incendin," he said.

"The kingdoms? You cannot know what we face, the dangers that we have kept from our shores. Because of what the Sunlands has done, your kingdoms have remained safe." She shifted her attention to Tan. "You didn't even know the threat of Par-shon existed and now suddenly, you think to stop them?" She snorted, then sneered at Cianna. "And you, too weak to make the desert crossing, abandoning the ancient ties of our people."

"Enough," Tan said. He infused a shaping of spirit into his words.

They all looked at him.

"We did not heal you for you to insult our people," he said.

"Then why did you heal me?"

"I…" Tan paused. He had healed her thinking she could help, that by healing Cora, they might better understand what drove Par-shon, perhaps find an ally in a warrior shaper. Now that he knew she was from Incendin, he wondered if he would even be able to get through to her. The divide between the kingdoms and Incendin might be too wide for them to reach agreement, but if they didn't, both would eventually fall to Par-shon. "I saw what happened to you in Par-shon. I know what you've been through. I only wanted to help."

"Help?" snorted Cora. "Help would have been the kingdoms offering aid rather than attacking centuries ago. Help would have been leaving me to die in Par-shon rather than bringing me here." She raised her chin, a smug smile playing at the corners of her lips. "If you would really help, then you would release me so that I might return to the Sunlands."

"You will have the freedom of this place," Roine said. "But no more than that until I decide what will become of you." To Tan, he said, "She will be your responsibility, your first as Athan."

He took his leave before Tan could reply. Cianna lingered just long enough to shoot Cora one more glare. Fire seethed from her skin, practically leaving her body glowing with heat as she made her way out of the small room.

Tan sighed and closed the door with a shaping of air.

Cora turned back to the hearth and said nothing more.

Chapter 8

Shaping Spirit

TAN TOUCHED AMIA'S FINGERS as they laced through his while she watched Cora. The Incendin shaper sat in the chair near the window, staring out upon Ethea. Her face was blank and she had not spoken since the confrontation with Roine and Cianna the day before. A warm breeze blew in, as it so often did around Tan, especially now that he had bonded to Honl.

"We were right to heal her," Amia said.

Cora's hands were clasped on the table and she twisted her fingers every now and again. It was the only thing that told him she wasn't as mute as when he had first found her. The breakfast he'd set in front of her was uneaten.

"I know that we were," he said. "I only wish that the others would see it the same way."

Roine had not returned. Tan knew that meant nothing in particular.

Roine would often be gone for days at a time, but this felt different. He had expected to hear something by now, if only to send word of what he planned with Cora. This silence felt almost stifling.

"The others think of what they've been through at the hands of Incendin," Amia said.

"You've been through the same."

"Had I known that she comes from Incendin, I don't know that I would have worked as hard to save her. Perhaps it was best that I didn't know. This way, she was given a chance. No one deserves what was done to her."

"You still would have tried to heal her," Tan said.

Conflicting emotions crossed over Amia's face. "Maybe."

"We can use them," Tan said softly. "We will have to if we intend to survive Par-shon."

"Only a few know what Par-shon is capable of doing, Tan, but all have seen what Incendin will do. They have seen the way that they attack, they have seen the city nearly fall, and the way they hurt and kill and twist..." Amia took a deep breath and shook away the tension that had started to fill her. "It's why you're the only one who can do what's needed."

He sighed. "I'm not sure that's even true. I don't even know what's needed. We've healed Cora. The Aeta summoned... someone. The First Mother claims she called them here for safety only, but I no longer know what to believe with her. And we still need to worry about what Incendin might do. In spite of all of that, it's Par-shon I fear."

"As you should."

Tan jumped.

"You are a shaper," Cora said. "You understand what it means to use the power of the elements. But you are also bonded, so you know too what it means to share in that power, to have your elemental burn through you, to *choose* you."

If Tan had any question about what type of elemental Cora had bound to, the way she described the power as burning through her erased it. Which elemental had she bound? Saa was found throughout the kingdoms and he'd sensed it while in Incendin, but the elemental had greater power in Par-shon. Possibly even greater power elsewhere. Tan hadn't seen evidence of inferin or saldam, but that didn't mean they couldn't exist in Incendin. From working with wind, he knew that different lands had different elementals. It was only in places like Ethea, places of convergence, where all the elements came together.

"I know what it was like to have my elementals nearly taken from me. That's why I wanted to help you. Others need to understand. They might not be able to reach the elementals, but they need to understand why the bonds can't be forced." It was no different than what Althem had done when he'd used spirit to force the kingdoms' shapers to do what they would not otherwise have done. They might not understand the elementals, but they could understand that.

Cora frowned. "You said elementals."

"Yes," Tan answered.

"You have bonded more than one?"

"I speak to all elementals," he reminded her.

With a soft summons to Honl, he drew upon the power of the wind elemental ashi. Warm wind gusted through the window, drawn from the south, from the heated lands of Incendin. Ashi were elementals of warmth and sun, drawn to the draasin. Tan was no longer surprised that he would bind to one. Were he ever to bond to an earth elemental, he suspected it would be much the same, tied to fire in some way. Everything about his shaping was tied to fire.

Cora breathed in the air, letting it trail over her face. She shaped wind, pulling on it, and the shaping danced across her skin. "How is it that ashi is here?"

Tan decided against sharing that Ethea was a place of convergence. He needed to convince Cora to trust him, but that didn't mean placing the kingdoms in jeopardy. Sharing every secret he had would do that. "It is my bond," he said simply.

"But you are of the kingdoms. You should bond ara."

Tan shrugged. "I may be of the kingdoms, but I've bound ashi."

Cora released her shaping and looked back out the window, again falling silent.

When she said nothing more, Amia touched his hand. "She needs time. Most of us do, Tan." She caught his eye. "Yes, myself included. What you suggest… it is difficult to move beyond what has happened in the past. Even Roine finds it difficult to understand, and he's faced Par-shon."

"We don't have time," Tan said. That was the problem. "And somehow, we have to find a way to use Incendin against Par-shon." He said the last softly, quiet enough that only Amia could hear. With a shake to clear his thoughts, he rose to his feet. "I need to walk. Can you stay with her?"

Amia smiled tightly, understanding the request he didn't make. Should Cora attempt to shape and overpower her, Amia would need to separate her from her shaping ability, much like the First Mother had once separated Tan.

"You restored me. I will not harm her," Cora said without looking back at him.

He considered telling Cora that Amia was probably too strong for her to harm. After watching her work with the First Mother the last few days, he'd seen the way her spirit shaping had grown. He doubted that there was another shaper who would be able to overpower Amia were she to attempt to confine them. "Thank you," he said.

Tan left Amia sitting with Cora, neither speaking.

He hurried from the small house and out to the street. The day had grown long, the sun already well past its zenith and starting down again, leaving a slight chill to the air. The people he passed were all dressed in heavier clothes. Some still wore scarves wrapped around their faces, though the smoke and dust from the attack had long since dissipated.

Pausing at an intersection, he surveyed the street. The homes here had not been damaged in the attack, not from the draasin or by the lisincend coming into the city. That didn't mean there weren't signs that the city had changed. Even here, workers replaced wooden framed buildings with stone, working by hand rather than shaping it into place as happened elsewhere. Most felt stone would have withstood the attack better. Tan doubted it would have made much of a difference. Had Enya chosen, she could simply have melted stone. Only the golud-infused stone would have survived.

What would it take to convince the others to look beyond Incendin? Roine may have placed a title upon him, but that didn't mean the other shapers would suddenly look to him for guidance. He was too new, too young, and he suspected there were some—perhaps even his mother—who distrusted him because of his bond to the draasin. Few knew how he had nearly transformed into one of the lisincend, but had they known, that would give them even more reason to distrust him.

Yet he needed to try. How could he manage to convince them if even those closest to him—his friends as well as the one he loved—weren't certain that what he suggested was right? Worse, if they learned that he housed the draasin, the creatures that had once attacked the city, in the tunnels *beneath* the city, he might lose any credibility he had.

Tan let out a frustrated sigh.

And then there was what he had sensed when the shaping had gone awry. There hadn't been the time to try and see what had happened to Elle since then. What if Elle really was in danger? He had sensed her, that much he felt certain about, but his mother hadn't been able to reach Doma to know if she was safe. Didn't Tan owe it to her to learn? She was more than simply his friend. She was family, and he'd lost enough family already.

That, more than anything, decided for him what he needed to do next.

He made his way to the archives and quickly reached the lower level and the tunnels. He wanted to be in a place of safety were the shaping to get away from him again. With Amia needing to watch Cora, there was only one place he could think of that would provide what he needed.

When he stopped at the massive door and pressed a shaping of fire and spirit onto the rune, he waited for Asboel before entering. The draasin had been hunting before but had returned. Had Asboel known that Tan would need him? Did the bond grant him that strong of a connection to understand what his bond pair required of him? Or had Asboel simply planned his return?

Can it not be both? Asboel asked as the door came open. Bright golden eyes stared out into the tunnels, the weight of his gaze taking in Tan and seeming to pass judgment.

Will you do this? Tan asked him.

You were reckless. I felt the effect of your shaping. It is good that you can draw upon the others for strength.

Tan entered the draasin den, the door closing behind him on a shaping of wind. He glanced around, noting that as before, the other draasin were not visible. *Do they fear me?*

Not you, Maelen. Sashari prefers they rest. Besides, I would not want you tempted to name them.

Asboel kept something from him, but Tan opted not to pressure him. Likely the request for the draasin to bond still troubled him. Tan still wasn't certain whether it was the right thing for the draasin to do, but it offered protections to them that they wouldn't have otherwise. Asboel should know how valuable that protection could be.

The draasin made a strange sound, something between a bark and rumbling roar. It took Tan a moment to realize that Asboel was laughing.

You are right about the value in bond, Maelen. It is no longer me you must convince.

Sashari?

Enya as well. She remains distant. Tan sensed the concern within Asboel. *Sashari might be the easiest. She has seen from you strength and sacrifice. You are much like the draasin in that.*

Tan smiled at the compliment. *You know why I've come?*

Not clearly. Only that you fear for the Child of Water.

I sensed that she was in danger. I need to help her if she is.

She has Water to help.

What if Water has been taken from her?

Then she was forsaken. It is not for you to fear.

Tan couldn't accept that as an answer. *She is family.*

That was a concept the draasin knew about quite well. Family was important to Asboel, the bond between he and Sashari much like what Tan shared with Amia. And then there was Enya. Tan had seen what Asboel had been willing to risk to save her. Not only allowing the bond but stopping her when she withdrew fire, risking himself to save her. Asboel rarely spoke of the importance of his family, but everything he did was to protect them. After a thousand years frozen in a lake, Tan could understand.

Will you help? Tan could think of no place safer than with his draasin companion.

You are always safe with draasin, Maelen.

Asboel crawled to the back of the den, his massive body curling around in front of the pile of stacked rock, and settled down, wrapping his tail around him as he did. He lowered his head to his forelegs and watched Tan.

Tan moved to the center of the den and unsheathed the sword, resting the point into the stone. He thought about what he had done, the way he had shaped through the sword the last time. This sword was different from the others, probably the reason why he was drawn to it as he was. The runes glowed with soft light that came from within the sword itself.

With a shaping of spirit, he pressed out through it.

The runes on this sword did more than augment his power, they helped him link all the elements, bind them with spirit more easily.

He sent the shaping wide, letting it spread away from him. It washed out through the archives, skimming over the draasin so that he was left with a vague awareness of them. The shaping went out from there, stretching to the streets above, sliding over people in homes or making their way along the streets. With it, Tan had a sense of their hearts, of their thoughts. It was indistinct, but there, and easy for him to touch. Fear simmered near the surface of many, and it did not take much strength to recognize the source of the fear. Memories of the last attack were too fresh and raw. It was this fear that told him that reaching an alliance with Incendin would be difficult, if not impossible.

Tan passed a soothing sense through the city, easing the fears and anxiety of those living within with nothing more than the barest touch. The First Mother had taught him this shaping, though he had not known it at the time. It was the way she shaped her people.

The shaping faltered. Tan pulled on more spirit, dragging it through the sword. He pulled on the elementals around him for strength: Asboel, Honl, the nymid and golud in the walls, letting spirit bubble from him.

The shaping raced throughout Ethea. Tan felt shapers and people. Awareness filtered through him. There was Zephra and Roine. He sensed Cianna and Vel. Amia was there, as she always was, but with spirit shaped as he did, she pulsed brightly within his mind. She seemed to recognize what he did and fed her strength through the bond between them.

It still was not enough.

How had he detected Elle before? Not simply by shaping spirit. What he had done had been more than spirit. It had involved each of the elements, forging them together as he drew through the sword for strength.

Tan added fire and wind to the shaping, drawing both upon himself and his bonded elementals. The nymid aided his water shaping. Golud helped with earth shaping. He bound these together, pressing the shaping through the sword, mixing spirit with it.

The shaping was powerful, more powerful than any he had ever worked unaided by the artifact. With it, he felt that he touched—if only barely—on the power of the Great Mother. The sword flared with blinding white light, filling the den. Tan understood now why Asboel had blocked the entrance to the other part of the den.

Spirit flowed from him.

It washed over the kingdoms and beyond. The shaping moved past the borders, giving Tan awareness of the scar left behind by the barrier's fall. It weakened as it moved through Incendin, leaving him with a sense of the people there, but nothing more. Like the people within the kingdoms, they were frightened. The shaping passed out of Incendin and into Doma.

There, distantly, he heard someone calling his name.

Elle, he answered.

He sent her name on the shaping, letting it move beyond through the distance, travel beyond what he would normally be able to send to her.

If she was in Doma, he would reach her even if Zephra could not.

Tan. There was a sense of relief in her voice. *I thought it was you but you disappeared. Be careful if you come to help… danger.*

He missed part of what she said. The connection was thready now, and growing weaker as his shaping failed. *Par-shon?*

They have come to Doma.

The sense of Elle faded for a moment. Tan pulled harder on the shaping, using the strength he had remaining.

It burns, Tan. Falsheim…

The runes glowing on the sword blinked out. Tan stumbled to the stone, but Asboel was there, catching him with a curl of his tail and lowering him to the ground.

Rest, Maelen.

His voice seemed to come from far away.

She's in danger, he managed to say.

The hunt will come when you recover. You were the one who taught me that.

Tan took a slow breath and felt himself beginning to relax. His strength began to return, more slowly than usual. He realized that he had drawn too much upon the elementals. A shaping like that risked weakening them and he needed to be careful with these shapings or he would endanger them more than even Par-shon could.

CHAPTER 9

A Mother's Passing

WHEN TAN AWOKE, Amia was crouching next to him. He sat up with a jolt and realized that he still rested in the darkened draasin den. His head throbbed and his body ached, muscles twitching almost as if he had finished running a great distance. He looked over to see Asboel blocking the door.

"How are you here?" he asked Amia.

The door should not have opened to anyone other than a shaper of fire and spirit. It was part of the reason Tan thought the room safe for Asboel, but if Amia could enter with nothing more than spirit shaping, he might have been wrong.

She touched his head and a shaping passed through him. "You're unharmed."

"It was my shaping," he said. "There wasn't anyone attacking me."

"That was dangerous, Tan," she admonished.

He sat up and crossed his legs. The sword rested on the ground, runes once more glowing softly. Since claiming the sword from the lower level of the archives, he had passed out twice using it. Maybe he'd chosen poorly.

It is the shaper, not the tool.

Asboel made the soft chuckling sound deep in his throat. Amia turned and smiled.

You sent for her?

At least he knew that the den remained safe.

I sensed her concern.

Through the bond?

Asboel snorted. *It has changed since the attack. It is stronger.*

Because we chose the bond?

We must always choose the bond. I think there must be another reason.

Tan shifted his focus to Amia. "I had to know about Elle. And I found her."

Amia nodded. "I heard."

"Then you know she's in Doma. You know that Par-shon has attacked."

Amia hesitated, the hand on his arm tensing for a moment. "I know that she said it was dangerous in Doma, Tan, but I'm not sure she was talking about Par-shon."

He looked to Asboel but the draasin could not help, not in this. "What do you think she was talking about, then? You don't think she's in danger?"

Amia shook her head. "That's not it at all. I know what we were able to hear. She said that it was dangerous in Doma, but then she said Falsheim burns. That doesn't sound like what Par-shon has done. They stole your bonds. The burning of cities is what Incendin does."

"Why would Incendin attack Doma? They have too much to worry about with Par-shon—"

"We know what Incendin wants with Doma. They want Doman shapers. They want to have the strength they'll need when they're attacked."

He couldn't shake the feeling that it wasn't Incendin, but rather that it was Par-shon, and if Par-shon had crossed the sea and began to attack Doma, they were closer to attacking the kingdoms than anyone knew, but he wasn't confident in his belief. He had to understand.

"It doesn't change the fact that she needs help," he said.

"All of Doma needs help if Incendin has attacked, not just Elle," Amia said.

"And we'll get them the help they need," Tan said. "But I need to reach her first."

He stood and started toward the door. Asboel eyed him for a moment, steam easing from his nostrils in a slow hiss. Tan felt the draasin moving within his mind, as if trying to determine his thoughts. *This hunt could be dangerous. If it is Par-shon, you cannot be there. If it is Incendin, then I will call for your help.*

I will leave the hunt to you for now, Maelen.

Asboel moved away from the door and Tan stepped through, back into the tunnels. Amia followed, trailing slightly behind him, staying silent.

"What happened with Cora?" Tan asked.

"When Asboel sent word for help, I asked another to stand guard for me."

"Roine?"

Amia shook her head but didn't answer.

They sealed the door leading to the lower level archives closed before Tan led them out, back to the house holding Cora. If Incendin attacked Doma, she might be able to provide an explanation as to why.

When they reached the house, the chairs near the hearth were empty, as were the chairs by the table. For a moment, he thought Cora had left, then he found her crouching in the corner, eyes focused on the fallen form of the First Mother.

"That's who you asked to stand guard?" Tan asked.

"She would not allow her to leave," Amia said.

"Then what's happening here?" he asked Cora.

The Incendin shaper looked up from the First Mother and met his eyes. "She is gone."

"Gone?" Amia said, rushing past Tan and touching the First Mother's neck. A shaping built, washing over her. Tan didn't need to be the one shaping it to know that the First Mother was dead.

"What happened to her?" he asked Cora.

She stared down at the First Mother. "I don't know. We were speaking of shaping. I had thanked her for what she did to heal me. And then her eyes went wide and she collapsed."

"I can't tell," Amia said.

Tan studied Cora. He didn't think that she would have attacked the First Mother, but what did they really know about her? She was an Incendin shaper, and a warrior shaper, able to shape each of the elements. Had she tried overpowering the First Mother to escape?

But if that were the case, why had she remained when the First Mother was gone?

Tan knelt next to the First Mother's body and pulled on a soft shaping of water and spirit. This washed over her, and he sensed the weakness within her, the same weakness he'd seen in her eyes and the slow way she had moved toward the end. It had been her time.

Tan thought of all that the First Mother had taught him since imprisoned. Not only runes, but parts of history, of shaping. Her knowledge was vast and great, more than he fully understood. "I'm sorry," Tan said to Amia.

Tears glistened in her eyes. She had lost so much of her people. First her family, then what she knew of the Aeta. Now, when she was finally learning from the First Mother, to have that taken from her seemed a cruel twist of fate.

"Who will lead?" she whispered. "There was a part of me that always thought we would eventually release her and allow her to lead the People. Now that she's gone, who will that be?"

Tan didn't know how to answer. Maybe there wasn't an answer. "Another will come forward," he said. "The People have survived for hundreds of years. They will survive this."

"She knew this was coming," Amia whispered.

It made a certain sort of sense. It would explain why the First Mother had called for a Gathering. Had she not been failing, she would have expected to eventually be freed, allowed to lead the People. Now she would not be there to choose her successor.

Amia stared at the First Mother. "She deserves to be mourned by the People. They deserve to know she is gone."

"Are you certain they don't already?" he asked.

"It depends on her last sending. She shielded me from them."

"Because you are no longer Aeta?" he asked. It sounded harsh, even to him, but it was the choice that she had made.

Amia nodded. "I am not," she agreed, "but I will ensure the People have her to mourn."

"And I need to go to Elle," Tan said. He should be here for Amia, but he couldn't leave Elle, not if she needed help. He wasn't sure he would be able to reach Falsheim safely, but for Elle, he had to try.

"You need to go," Amia urged. "But you need to be safe. You will take him?" she asked, implying Asboel.

"It's too dangerous. If Par-shon has attacked—"

"It was not Par-shon."

"And you heard what Elle said," Tan reminded.

Cora stood and cleared her throat. Cora looked from Tan to Amia, waiting for one of them to speak. "Where has Par-shon attacked?"

"Doma," Tan said.

Cora sniffed. "Doma means nothing to Par-shon. There are few shapers there, and those who remain can no longer speak to water."

"There is one who can," Tan said.

Cora studied Amia, tapping her lips as she did. "She doesn't believe it was Par-shon."

"No. She thinks Incendin attacked, as they have attacked many times before. Many shapers have been dragged away from Doma, forced to serve Incendin."

Cora tipped her head as she considered Tan. "Is that what you believe, warrior?"

"I have seen Doma attacked by Incendin. I know what I've been told by those who lived it. And I know what the First Mother did to provide safety for the Aeta."

"The Sunlands needed protection," she said, as if that was enough to explain what Incendin had done in the name of providing its protection.

Tan pressed his lips together to fight the urge to say something about the type of protection that Incendin had used, the way they had stolen from Doma the ability to keep their people safe.

Amia touched his arm, soothing him with a spirit shaping. "She said Falsheim burns, Tan. *Burns*. That is the work of Incendin."

"I will go to see. That's all," he said. "Then I will return and get help."

"Your mother said the crossing was too dangerous," Amia reminded him.

"For a wind shaper, but I do not intend to travel by wind," he said.

She stepped toward him and slipped her arms around him. "Please…" she started, then shook her head, and pressed her lips together. "Just be safe," she said.

"Can you watch her?" Tan asked Amia, motioning toward Cora. "I will send a summons to Roine. He can have another take over, but I don't want to be here when they come, especially if it's my mother."

Amia stared at the body of the First Mother. "I will stay until another comes."

"You could take me with you," Cora suggested.

"Not if Incendin has attacked," Amia snapped.

Cora looked at her with a quizzical expression. "What you describe is not the Sunlands I know. Let me come. Perhaps I can help broker peace."

"Or harm Tan and escape."

"I owe him a life debt. He has little to fear from me. But you may bind me, if you will. You are strong enough in spirit to see it done. And I've felt his strength with shaping. He will be safe."

Taking Cora would avoid the need to explain to Roine what he did. If he was only gone for a little while—long enough to determine what was happening in Doma and to see if he could find Elle—there would be no reason Roine would need to know.

He hated that he was beginning to keep secrets. First the draasin beneath the city, and now this. Where would it end?

Amia watched Tan. "Are you certain you should do this?" she asked.

"Not at all," he answered. "But I don't know what else to do."

She turned to Cora and performed a massive shaping of spirit. Tan sensed the way she wrapped Cora's mind, binding it so that she was restricted from shaping. When she was done, she pressed the connection to the shaping through their bond, giving control to him.

Be safe, she said.

He leaned toward her and kissed her on the cheek. *I will not be gone long.*

Bring Elle back with you if you can.

That is my intent.

Promise me that if Incendin attacks, you will not hesitate to do what is needed.

Tan considered this request the longest. *I will do what is needed,* he answered.

Somehow, he would find a way to use Incendin. If only he could figure out how.

Chapter 10

Doma

IN THE UNIVERSITY COURTYARD, darkness surrounded Tan and matched his heavy heart. The sudden loss of the First Mother left him feeling uneasy about leaving the kingdoms without knowing what happened, but the memory of Elle and the fear he'd heard in her voice drew him away. He needed to help her. With his abilities, he should be able to reach her quickly and then return.

Cora stood next to him. "What happened here?"

"First, the draasin. The archivists were spirit shapers who twisted a shaping placed on the draasin, preventing them from hunting man, and forced one to attack the city. The second attack was when King Althem—also a spirit shaper—allowed the lisincend to enter the city."

"That," Cora began, staring at the university again, moved back a step slightly, "is a lot to take in."

Tan nodded. "Imagine living through it."

"The draasin are shaped to not hunt man?"

"Were. The shaping has been lifted. It placed them at risk."

"You weren't worried about those living in the kingdoms?"

He frowned, surprised by her line of questioning. "They are elementals. They're not meant to be controlled."

"What of the bond?"

"You were bonded. Do you really think the bond was meant to control the elementals? It's a path to understanding, to knowledge. Which is why what Par-shon does bastardizes the connection the Great Mother gives. No one deserves that, not even Incendin."

Cora rubbed a hand along her jaw. "You have seen what the lisincend will do to your city and still you would say this?"

Tan sighed. "I've been consumed by fire, very nearly transformed, so I understand the power burning through the lisincend, the primal urge to release fire. They are dangerous, but it's because they have no control. They allow fire to rule. I understand what happened to them, but do not have to agree with it."

Cora stared at him for a moment. "You are a surprising man, Tan."

They stopped in the shaper circle and he readied his travel shapings as he considered where to go. He didn't really know where to find Elle, only that from what she said, she was somewhere in Doma. Traveling with a warrior shaping and adding spirit would not work, but he could leave spirit out of the shaping, use Roine's shaping to travel.

He pulled the elements together, leaving spirit out. As he drew the shaping toward him, he grabbed Cora's arm and held her.

They lifted from the ground, the wind whistling around them. His ears felt hot from the power behind it. There was a sense of earth and water mixed in, making him much more aware of the shaping than when he added spirit. This felt as if he fought the lightning, as if the storm raging around him might overpower him if he weren't careful.

Tan pushed toward Doma. It didn't take long to travel, but not having spirit involved slowed their progress. He felt it as they crossed the mountains of Galen, crossing the remnants of the barrier, before streaking across Incendin. Tan tensed as they passed over Incendin, fearing what Cora might try, only relaxing as they moved into Doma.

Doma here was different. The mountains separating it from Incendin rose up behind him, the dark green of the pines growing along the slopes and making the mountain almost black in the night. Somewhere to the south, the sea crashed with steady waves. Udilm would be there, and somewhere, Elle. Tan lowered them to the ground overlooking the sea.

Cora stepped away from him. "You do not shape that with confidence," she observed.

"I've never made that shaping before."

She shot him a sharp expression. "You risked yourself traveling with a shaping you have never used?"

"Normally I add spirit. It's more precise. But I don't know where I'm going."

"Foolish, still," she said. She shook her head, frowning as she looked around. "I have been to Doma once before. It is… different than the Sunlands. There is so much water all around."

"Yes, and with the water the udilm prevented the lisincend from attacking for as long as they were able," Tan said. "Doma thought udilm abandoned them, that their shapers could no longer speak to the great water elemental, but that was never the case. Par-shon *took* those who could speak to udilm, stole them away for their bond. It made Doma more vulnerable to both Incendin and Par-shon. So when Incendin came for Doma shapers, there was nothing left to stop them."

Cora ran a hand through her hair, and tipped her chin forward. "You understand that this was done and why this was done. I do not hear anger in your voice."

"Anger would not serve anything. Would anger return the Doman shapers Incendin took? Would it bring back those who can speak to the water elementals?"

Tan stretched out with his earth sensing, questing for signs of where they were and looking for anything that would help him reach Elle. The sea was to the south, not far from where they were now, and he heard the steady sound of waves crashing along the shores. Tall grasses grew in wide fields, spreading out all around them. Some seemed intentionally grown, almost as if they were crops placed by farmers. A few trees scattered across the field. Animals scurried along the grasses, and through earth sensing, Tan noted mostly mice, squirrels, and a few small deer. He sensed no people nearby.

He pressed farther out, using earth to reach as far as he could. To this, he added a touch of spirit, enough to give his sensing even more strength. Immediately, he wished he had not.

"Come on," he said.

"Where are we going?" Cora asked.

"There's a village nearby."

Tan started forward on a shaping of air, pulling Cora up onto it with him. He was silent as they traveled, fearing what they would see but knowing what he had sensed. Could Amia have been right? Could this have been Incendin's work?

They crested a small rise with the ground disappearing on the other side. Down below him, he sensed the village. Once, it had been a vibrant village along the seashore, but now it was something else, empty and abandoned. Some of the old inhabitants were still there, but fire had claimed them, charring flesh and stealing life.

"What is it?" she asked.

"Fire destroyed this village," he said.

Cora shook her head. "There would be no purpose in destroying a village like that. Fire would not—"

"My village was destroyed by the lisincend. Did you know that?" he asked. His voice had gone hushed, soft, and carried a dangerous edge. "The lisincend trailed the Aeta, wanting them to aid in the transformation. When they couldn't find the Aeta, they destroyed everything within my village. Nothing remained."

Cora stiffened. "How is it that you survived?"

"I wasn't there at the time. Theondar had taken me from the city while searching for something, otherwise I would have been there and would have died as surely as everyone else." Tan took a deep breath. "So you cannot tell me that fire would not do that to a village. I've seen the destruction the lisincend cause."

Cora pushed past him and started down what looked like it had been the main street. Some of the homes remained intact here, and those near the center had been burned, though the flames didn't reach all the way to the rooftops, as if they had been quenched rapidly. Patches of ground heaved, leaving jagged rock flung through the village.

A battle had taken place here. Had Elle been here during the attack? Had she learned to speak to her elemental well enough to get those she cared about to safety? If she had, what had happened to her in the time since then?

Cora went into one of the homes and ducked back out quickly, one hand over her mouth. Her eyes told him everything that he needed to know.

"Are there any survivors?" she asked.

He stretched out with an earth sensing mixed with spirit. Through the connection, Tan could tell that none lived. "None that I can tell."

"The dead deserve their final resting. Do you know if Doma buries their dead?" he asked.

"Some bury, some send them out to sea," Cora said.

He looked toward the water's edge. The distance was probably too far for him to ask the sea to move inland to do the work, but he might be able to shape earth. Sand and wind would cover the village more than he ever could.

Tan made his way to the rise overlooking the village. He reached out through the earth, starting with sensing, using the knowledge that his father had long ago taught him. There was a stirring there, deep beneath him. It was like golud, only different. Tan knew little about any of the earth elementals but could recognize when one was present. With a rolling request, he sent word to the earth, asking for the sand to swallow what remained of the village, to do what eventually would be done in time with more urgency. To the earth shaping, he added wind, letting ashi swirl around, sending sand toward the village in an unrelenting sheet. Between the two, the village was hidden, disappearing beneath a massive dune of sand.

No fire was used. With what had happened here, Tan would not use fire against them even though it was the easiest elemental for him to reach.

"You waste your energy on such a shaping?" Cora asked.

Tan stared at the dune. Lumps of sand revealed the peaks of houses beneath, but the dead within would have their peace. "I waste nothing," he said.

"Your energy is finite. All shapers have limits."

"I draw on the power of the elementals around me," he said. "They aid nearly all of my shapings."

"That was golud?"

"Probably not golud, but earth nonetheless. And ashi helped as well. So don't worry. I will not weaken myself too much before we can reach safety." Tan stared at the remains of the village. "Besides, giving those people the peace they have earned is not wasteful. The only thing that would be wasteful would be had they died for no reason. I will see to it that is not the case."

He stepped away from Cora and sent a shaping into his sword, using it to call to Elle.

Elle. I have come to help.

Then he waited. She would be here, somewhere, if only he could find her. Now that he was in Doma, he should not have to reach quite as hard to speak to her. Distance mattered with a shaping like this, especially when it was to someone he did not share a bond with. Amia was there, deep within his mind, but he would have to strain to speak to her. It was the same with Asboel, though the fire elemental had more strength speaking through the bond, and Tan had practiced reaching him even from great distances. But Elle and he were not bonded. They shared the ability to speak to elementals, and they were family, but there was nothing quite like the connection he shared with even Honl.

When she didn't answer, he tried again. *Elle!*

Tan waited for an answer, but there was none.

Much of the night passed with him sitting atop the rocky shoreline, staring out at the sea as he continued to attempt reaching Elle. Cora rested nearby, keeping quiet for the most part. Now she slept soundly, her steady and rhythmic breathing mixing with the crashing waves along the rocks beneath him.

He didn't know what to make of the fact that Elle hadn't answered. Maybe it was nothing. She could be sleeping or simply unable to hear him, but he had the feeling that something blocked their communication. Par-shon knew some secret of using runes to prevent shaping and communicating with bonds, so if she *had* been abducted by Par-shon, then it was possible that she couldn't reach him. But why now? Earlier, she had spoken to him, why had Par-shon only now blocked her reaching him?

The other possibility was equally dire for her. What if Amia was right and that she spoke of Incendin shapers? If Incendin attacked—if Incendin were the reason for Falsheim burning—then Elle might have been caught up in it. If so, and if Falsheim burned, he had to prepare for the possibility that she had died with it.

Morning came slowly as he continued to toss through the possibilities of what had happened, never coming up with anything more likely. The sun rose in streaks of orange and red skimming across blue water. Swells peaked with white crested before slamming down on the rocks below, the steady rhythmic washing of the waves rolling over him.

He sat up and breathed out heavily. Cora was already up and letting her legs dangle from the rock as she stared out at the sea. A cool breeze blew in off the water, a mixture of ara and wyln. He recognized the wyln now that he felt it. Honl was there with him, swirling around him, flowing through each breath, but ashi did not blow here.

Cora cleared her throat and looked at him with a pained gaze. "Did you reach her?"

"No."

"Will you return to Ethea now?"

The hard edge that she had worn since awakening from healing had softened the longer they were away from Ethea. Tan thought it possible that had nothing to do with it, that she had struggled with what had happened to her, but couldn't know. Her bond was gone, possibly never to return. When he'd sealed off the injured end of it, there had seemed no way to do it without opening her to other injury. For all he knew, she would never be able to bond to elementals again.

"Not yet," he decided. "She said Falsheim burned. If that's true, then I need to see it."

"And then you'll return."

Tan nodded.

They sat together in general silence, only the sound of the breaking waves between them.

"Tell me about your bond," Tan said. The sun touched the top of the water in the distance, making it appear that even the vast expanse of water burned. It was times like these that he wondered if Asboel were right when he claimed that without fire, there would be no life.

"What is to tell? You know that it is no more."

"I'm sorry that I couldn't do more to save it," he said.

Cora sat straighter, and tipped her head as she studied him. "You actually mean that."

"Yes. Why wouldn't I?"

"You know that I'm from the Sunlands, and I've heard the horrors you blame upon my people, horrors that I cannot deny, yet you still claim that you feel sorry for the fact that my bond is gone."

Tan sighed. "It's my fault that you can't reach your bond anymore. You were injured, and had I not sealed it off, I think you would have died, but that doesn't change the fact that I couldn't fix it."

Cora laughed bitterly. "There were times I wish I would have died." She met his eyes. "This is not one of them, Tan, and you are not to blame for the loss of my bond. That is entirely Par-shon." She rested her hands in her lap, playing with her fingers. "Saldam. You asked about my bond. It was to saldam."

"Can you tell me about saldam?" he asked. Saldam was an elemental of fire, and one that he had not reached. Like so many of the elementals, they remained mysterious to him.

She chuckled. "You are bound to the draasin and you would ask about saldam?"

"I have learned that each elemental has different power. I've seen saa draw incredible strength. I've asked ashi to overpower ara. So I know that there is something to saldam."

She paused, lips pursed in thought. "Saldam is different than saa," she said at length. "It is not drawn to fire in the same way. It must be called."

"What does it look like?"

"Look? There is no way to describe it, really. They are a part of the world, but different from it. They are fire." She stared out at the sea and fell silent again.

"What happened to you? How did you come to be captured by Par-shon?"

Cora's answer came slowly, and she spoke softly at first. "I am much like your warriors, so I was chosen. It was an honor I could not refuse. Answers, scouting. That was all it was to be. When I traveled across the sea, Par-shon waited for me. They captured me and brought me to a room where they claimed I would die. When I did not, I was brought somewhere else. After that…" She trailed off, a distant look coming to her eyes. "I remember little after that. Pain. Awful and all-consuming pain. And then nothing until I awoke to see you passed out on the ground. And you were not of Par-shon."

"No. I am not of Par-shon."

"You haven't told me how it is that you escaped."

Tan thought back to what it was like when he was trapped in the place of separation. There had been a moment when he thought that he might die, when he thought that shaping would be stolen from him forever. Had he not learned how to reach for spirit, he might still be trapped there. And Asboel would be lost, Honl would be lost. Possibly even Amia.

"Spirit," he said. "The Utu Tonah did not plan for spirit. I was able to shape it, to press through the runes he placed on the walls all around the obsidian tower blocking my shaping, and destroy them. I think that it's because there's no elemental for spirit that he failed."

Cora arched a brow at him. "Are you so certain?"

"I've summoned spirit, but it's different than the elementals."

Her eyes widened slightly. "Yet there are those who shape spirit more strongly than others. Shapers like your woman. It seems to me the Great Mother created elementals of spirit in her own image."

Tan smiled but Cora didn't mirror it. He figured she hadn't meant her words as a joke. He could only imagine Amia's reaction if he suggested to her that she was an elemental who was bound to him. What would she say then?

The sun was well above the horizon now, and bright in his eyes. He stood and turned to the east, toward where he thought he remembered seeing Falsheim on the maps he'd studied. "It is time," he said.

"You will shape us the same as last night?"

He nodded.

"Then perhaps I should have remained behind. You have saved me only to bring me to my death."

Tan laughed and prepared the shaping, drawing on fire and wind, pulling strength from the earth, and then lifting them on wind. They streaked across the sky, moving quickly. It was different in the daylight than it had been last night. There was the same sense of movement, the same loud whistling in his ears, the thundering through his bones, but he could see where they were traveling, and moved quickly to the east. Then he saw it rising out of the distance: the walled city of Falsheim.

As Elle had said, the city burned.

CHAPTER 11

As Fire Burns

TAN LOWERED HIMSELF AND CORA to the ground outside of Falsheim, hiding them in a clump of burned trees. The city sat at the edge of the sea, a wide mouth of water seeming to rush toward the city itself, waves visible from overhead as little more than white capped swells. A massive wall rose up and around the city. From where he stood, it appeared as if the wall went all the way around, even across the sea. Buildings rose over the top of the wall, but none quite so high as the palace in Ethea, or the Fire Fortress in Incendin. A flat expanse of land stretched from a nearby river, the ground around it scorched and burned.

The wall itself had been blackened. Patches looked unharmed, but most of the wall had a layer of dark crust. Stone crumbled in places, supported by the surrounding wall to keep the entire thing from collapsing. A line of fire raced along the top of the wall, held there as if by a shaping. Something about the shaping pushed against Tan, as if to hold him out.

"This is not Incendin," Cora said. "The lisincend would not do this."

Tan didn't know. It reminded him more of the attack on Ethea than the attack on his home village of Nor, but both had been done by the lisincend. Why would this be different?

"There are new lisincend. They have wings and their power is twisted differently."

Cora sucked in a breath and her back stiffened.

"You expected something like that," Tan realized.

Cora clasped her hands together as she turned to him. "Shapers have attempted to grow closer to fire for as long as the Sunlands have been in danger." She studied the walls, her gaze skimming along the flames. Tan sensed saa within the flames, but something else as well, an elemental he didn't recognize. "It was from this desire that the lisincend were born. A small faction of the fiercest fire shapers wanted something different. They didn't want to simply embrace fire. They felt Fur and the others did not go far enough. They wished to become fire."

"They attempted a shaping using spirit, sacrificing the shaper to combine their shaping with spirit. It created this new lisincend," Tan said.

Cora let out her breath slowly. "Were they powerful?" She didn't hide the naked eagerness in her voice.

"Very."

"Do you know who was the first?"

Tan could still see the transformation of the fire shaper Alisz if he closed his eyes. He remembered all too well the power of her shaping as she drew it through the artifact, stealing the archivist's blood, his spirit, as she performed the shaping. "Her name was Alisz. There were others, but she was the first."

Cora's eyes tightened and her breathing quickened.

"You knew her, didn't you?"

"I knew her," Cora said softly. "What happened to her?"

Tan watched her reaction as he said the next words. "She attacked the kingdoms. And she made the mistake of making it seem as if she killed the draasin hatchlings. The draasin did not feel remorse when he destroyed her."

"She went too close to fire," Cora said, mostly to herself.

"She was a fool to taunt the elementals," Tan said. "Who was she to you?"

It didn't seem like Cora would answer at first. Then she sighed. "She was my sister."

Sister? And here he had told her about the way the draasin had destroyed her, describing it in more detail than someone who'd lost their sister deserved. What would it have been like for him to hear about how his father died?

"I'm sorry, Cora."

She rubbed her hand over her arm and sniffed. "You have lost those you care about to the Sunlands. Do not pretend you were not pleased to see her go."

Tan stared at the flames burning atop the wall surrounding Falsheim and his memories turned to what had happened in Ethea and Nor. "I won't deny that I shared in the draasin's pleasure of her death. She was dangerous," he said. "Fire burned too brightly within her. But that doesn't mean I can't mourn for you."

"You are a strange man, Tan."

He grunted. That was better than what some considered him. "Why did you say this wasn't Incendin?"

"This is not a shaping of the Sunlands. And we would not attack Falsheim. We've taken shapers from these lands, but that was to aid in our protection. There are few enough shapers born to the Sunlands, and most of fire. To hold Par-shon at bay, we needed other shapers of power. Were Falsheim destroyed, we would lose even that."

"How many warriors were there?"

"I was the last in a generation," Cora said.

Much like with the kingdoms. Even Incendin had experienced a change in their shapers. "Have you learned why?"

She shook her head. "There was one among us who sought that answer." She paused, turning to him. "He was once of the kingdoms as well. I learned much from him."

Tan felt as if his heart stopped for a moment. "Lacertin," he said, his voice catching as he remembered Lacertin's sacrifice, everything that he'd done to protect the kingdoms. All in service of the king who had died long before. He had forgotten to ask whether she knew him, but of course she would have known him.

"You know?"

"He returned to the kingdoms. That was always his plan."

Cora laughed bitterly, a low and harsh sound. "His plan?" she repeated. When Tan nodded, she laughed again. "All that time spent in the Sunlands, all that time he spent isolated in the Fire Fortress, and he worked against us the entire time?" Her voice carried with it an edge of respect.

Tan hadn't had the chance to ask Lacertin much about the time he'd spent in Incendin. He had died too soon. But he believed that Lacertin had loved his king, and he believed that Lacertin had worked on behalf of the kingdoms the entire time. "That's what he said."

"You believe him, even after everything he did?"

"I don't know all that he did, but I believed him," Tan said.

"Believed. That means he… he is gone?"

"Althem was a spirit shaper. Lacertin had served King Ilton as closely as anyone could. When he learned that Althem used his spirit shaping, that he might have been responsible for his father's death, there was nothing that would have stopped him from trying to repair what was done."

"How did he die?"

She spoke in a whisper, and Tan realized that Cora had cared about Lacertin. Knowing that he'd had that effect on someone else, even someone from Incendin, helped him understand Lacertin a little better. He had sacrificed so much on behalf of the kingdoms, more than any.

When Tan took too long to answer, she went on. "It was Alisz, wasn't it?"

He nodded numbly.

"You cared about him?" she asked.

"I didn't know him well," Tan said. "But I know what he went through, the sacrifices he made for the cause he believed so strongly in. He spent twenty years living in…" He trailed off, catching himself before saying something he might regret. Besides, he didn't know what experience Lacertin had living in Incendin. He had known Cora, had trained her, so it was possible that much of it was happy. "Anyway, he was incredibly brave."

"I didn't know him when he first came to the Sunlands, but there are stories of what he had to endure. The Fire Fortress can be a dark place and he was tested—some would say punished—forced to prove that he'd given up his allegiance to your kingdoms." Cora's eyes closed and she shook her head as she spoke. "He never spoke much of that with me. He was patient and particular about how things should be done, and the most skilled shaper I have ever met."

There was something to the way she spoke told Tan that they had been more than close, maybe as close as he and Amia were. "I wish many things could have been different."

Cora opened her eyes. Tears swelled within them. "I worried what he would think of my disappearance, but now I learn that he disappeared from the Sunlands as well." She forced a smile. "It's possible I didn't know him as well as I think I did."

Tan placed a hand on Cora's shoulder and squeezed as reassuringly as he could. "I would like to hear more about him when we're through with this."

She blinked away the tears, took a breath, and drew her back up straight. "I doubt there is much I could teach you, Tan. He did not speak to the elementals as you do."

"Not about that. I would like to know Lacertin. I didn't have the chance when he was alive." He hoped he could convince Roine to sit with him as well. It had taken until Lacertin's death for him to realize that he had the wrong enemy all along.

"Then you will hear of it."

Tan squeezed her shoulder again and then turned to the wall surrounding the city. The fire was important, he suspected, but why? What purpose would it have?

"You said saldam was not drawn to fire like saa?" he asked her.

She had to shake her head at the sudden change in topic. "Not like saa. I know little about saa, only that it comes to fire. It is a weak elemental. Saldam might not be as powerful as the draasin, but it sits above saa and inferin."

"I think you might be surprised. Did you see saa in Par-shon?"

"I had barely any awareness of my time in Par-shon," she said.

"Had you been able, you would have seen that saa is a powerful elemental of fire in those lands. So much so that it helped me escape." There, the power of saa had filled him, lending him strength, much like the elementals had when he had shaped through the sword while trying to find Elle.

"You think they try to call saa?"

"I'm not certain. If it's Par-shon, they have bound most of the elementals. I wonder if they think to summon the draasin using fire."

Cora's mouth tightened as she glanced to the wall and then to the sky. "Or maybe they attempt something different. Maybe they have used fire as a way to draw the draasin's bond to Doma. If they have you, they can separate the bond."

That could be possible, but he sensed nothing like the separation that he'd known while in Par-shon. Whatever they intended in Doma was different.

Honl, he said, calling to the wind.

The wind elemental flittered through the air and coalesced in front of him in the shape of a slender, translucent figure. *Tan. There is fire here. Not draasin fire.*

Can you tell me if there are those who would steal my bonds?

Honl hesitated. Tan waited for him to tell him how dangerous it would be, but Honl did not. He simply made a gesture something like a nod and drifted off, blowing toward the city.

"Do you think the wind will be able to tell us whether it is safe to enter?" Cora asked.

"I don't know. I don't sense anything around us to fear."

"That doesn't mean there's nothing there. There are ways of masking yourself from earth sensing," Cora said.

Tan had done that once before when attempting to hide the draasin from the kingdoms' shapers, using golud for assistance. Obscuring someone from him would require an earth elemental, but then Par-shon bonded earth elementals. If there were shapers here that he missed, they were in more danger than he realized.

Without waiting another moment, Tan shaped a travel shaping, slamming spirit into it. He grabbed Cora and pulled her toward him as he drew it down upon him. The blinding flash of light from his shaping struck with a thunderous explosion, fast enough and strong enough to disturb the earth shaping hiding three shapers along the wall around Falsheim.

As the shaping lifted them, Tan unsheathed his sword and pressed out through a new shaping of fire and spirit through the sword, sending a lancing of white light that split and struck the three shapers atop the wall.

Then Tan and Cora were carried away.

The shaping lowered them to the ground near the village they had buried.

"What was that?" Cora asked.

Tan jerked his head around. He still clutched his sword and held a fire shaping ready to unleash through it if needed. "That was a traveling shaping. Sorry we couldn't do it that way before."

"That was smoother," Cora agreed, "but that's not what I'm asking. Your sword. What did you do to those shapers on the wall?"

"You saw them?"

"Only after you unleashed your lightning. It unsettled whatever obscured them. What did you do to them?"

"I released the bound elementals."

She looked at him strangely. "I would not have expected that from you."

"Why? I've made my feelings about the way the elementals should be treated quite clear."

"Not that. But you killed those shapers."

Tan grunted. It would have been easy to kill them, but he had not. It wouldn't have taken anything more than spirit with enough force and he could simply convince their hearts to stop beating. The shaping would be easy and similar to one that the First Mother had been demonstrating.

"We need to return to Ethea," he said.

"You're not going to rescue your friend?"

"I will rescue her, but I can't do it alone. I came to find out if it was Incendin or Par-shon attacking in Doma. It is clear now that it's Par-shon."

"And you've killed their shapers."

Tan shook his head, waving the sword as he spoke. "I didn't kill them. I released the bond to fire they held."

"You can do that?"

"They aren't shapers, Cora. What they use is stolen power. It was not freely given."

Tan studied the water, listening to the way the waves came rolling in. *Udilm. You will tell Tan if Elle remains safe. Tell her that I will return.*

He sent the request on the waves, not expecting an answer. The udilm were difficult for him to reach and the only time he'd spoken to them had been when he had nearly drowned. But he could hope they would listen. That the udilm would get word to him if Elle was not safe. And since he couldn't reach her with spirit, he hoped they would let her know that he was coming back for her.

After taking another look around Doma, Tan pulled Cora to him and shaped a return to the kingdoms.

CHAPTER 12

Choices and Changes

THE SENSE OF HIS BONDS FLOODED back to him as he arrived in Ethea. Honl was there, weak, but returning after being with him in Doma. Asboel hunted, flying somewhere over the northern part of the kingdoms, remaining out of view as much as possible. And Amia. She would know that he had returned. He sensed that she was frustrated, but could not tell why.

Ferran jumped from the top of the university, and landed with a solid *thud*, the earth cushioning his landing. Tan realized that he still needed to figure out what Par-shon had done that allowed their earth shapers to fly. It was a trick that might be useful. As powerful as Ferran was with earth, he might be able to use it.

"Theondar searches for you," he said, nodding deeply to Tan. It came across as something like a bow. He glanced at Cora, and tipped his head toward her as well.

"Do you know where I can find him?" Tan asked.

"He went with Amia to the palace. The First Mother of the Aeta passed last night."

"Thank you," Tan said to Ferran.

Ferran bowed again and turned back to the university. Tan started toward the street, but hesitated. *Golud. Can you assist with the building here?*

With golud, Tan never knew if the elemental answered, but the ground rumbled slightly, so he took that as assent.

"Why did you not share with him what you knew?" Cora asked.

"In time," Tan said.

They turned onto the street and hurried along it, forced to push through the throng of people making their way through the city. A few horses pulled carts, a sight that hadn't been seen in Ethea in months. Now that the streets were again passable, life began to return to normal. In time, people would forget what had happened here. They might remember the aftermath, the fallen buildings and the vague recollection of the work involved in the cleanup, but they wouldn't remember the terror they felt when the draasin had attacked, the same terror they had felt when the lisincend prowled the streets. To Tan, that was a good thing. No one *needed* to remember those events. Maybe by then, the draasin wouldn't need to hide.

The palace rose up from the center of the city. Walls of white stone contrasted with his memory of the obsidian tower in Par-shon. A wall had once circled the palace, but it had fallen in the attack and Roine had elected not to rebuild it. He said that he would let the next ruler decide if they wanted it in place. The wide courtyard that once had been shaped into existence, marking the four different kingdoms surrounding Ethea, was razed, replaced by freshly planted trees and a wide patch of terraced grass. It was not quite as impressive as what Tan had seen when first visiting, but it felt more a part of the city now.

A large plaque on the lawn marked where Lacertin had died. The five-pointed star, the symbol of the Order of Warriors, marked the top. That was a new addition, and fitting. He pointed it out to Cora, who stood with a bowed head in front of it until Tan was forced to drag her along.

Tan paused at the door to the palace. This was his first visit as Athan. The title hadn't weighed on him before, but then, he hadn't really given much thought to what Roine would expect of him when bestowing the title. Already Tan had violated one of Roine's commands when he brought Cora out of the city. What else would he do?

They found him in the hall, staring at a painting, a deep frown pinching the corners of his mouth. "You are already becoming more like me than I care for," he said and indicated Cora. "You were to keep her within the city."

"Amia placed a shaping on her, restricting her."

"She forced a shaping like that? I thought Amia would not—"

"I requested the barrier," Cora said, interrupting. "If it was the only way your Athan would allow me to accompany him, I accepted it willingly."

Roine studied her with dark eyes, frowning as if working through a puzzle. "You are still restricted?"

"I have no need of shaping," Cora said.

"Then it will remain. When you decide it should be removed, I will ask that Amia remove it. So long as it remains in place, you are free to move about the city."

Tan hadn't expected that reaction. Since assuming the title of king regent, he had changed, harder in some ways, and more decisive in others.

"And you," he said to Tan. "You went after Elle?"

"I didn't find her."

"What did you find? Amia said you sensed her with a powerful shaping, though I didn't need for her to tell me about it."

"You felt it?"

"I think all of the kingdoms felt that shaping. I've never known anything like it. So much power, but *warmth*. I recognized your touch within it, Tannen."

Cora turned sharply to look at him. "I felt that as well but didn't know what it was. That was you?"

"It was how I attempted to reach Elle."

"It was after that shaping touched me that the First Mother died," Cora said.

Roine glanced at Tan.

"It had no purpose other than sensing," Tan protested. He didn't mention the light touch he'd placed on the city, the one that reminded him of the way the First Mother shaped her people. "That wasn't what took the First Mother's life. I think she knew her time was coming to an end. She was old, probably older than any of us realize. I think she held out as long as she could, hoping that she could pass on what she knew to someone. That it ended up being Amia… well, that was what she wanted all along, I think."

"There wasn't any way to heal her?" Roine asked.

"I think she wanted it," Tan repeated. He thought about the way she'd looked at him from the hall the last time he'd seen her. There had been a sense of contentment about her.

"You think she simply ended her own life?" Roine asked.

"I think she chose her moment," Tan said. "She had summoned the Aeta to gather. She had built a renewed relationship with Amia. And she had the opportunity to pass on what she knew."

"There wouldn't have been time for her to pass on everything," Roine said.

"You don't know the shapings they were layering on Cora. I think most of them simply meant to teach. I became lost within an hour, and it went on for days. By the end, Amia was working alone as much as she was working with the First Mother."

"Now that she's gone, we have no way of knowing what the archivists intend," Roine said.

"Not without someone to lead the Aeta," Tan suggested.

"You think Amia would lead them?"

Tan didn't know, not with any certainty. Amia didn't *want* to lead, but she also didn't want the People to be directionless. Most of the families had no idea what the First Mother had done, just as most of the families had no idea about the archivists. They wanted only to protect a secret they thought the Aeta *must* protect, but now it was known that the Aeta had spirit shapers among them. There was no secret to keep.

He felt Amia coming toward the palace. "I don't know if she will lead them," he answered. "But she would be the right person to do so."

When she reached Tan, she wrapped him in a tight embrace. "Where is Elle?"

"Doma, I think. I still don't know."

"And Falsheim?"

"It burns, as she said."

Roine frowned. "So Incendin has taken to attacking Falsheim? That doesn't make any sense."

Cora snorted. "It is what I said."

"Not Incendin," Tan answered. "Par-shon."

Amia released him and stepped back. "You saw them?"

"Not at first. We made it to Falsheim and saw a line of fire along the wall. It wasn't until Cora suggested they might be obscuring themselves from us that I noticed their bonded shapers atop the wall. I freed three elementals from their bonds."

"They will only form new ones," Cora said. "That is the way of Par-shon. They aren't limited the same way that we are. They don't have to wait for their shapers to develop from sensers, to learn control. They have only to force a bond on the shaper and the elemental can be used. It takes time to learn to control it, but they are powerful even when newly bonded."

"Finding the bond will take time," Tan said.

Cora laughed bitterly. When Tan shot her a look, she only shrugged. "You have not fought Par-shon long enough to understand. They have ways of finding the elementals. They can trap them. When that power is trapped, they only need to stamp their bond upon it."

Tan had seen one of the Par-shon traps, or at least something that he suspected was their trap. It had been how they had nearly captured Asboel. Had it not been for Tan's bond to the draasin, he wouldn't have known what they intended. Had Tan not discovered how to shape spirit, Asboel would still be trapped.

"You have seen one."

"Yes, but it was… massive," he said. "It stretched for miles. That kind of trap would be too elaborate to easily replicate."

Cora cocked her head. "Miles? That would not be for any… ahh, they used it for the draasin, didn't they? It would take much strength to confine one of the great elementals. You should see the ships they use and how they filter the water for udilm. It is much the same."

Tan was horrified by the idea of Par-shon sweeping through the sea, as if simply attempting to fish for the udilm. "And what of golud or ara?"

"For golud and earth, they bore into the ground. When they bore deep enough, they insert these long, slender rods bound with their runes. This contains the earth. I have not seen how they confine the wind, but they have enough wind shapers that they have a way."

"If they can simply farm the elementals, why bother separating shapers bound to the elementals? Why risk that?"

"Because they can," Cora said. "And because the risk of leaving even one shaper bound to one of the elementals is too great."

Tan wondered if Roine would argue with what he said next. "Parshon has claimed Doma. They need our help."

"Tan, that is a discussion for another time."

He shook his head. "You think Cora should not hear this?"

Roine pulled Tan down the hall, leaving Cora standing with Amia. "I think you should be careful who you're sharing with, Tan."

Tan glanced back at Cora. With her dark hair and dressed as she was, she could come from anywhere in the kingdoms. "She's no threat. Maybe she was once, if Cianna's reaction to her means anything, but she's certainly not now."

"Only because Amia's bond restrains her."

It was more than that. Tan didn't think that Cora would harm him were the bond removed. There was a part of him that thought she might actually be helpful. What might she know that he could learn? The kingdoms and Incendin had battled for so long, it was easy to forget how similar their people actually were. And she was a warrior. In that, they were more alike than they were different.

"She is from Incendin," Roine said. "I've battled Incendin my entire life, Tan. My *entire* life. Do you really think we've done that over a misunderstanding?" Roine clenched his hands into fists. "There are fundamental differences between us that can't simply be overlooked. A common enemy will not change that."

"You would have us continue to battle Incendin? You would have more shapers lost?"

"I would have *no* shapers lost!" Roine's voice began to rise with his irritation, and his jaw clenched as he worked to lower it. "I allowed you an attempt to save the lisincend. I think you needed to see for yourself that it would fail. But what you're suggesting is entirely different. How many lisincend remain within Incendin? How many hounds? Do you think they would abandon the hunt because they want our help facing Par-shon?"

"Someone leads them—"

"Yes. Their king leads them, but he has offered nothing but broken promises." Farther down the hall, they were nearly to the massive chamber where Tan had once met King Althem. The portraits along the wall were of the more recent kings, and Roine stopped in front of Ilton. "Let me provide you with some context. You were too young to remember, but there was a peace accord once. Ilton managed to convince their king to agree. For nearly one month, it survived. In that month, the shapers along the border tried to overlook the steady attack from Incendin hounds or the regular appearances of their shapers, almost as if testing our responses. Had we not managed to secure the border with the barrier, we might never have had peace. But we did. For nearly twenty years, because Incendin could not enter our lands. That is what Incendin responds to: power and threats. And if we risk our shapers for Doma, we will lose power and we may have fewer threats remaining."

Maybe Roine was right and he didn't know Incendin nearly as well as the king regent did, but he had come to know Cora, if only a little. She had not been lying to him when she spoke of the loss her people had suffered. She had not faked the emotion he'd seen from her when she learned of Lacertin.

"Look at her, Roine. Does she look like one of the lisincend?"

Roine raised his hand before catching himself. "Alisz did not either, but you saw the monster she became."

"The same monster I nearly became," Tan reminded him. "Cora is not unlike you. She's a warrior. She lost her bond. And she knows what it's like to face Par-shon. There are many things we can learn from her."

"Tan, we have enough problems protecting the kingdoms to risk it—"

"She knew Lacertin," Tan said. Once, that would have turned Roine even more against Cora, but his attitude about Lacertin had changed near the end. Even Roine could not argue with the sacrifices that Lacertin had made.

"How?" Roine asked.

That he would ask was the start. "She studied with him. They were more than that, I think, but I didn't think it was my place to ask."

"Does she know what happened to him?"

"I've told her."

"Tan, you have proven yourself to me time and again, so I know better than to fully discount what you have to say, but we face the real risk of dealing with both Incendin *and* Par-shon. We will need everything we can to face them."

Maybe there wasn't a way to get through to Roine, not without showing him what Par-shon could do, but Roine had seen that. He had been there the day Par-shon had attacked; it had been with Roine's assistance that they had survived. Had he *not* come to help, Par-shon might have won.

"I'm not saying we align ourselves with Incendin. Only that we need to *use* them. They have experience facing Par-shon. We can take advantage of that."

Tan looked down the hall to Amia and wondered if it needed to be more than that. She wasn't from the kingdoms originally. She owed nothing. What she did, she did on behalf of Tan, wanting *him* to be safe, to be happy. Yet she had helped the kingdoms as much as any shaper since he had met her. If not for her, Incendin might have the artifact.

Now, when he looked at Cora, he saw another outsider, another person with a unique perspective, but one who understood the dangers they faced in Par-shon. She was a survivor. If they could move beyond the fear of Incendin, they could learn so much from each other.

"Doma is the first to fall on this continent," Tan said, "but Doma won't be the last. Once Par-shon reaches Incendin, they will only be a border away. We need to do whatever we can to protect ourselves from them."

Roine clasped Tan on the shoulder. "The kingdoms has survived for over a thousand years. We will weather this as well." He took a deep breath, glancing past Tan. "And Incendin moves again. For now, let them attack Par-shon. Let them bloody and weaken themselves. We can grow stronger, set our barrier. We can have the time we need."

"How do you know that Incendin is moving?"

Roine's mouth tightened. "You're not the only shaper who doesn't listen to me."

"Mother?"

Roine nodded slowly. "Zephra has shown that Incendin readies for attack. Because of that, *we* need to be ready. Now. Know that we will do everything we can—and *I* will do all that I can—to keep the kingdoms safe, but we can't sacrifice our ideals to do so."

With that, Roine gave Tan a firm nod and took his leave.

Tan wasn't certain what ideals the kingdoms valued. He didn't know what they risked. From what he'd seen, the kingdoms had committed many of the same atrocities as both Incendin and Par-shon. The archives contained records of these events, records detailing how the elementals had once been forced to serve, much like what Par-shon did now. They may have used a different term, but did harnessing make it any better than the forced bonding that Par-shon did?

Tan sensed Amia waiting for him as she waited with Cora. He

didn't know what he needed to do, only that if he were to serve the kingdoms—if he were to be the Athan that Roine had bestowed upon him—he might be forced to act in ways that went against the king regent.

The change he knew would be needed for them to survive would be hard, but it had to start somewhere. He thought of all the changes he had gone through since leaving Nor, how different he was from the naïve boy who had left his village with the intent to lead the king's Athan through the mountain passes. Each choice had seemed so small at the time, but looking back, he recognized how significant each one was. Now he was a warrior, able to shape all of the elements, able to speak to the elementals, and a rider of draasin. Now he was the Athan. But each step had taken change. Each one was only a small change, but it led to such a great effect.

Tan considered the door Roine had vanished behind. What changes would the king regent have to make? And the other shapers, could they change as well? What changes would Tan still have to undergo? Even were he to want to avoid them, could the kingdoms afford it?

CHAPTER 13

A New Bond

THE AIR AROUND TAN WAS HOT and dry, burning with the elemental power of the draasin. Asboel streaked through the air with his powerful wings pumping, his breath steaming out from him in great gusts. Tan focused on what Asboel could see beneath him, the steadily changing landscape now becoming increasingly barren.

"We're going to cross into Incendin soon," he said to Cianna, who rode behind him.

Tan suspected Asboel knew his reason for bringing Cianna with him, more than simply for her to meet the draasin. For them to survive Par-shon, they would need to have strength equal to Par-shon. That meant shapers augmented by the power of the elementals. Everything he'd learned searching through the archives had told him that shapers had once bound to the elementals, though some had been harnessed rather than given freely.

"You shouldn't have brought me," Cianna said.

Tan twisted to see a wide smile on her face.

"I might be tempted to take the bond from you myself."

"I doubt he'd allow it, but you could try," Tan suggested.

Cianna laughed. Her flaming hair was wild in the wind and she seemed not to care. The longer they flew, the more comfortable she became, to the point where she no longer even held onto Asboel's spikes, clinging to his back with only her knees, riding him much like a skilled equestrian.

Perhaps I should have chosen her, Asboel sent as they crossed the remains of the barrier.

Tan felt the barrier as a soft tingle across his skin. Each time he passed over, he had felt its lingering effects wane further. Now, for the first time, he noted that it was stronger than it had been. Roine was rebuilding the barrier.

You would have her assume the bond?

She is bold.

Tan had already seen Asboel's approval of her shaping ability and now sensed a new appreciation. It was this reason that he'd chosen Cianna for what he intended. *And Sashari? Does she approve?*

Asboel looked up to Sashari as she soared high overhead. The female draasin was smaller than Asboel, but quicker and nearly as powerful. Tan had not seen her in battle, but the fierce way she protected the hatchlings made him suspect that she would be as formidable as Asboel. Had the draasin bonded a thousand years ago, the ancient shapers might have better understood them rather than feared them.

Understanding does not eliminate fear, Maelen. Sometimes understanding only furthers fear, provides justification for it.

Small steps, Asboel. We must begin with one. Then another. In time, we can reach the rest.

Cianna yelled with delight behind him as Asboel banked, twisting back toward the kingdoms. They wouldn't push too far into Incendin until they knew more about what the movement of within Incendin his mother had seen meant. As much as Tan wanted to investigate Incendin himself, he would honor Roine's request for now and remain within the kingdoms while trying to figure out how he could help Elle.

He still had not reached her again, and this in spite of trying twice more. Neither time had produced anything resembling the flare of connection he'd achieved when he first managed to reach her. Tan didn't know what it meant. Possibly nothing. But what if Par-shon had captured her? What if she had bonded and they were separating her from it?

Tan felt Cianna move and looked back to see her standing on Asboel's back. She had her arms outstretched and a look of joy spread on her face.

"What are you doing?" He had to yell over the wind.

Cianna only laughed. "If I fall, it will be worth it. I never thought to ever see one of the draasin and here I am standing atop his back, *flying*!"

Tan pulled her back down so that she settled between the spikes again. "Now you're sitting."

She only laughed at him.

She is fearless, Asboel noted.

She's having fun, Tan said. *But there are other ways to express it.*

Asboel snorted and sent flame shooting from his mouth. They arced in a wide circle. As they did, a massive shadow drifted toward them. Tan looked up to see Sashari dropping quickly before spreading her wings and catching the wind, slowing as she did.

Sashari would allow her to ride, Asboel said.

Tan sensed that if Cianna didn't take this opportunity, it would be lost. "You're to switch to the other draasin," he told her.

"He's offended by my presence?"

"I don't think so. Impressed is more accurate. But she's jealous she has no rider."

Cianna grinned at him. "How do you expect me to reach her?"

"Jump."

Cianna stood and faced Sashari as the other draasin dropped below Asboel. With barely a hesitation, she jumped, pressing with a shaping of fire to guide her over to Sashari, landing smoothly atop her back. Cianna settled in and Sashari soared, climbing in the air with a powerful beating of her massive wings.

You chose well, Maelen.

Was it that transparent?

I know you. I know what you would ask of the draasin.

They soared above the forested mountains of Galen. Somewhere below them was the lake where Tan had once freed Asboel. Now that place of convergence had been abandoned, but the memory of the draasin was still there.

I don't know that it will even work. Not all are able to speak to the elementals.

All have the capacity to know the Mother. That is all that is required.

You think any can learn spirit?

Asboel flicked his tail, a gesture Tan had come to know as a sense of frustration. *Not spirit. The Mother is not spirit any more than the draasin are fire.*

Tan wondered what that meant as they flew over Sashari. She seemed intent on either dumping Cianna from her back or impressing her; she banked and swooped, each time in ever-impressive tricks. Every time Tan saw Cianna's face, the smile had spread.

You once told me that the draasin are fire.

The draasin are fire and are not. Much like the Mother is spirit and is not.

You're confusing me, Tan said.

Only because you don't have the capacity to understand. At least you recognize your ignorance.

Tan considered what Asboel told him as they started back toward Ethea. Asboel would leave them outside the city, trusting Tan to return them the rest of the way. He still hadn't learned how the draasin got into the tunnels beneath the city. If he truly wanted to know, Asboel would likely share, but for now it didn't matter.

Will it work? he asked Asboel.

The massive draasin started their descent. He let them coast, wings tilted in such a way that the wind buffeted off it, bringing him to the ground with speed and control. Claws gripped the ground as they landed.

It will depend upon Sashari. She was willing to meet. That was a start, I think.

There may not be time for delay. The risk is great for all if we don't begin to reforge the bonds that were lost.

You will not stop with the draasin, Asboel noted.

To save the elementals, I don't think I can. Tan thought about his ability, about how he possessed gifts so rare, they might never have been seen before. There was a reason the Great Mother had given them to him. *This is my purpose, Asboel. This is the service the Mother demands of me.*

Asboel said nothing for a while. Then, *You have earned our trust, Maelen. I will tell her what you said.*

The landing was in a rocky overlook to the west of the city. The air was still and cool, carrying a hint of rain. A few scrub trees grew along the rocks, but nothing else. Ethea could be seen, but it was distant, far enough that those living within the city wouldn't fear the sight of the draasin soaring overhead. Eventually, the rest of the city would come around to the idea that the draasin were not the enemy, but Tan knew it would take time.

Asboel tilted his head back, watching as Sashari landed next to him. She was nearly as long as Asboel, but leaner and sleeker. Where he had a thickened scaly hide so red it was nearly black, she had streaks of gold and bright red mixed along her flanks. Much like Asboel, massive spikes protruded around her back and neck. Her tail had barbs, though they were not as pronounced.

Cianna jumped from Sashari and bowed to the massive draasin, making a point of maintaining eye contact as she did. Sashari snorted, smoke billowing from her nostrils, and then she leapt to the sky in a quick fluttering of wings.

Hunt well, Asboel, Tan said.

Always, Maelen.

Asboel lifted to the air and followed Sashari. They circled around to the north before fading from sight. Both Tan and Cianna watched them until they disappeared to nothing.

"Thank you for that," Cianna finally said.

"I promised that I would."

"There is no other reason?"

Tan shrugged as he prepared a shaping that would bring them back to Ethea. "Does there need to be another reason?"

Her smile split her face again, and she reached up to smooth down hair that flew wildly around her. "Not really. But I think there is."

Tan hesitated. Cianna deserved to know his intention, especially if she was to be a partner in what he had in mind. For all he knew, she might refuse if Sashari offered to bond. And there was no guarantee that the draasin would even agree to it.

"With Par-shon threatening in Doma, we will need shapers of strength to keep the kingdoms safe," he said.

"You look beyond Incendin already? Theondar says—"

"Theondar is wrong," Tan said, interrupting her as gently as he could. "He sees only the threat he knows, not the one that he doesn't understand. That doesn't make them any less dangerous."

Cianna crossed her arms over her chest. Heat radiated from her as it usually did, sliding away and dancing around him. Connected to fire as he was, he barely noticed anymore. "What does this have to do with me? You think I should ignore what my king has asked and help you rescue your friend in Doma?" She arched her brow. "Don't think I haven't heard about your little trip there, especially after that shaping you sent throughout the city."

"How many know about that?" he asked. He hadn't intended for everyone to be aware of his actions, but if he'd used enough power to reach Elle, he should have expected something like this.

"How many? I think all of Ethea felt what you did. Most probably didn't know what it was, but likely they felt it. The shapers knew. Those who were unsure that you should be Athan are now convinced. I don't know the last time I felt a shaping that strong."

The last time would have been Althem, but Tan didn't want to remind Cianna of that. "I needed to know if she was safe. When we were trying to heal Cora, I heard her."

Cianna raised her hands to fend off discussion. "You don't have to convince me, Tan. I've been with you enough to know what you've risked. The others may need more convincing, but this was a start."

Tan glanced down at the ring Roine had given him. "They probably think Roine mistaken in giving me this title."

Cianna laughed. "You can be stupid sometimes, you know that?"

"What?"

"It doesn't take a skilled shaper to recognize how powerful you've become. And to think it has only been a few months since you first came to the city! Besides, Ferran voiced support. For most, that was enough."

That the earth shaper would support him meant quite a lot. He had been one of the first masters Tan had met. When he'd met him, Ferran had been focused on trying to understand where each student came from, testing to see if anyone had ties to Incendin. Now he seemed different. He was focused on repairing the university.

"Only Ferran?"

Cianna grinned again. "I supported you too, but there is little love for fire."

"I like fire just fine," he said.

Cianna studied him. "There aren't many who understand it. I think what you've been through has shown you the dangers of fire, but also its uses. There is power to it, but destruction. Using fire means balancing between the two. You have to be willing to risk everything for the reward."

"That sounds like what the lisincend would have claimed."

Her smile faded. "I didn't say you would do anything. I know how it nearly consumed you. You're lucky you speak to water, that the elementals restored you. Others would not be so lucky."

"You knew of Cora before. What was she?"

"Those of us from Nara have known of a fearsome shaper for many years. Corasha Saladan is a name many knew. I did not know she was a warrior too, but her ability with fire is renowned." She crossed her arms over her chest, her eyes hardening. "Had I known it was Cora you returned from Incendin, I would have killed her the moment she stepped foot in the kingdoms."

The Cora that Tan had come to know didn't strike him as anyone he needed to fear, but then again, Tan didn't know her reputation or what she'd done.

"Thank you for supporting me. I will do what I can to prove I deserve it."

She laughed. "Do you really think you must do more? It seems you've already done enough. You have shown me the draasin and convinced it to let me ride. That is enough."

"There is more, if you would be willing."

Cianna clasped her hands in front of her, her eyes twinkling as she nodded. "Of course there would be more. I think I've already said I'm not interested in working against Theondar. He has made it clear that a rescue in Doma is too dangerous. In that, I happen to agree with him."

"Rescue isn't what I have in mind for Doma," Tan started, "but that's not what I want to ask you about." Her brow raised as she waited. "You are right that there was another reason I brought you to meet the draasin. You saw what we faced when the Par-shon shapers attempted to separate me from my bond with the draasin. And you saw again what we faced when their shapers came to Nara. There are countless more from Par-shon—"

"You've said this before, Tan. I understand the danger. We are working to get ready, to rebuild the barrier. Theondar has many ways that he is attempting to protect the kingdoms."

"As am I," he said. "If Par-shon manages to somehow bond one of the draasin, they will have enough elemental strength to overpower us completely. There might be nothing we could do to stop them."

"You have kept the draasin from them," Cianna said.

"The hatchlings only. They are young and still weak. In time, they might be strong enough to help him in his plans, but now they are more helpless than anything. It's the others I worry about. If he forces them to bond, not only the draasin will suffer, but the kingdoms as well."

Cianna cocked her head, studying Tan. "I take it from what you're implying that you expect me to form a bond with one of the draasin? That's why you brought me here?"

Tan sighed and stared at the sky. The sun was falling, leaving swirls of orange and red streaking across the horizon, much like what he saw when looking through Asboel's eyes. The sense of Asboel was there, distant but content. He was safe. Sashari was safe. Tan suspected that Enya was also safe, but he heard so little about her. Asboel would have warned were she in danger, wouldn't he? Or would Par-shon manage to draw her?

"The bond offers the draasin protection," he said. "They can't simply be forced. It would have to be taken from the bonded." And doing that meant creating some way of separating the bond, either like what they had seen in Incendin, or by what he had nearly experienced in Par-shon. Either took time. Possibly time enough for the draasin to be rescued were they captured.

"Zephra nearly died when the bond was stolen," Cianna said.

"There is risk. My mother nearly died. Vel, Cora, and…" he wasn't sure what to call the other man, as the healers still hadn't learned his name, "well, they nearly lost their mind. I don't know what would have happened to me had the bond failed, but I know how painful it was for me, so I can suspect."

"Why would I do this thing?"

"Because there is value to you. Think of the shapings Zephra can work, how much she has learned from the wind. I would not be the shaper I am now, as ignorant as I still am, without the guidance of the elementals. And because it is the draasin." This was the most important reason, at least to Tan. "They were gone from the world for so long. If Par-shon claims them, they might truly be lost. If they are, they would never return."

Cianna took a few slow, thoughtful breaths, pacing from side to side across the rock. A warm breeze began blowing, whispering around them, blowing in from the south. Ashi seemed interested in making its opinion known as well.

"If I were to accept, she would allow me to ride her again?"

Tan laughed. "I think she would demand it of you. They thought you 'bold.'"

Cianna grinned again. "Only because you are so timid by comparison. You are a warrior. And a draasin rider. You could not be hurt!"

"You might be surprised," he said.

Cianna's face turned serious, her eyes narrowing. Heat surged from her skin. "You may tell her that I would accept the bond were it offered."

Tan felt relief wash through him. He had not been entirely certain that Cianna would accept. She had seen how his bond with the draasin had changed him, but there was such strength and understanding to working with the elemental. As much as any who shaped fire, Cianna understood. It was why he had thought of her first. And if Sashari agreed, it left only Enya to figure out until the hatchlings were older. They could bond when young, but that type of bond felt no different to him than a forced bond.

He focused on his connection to Asboel and realized that the draasin was actually nearer than he thought.

Sashari will accept the bond if the Bold One agrees.

Tan took in Cianna's unruly red hair, her slight frame, and the playful heat to her eyes. Bold One suited her. *She was uncertain. She fears what it means for her.*

As does Sashari. Were it not you asking, Maelen, Sashari would not have considered. She recognizes your intent through the fire bond.

I hope I am not wrong.

As do I, but I see wisdom in your request.

How will they bond?

Asboel made a strange clicking sound, something like a chuckle. *It has already begun.*

Tan saw Cianna's eyes go wide. Her body became stiff and she stood frozen in place. She still shaped, though, massive amounts of heat coming off her skin and misting in the air.

"I can hear… something," Cianna whispered.

"You will need to call to her," Tan urged. He suspected that if he were to give Sashari's name to Cianna, it would hasten the connection, but doing so felt a violation of sorts. The name must be given willingly.

Cianna shaped fire, and it built within her. As it did, heat and steam and power radiated from her. Her lips moved, as if she spoke, but no words came out. Cianna's face contorted as she worked with Sashari, and then her eyes snapped open.

"Sashari," she breathed. The word left her lips on a shaping of fire and disappeared.

Spirit bloomed briefly, like a flash of light, and then faded. Had Tan not been able to shape spirit, he doubted he would have ever sensed it. It was beautiful and natural and so very powerful, nothing like the cruel and ugly bond forced on the elementals by Par-shon.

Sashari landed suddenly, almost crashing to the ground. She twisted her massive head and stared at Tan, briefly bowing it toward the ground. Raising it again, she turned to Cianna.

Cianna seemed to listen and then climbed onto Sashari's back, the wide smile never leaving her face. Tan had the distant sense of their connection. Were he to focus with a shaping of spirit, he thought he might be able to reach and listen, but it was not his to share.

They took to the air, and Cianna laughed as they did. It was good that Cianna could experience the joy of the bond for now. Soon enough, he suspected there would be a different need for the bond, a different test.

Sashari is pleased, Maelen.

Tan stared after them. *Do you think Enya will ever accept a bond?*

Enya will need time. She fears the connection we share, as she fears your kind. In that way, she is young. We must shield her.

I will do all that I can to protect her, Tan said.

I know that you will. You are Maelen. Now, while Sashari plays, I must return to the hatchlings. They grow restless and hungry.

They seemed content to eat your ears.

Asboel snorted high overhead, the plume of smoke from his nostrils becoming a thick cloud. *Careful, or I will let them eat yours.*

Remember, I am Maelen. They will find me more challenging than I'm worth.

This is true. Best that I find them a soft cow.

Tan laughed as he took to the air on a shaping of wind, augmented by Honl. He added a hint of fire. He reached Asboel as he circled overhead.

We will hunt soon, Maelen.

Tan feared that they would need to hunt, and feared where it would lead them.

CHAPTER 14

A Mother's Return

AMIA SUMMONED HIM upon his return. He had recognized her hesitation when he suggested that he would take Cianna with him, but she understood the reason. There was no need for the irritation Amia felt toward Cianna, but it didn't change the fact that it existed. The shared connection to fire was a part of it, but Tan suspected there was more he didn't fully understand.

"It worked," she said, studying his face, when he reached the door of their house.

Tan nodded, entering the house and pulling the door closed behind him. The room smelled of cut flowers and spices. A large wreath of woven flowers draped over one of the chairs. A weary expression on Amia's face told him that she had been working the entire time he had been gone, only he didn't quite know what she had been working on.

"I didn't know if it would work," Tan admitted. "How to convince an elemental of the need for a bond? But Cianna has always served fire in a way the draasin respect. She will be a good match for Sashari."

"Where is she now?"

Tan glanced toward the window. "Out. Somewhere out there. She travels with her now. They will need to explore the bond and come to understand what it means for them."

"I sense that you're relieved."

Tan was. He hadn't realized how worried he had been about the draasin, but knowing that he wasn't going to be the only one to protect them gave him more confidence that they could keep the draasin safe from Par-shon. "There is much more to be done. Roine isn't willing to help rescue Elle, but I haven't been able to reach her anyway."

"I've tried as well. I thought the connection between us would facilitate me reaching out, but there is nothing but silence."

She didn't say it, but Tan knew Amia thought Elle was dead.

"Other than my mother, she's the only family I have left," he said.

Amia made her way over to him, and embraced him. They stood together for a moment, their shared connection giving more reassurance than the physical contact.

"You're preparing for the First Mother?" he asked.

Amia nodded. "The People gather outside Ethea. Nearly a dozen families in all."

"Only a dozen? That doesn't seem right. How many were there?" When Tan had originally met the First Mother, when they'd gone to the Gathering, there had been at least six families already there, with more arriving as they waited. How had the Aeta lost so much?

Amia shrugged. "When I first went to the Gathering, I remembered it as a time of celebration. A thousand or more of the People would come together. We would have songs and commune by the great fire. There would be trading, but mostly there would be stories, tales told of the People, of the lands we'd crossed since last we gathered. The Mothers would meet and celebrate. Daughters would be raised." Her hand went to her neck as she remembered. "It was where I first learned what I could do. What I would be. I remember… I remember the way she took me aside when I was barely more than five. I think I knew even then. She shaped me, layering it overtop my mind, freeing me."

Amia closed her eyes and wrung her hands together as she remembered. "My mother could never teach. She was a skilled senser, but she couldn't teach what I needed. The First Mother provided those lessons." She sighed and fell silent for a moment. "It was more than that. The Gathering was a time of communion. During that time, we would be more than caravans and families. We would be one, a People."

Her eyes glistened with tears. "We are the landless. Wanderers, but during the Gathering, we had a place. None would admit it, but those would be the best days of the People. Always before, the First Mother would call the Gathering. It was how we knew to come together. Now there is no more First Mother. She has called her final Gathering."

Tan hugged her again, holding her against him as her tears came in steady sobs. Amia had worked so hard to hide those tears, almost as if she feared what would happen were she to let them out. Tan was glad she felt safe enough with him for the tears to flow freely.

"Will you go?" he asked.

"I am no longer of the People," she answered. "I don't know if I could ever return after what happened."

"You know that I—"

She stopped him, pressing a finger to his lips. "I know you will," she said, stopping him before he could tell her how he would support her. She took a deep breath and shook her head as she changed subjects. "I prepared a wreath to travel with her body."

"You'll be the one to bring her body to them?"

"Roine offered another, but I think this should be me. I might have chosen to leave the People, but that doesn't mean I can't grieve." Tears still welled up in her eyes. "I don't want to do this alone," she said.

Tan kissed her forehead. She had lost so much, he knew losing even more was what she feared the most. "You will never be alone."

Amia swallowed and rested her head on his chest. They stood there as the remains of sunlight faded, leaving the room shadowed, and neither spoke.

A shaping to carry the First Mother outside the walls of the city felt somehow wrong, so they took her by more conventional means. Roine provided a wagon and a team of horses for them to ride out to the Aeta.

The mother laid upon a finely woven blanket, a pillow propping her head up. Amia had dressed her in a colorful gown she'd acquired for the burial. Her hands were clasped across her chest. In death, she looked peaceful—and older than she had ever appeared while alive.

They rode in silence. Amia, who had much more experience with horses, steered. Living in the mountains of Galen, he hadn't the need to ride. Horses were of little use, at least climbing the upper slopes. The only horses to be found in Galen were in Lord Lins' stables. When his mother took charge of his household, Tan had been tasked with cleaning the stables. It had been menial work and his mother's way of motivating him to leave Nor and head to Ethea where he could study at the university.

When they passed the walled border of Ethea, Tan paused to look at the city from this direction. He had only come in by ground a few times. Since learning how to shape—really, even before then—he had traveled to and from Ethea in a much different way.

A smattering of farms ringed the city. This late in the year, most of the fields had already been harvested, the grain stored for the coming winter. Other plants grew: some vegetables, rows of tomatoes, the tufts of fall carrots poking from the ground, and a pumpkin patch that still had bright orange pumpkins growing from vines. Beyond the farms, the landscape changed over the sweeping fields of grass as they rolled into the outer edge of Ter.

As he stared, he realized that these were the people who needed protection from Par-shon. Those living within the city had shapers for protection, but outside the walls of Ethea they were vulnerable, much like his home village had been vulnerable when Incendin had attacked.

Amia broke the silence first. "Do you think it's safe to leave Cora in the city alone?"

Tan was surprised that was the question she chose to ask. "Roine gave her access to the city. The shaping holds."

"You're not going to do what Roine wants, are you? You intend to try reaching Elle once we are done with this." She shifted the reins in her hands.

He considered how to answer. "I wasn't sure before. Roine wants to prepare for an Incendin attack, but…"

"You worry about Elle."

He nodded. "Either she's alive and still in danger or she's already gone. I need to know which it is."

"Who will you bring with you?"

He was thankful that she didn't try to talk him out of it. That didn't mean that she supported his plan, only that she wouldn't fight him on it. "I don't know. Roine won't help, and he'll be angry if I ask any of our shapers to go." He didn't say it, but bringing Amia with him only risked her capture.

"You're considering Cora."

He wasn't sure whether that would be safe, either. Doma was too close to Incendin. If he released the spirit shaping restricting her and tried to rely on her for help, what would compel her to stay? She knew how to travel and had studied with Lacertin, so there were probably other tricks she knew.

"I don't know. I can't simply wait here knowing that Elle needs help."

Amia smiled. "I wouldn't love you as I do if you could."

He took her hand and they continued onward.

The road curved several miles from Ethea, and Amia veered the horses and the wagons away from the road and through short grasses. "We are not far now."

Tan heard the sounds of the Aeta long before he saw them. The occasional gusts of wind caught their bells and sent their musical tinkling into the air. A mournful lute sung softly. The smoke from the great fire at the center of the circle of wagons trailed into the sky, the flames burning within the fire pulling on Tan's senses.

They passed over a small rise, and then he saw the wagons. They formed a wide circle ringing a massive fire. Roine's offer of protection meant that they could camp here, that they would remain safe within the borders as they held a Gathering. Tan wasn't sure what he had expected, but what he saw looked no different than what he'd seen at the Gathering in Doma.

"Is this all there are?" Tan asked.

"These are the families who remain," Amia said. "The lisincend claimed mine. The archivists destroyed one. Several were claimed when the lisincend attacked the last Gathering. Perhaps more will be coming, but this is all for now."

She stopped the wagon outside the circle. The grasses had been trampled flat here, creating a wide swath of openness between the grasses and the circle of wagons. An Aeta woman came from between two brightly colored yellow wagons and looked up at them. She had golden hair much like Amia and a slender band of silver around her neck.

"Daughter," Amia said, nodding to her. "I have returned the First Mother so that she may find rest among the People."

The Daughter said nothing as she approached the wagon and looked into the back. Her breath caught as she saw the First Mother and she closed her eyes. Tan felt her shaping build. It was weak, but there was no doubt it came from her.

A pair of well-muscled men appeared from around the same place that the Daughter had come from. They said nothing as they approached the wagon, simply reaching in and lifting the First Mother from the wagon and carrying her back toward the great fire.

The Daughter met Amia's eyes, nodded, and turned away, all without saying a word.

"We can go," Amia said.

Tan took her hand and squeezed. Tears had returned to her eyes.

"Are you certain you don't want to stay?" he asked.

She shook her head. "It is no longer my place. I abandoned the People when I made my choice."

"I'm sorry," he said.

"You have nothing to be sorry for. Choosing you is not the reason for my sadness."

Tan still wished there was something he could say, a way to provide Amia comfort, but he knew there was not. He squeezed her hand and simply sat next to her, riding together in silence.

Amia started the horses back toward Ethea, leaving the Aeta to mourn behind them.

CHAPTER 15

Request to Water

THE REST OF THE DAY HAD PASSED with something of a pall hanging over it. Amia stayed near him, and they spent the time in the lower level of the archives, each staring at a different book pulled from the vast shelves, both lost in thoughts of their own. Tan sensed the sadness in Amia and understood she needed time to mourn.

He considered going to Asboel. The draasin was in the den not far from him, and his nearness gave Tan comfort. But Amia needed him more. Even if they didn't speak, she needed his presence.

After a while, he decided to attempt another spirit shaping. He unsheathed the warrior sword and planted it in the middle of the floor, the tip pointing into the stone. He focused on its runes. He focused on its runes and began his shaping.

Spirit surged, growing with increasing intensity as he pulled on the shaping. Tan drew with even more force from his stores of spirit, and finally released the shaping, letting it sweep away from him.

As before, it stretched outward, first through the city and then beyond, to the surrounding kingdoms, and farther, as it reached Incendin, to the lands of Chenir that Tan didn't know, and faintly, into Doma.

He had the impression that he could sense anything he chose to. But he only wanted to reach Elle.

There was nothing but silence.

Tan withdrew the shaping before it faltered. He'd learned the limits of shaping through the sword, though each time he used it, the shapings became stronger, as if he were getting stronger.

"Nothing?" Amia asked as he settled back into his chair.

"There was nothing," he answered.

"The silence worries you more than hearing she was in danger," she noted.

"At least I knew she lived."

"She's strong. You told me that," Amia said. "And she can reach water."

Tan sighed, wishing there was some way that he could reach her. He had sent a message to udilm, but his connection to them was weak.

But could there be another way to reach her through water? He had assumed udilm the only way, but the nymid and udilm communicated. Had they not, he would still be in lisincend form. Udilm had refused to heal him, but they had called to the nymid, drawing their strength to him.

He stood, the suddenness of the motion tipping his chair back. "I've been going about this the wrong way," he said, pacing from one end of the room to the other. "I've been trying to shape spirit to reach her, but there's an easier way, one that doesn't require me shaping the entire kingdoms. She might have been able to speak to udilm, but I can speak to the nymid. If they can get word to her, then maybe I can find out what happened."

Amia set the book down and joined him at the shelves. Tan glanced at the cover of the book she'd been reading, noting that the rune on the cover said spirit. "I will come with you," she offered.

They made their way through the tunnels with a shaping of fire to guide them. Tan gave control of a shaping of fire to saa, letting the elemental control it as they walked. Cianna would need to know about the draasin den, he realized. He would have to come up with some way for her to reach Sashari. Now that they had bonded, he couldn't keep them apart. At least then he wouldn't be the only one sharing in the secret of the draasin den.

He stopped where water pooled between the stones, the same place Roine had once been healed after Althem had nearly killed him. He dipped his hand into it. It felt warm, much warmer than he would have expected. Was that because the draasin now called this place home, because they had made it their den?

Within the warm water, the green shimmer of the nymid swirled. Tan focused on the water elemental, then he breathed out a call. *Nymid. I need your help reaching the Child of Water.*

The response came quickly, washing into his mind with a surge of power.

He Who is Tan. We have felt your connection to the Mother.

My connection? I haven't...

Tan trailed off. Was that what he did when he had been shaping spirit as he had?

Should I not have used the connection? he asked the nymid.

The connection is yours to decide how to use, He Who is Tan. It is the gift of the Mother.

I heard Elle, the Child of Water. She was in danger and I tried to reach her.

The Child of Water cannot be in danger.

Tan tried to think of how to share what he needed with the nymid. Their understanding of the world was different than his, different even than the draasin. At least with the draasin, he understood how to show Asboel what he wanted. With the nymid, they were limited by his ability to explain.

There are those who seek to force the elementals to bond. They would take water from those like her and force it to serve.

Sorrow washed through the nymid. *The nymid remember. The nymid were once harnessed.*

Harnessed. They had used the same term the ancient shapers had used to describe their method of controlling the elementals. That could not have been chance.

The Mother would have me stop this. The elementals should be allowed to choose whether to bond. It should not be forced, Tan said.

You would not harness the nymid?

Tan hesitated, then opened his mind to the nymid, sending a shaping of spirit through the connection he forged. They needed to understand his motivation. The nymid were in as much danger as any of the elementals. If Par-shon discovered this place of convergence, Tan could only imagine how many would be forced to bond. All of them, likely. If he did nothing else, he would prevent that from happening.

Any bond should be freely offered, Tan said. *Much like the bond I share with the draasin and ashi.*

The nymid considered for a long moment. *You would bond with the nymid?*

I would only bond if it were freely given. He hadn't thought he needed to be bound to the nymid to ask that favor of them.

The pool shimmered and a face appeared there, coalescing in the bright green Tan had come to associate with the nymid. Of all the elementals, he had known this one the longest. It was because of the nymid that he still lived. They had saved him when Fur had tried to kill him and capture Amia. They had helped him rescue her. And the nymid had been the reason they were able to reach the artifact in the first place. Never before had he had a sense of individuality from them.

Only, that wasn't quite true. During his first experience with the nymid, he had spoken to one of the water elementals more than the others, one most interested in helping him. The face that shimmered to the surface somehow reminded him of that nymid, but that wouldn't be possible.

I need help reaching the Child of Water. She might be in danger.

Word has already spread from here. We will find the Child. The nymid swirled and surged out of the water, wrapping around Tan's arms, leaving a shimmering green hue to his skin. Then the elemental retreated back into the pool, swirling softly.

"What just happened?" Amia asked.

"The nymid search for Elle."

"Not a bond?"

Tan shook his head.

Amia knelt before the pool of warm water and trailed her finger through it. The shimmery green water suffused with the nymid slid up her hand and then receded back into the pool. "I didn't think it would take this long. You have known nymid the longest. I expected you to have bonded to them by now. What does it mean that they won't? You have bonded the draasin and learned to control fire. You bonded ashi and have begun to master wind." She looked up at him, pulling her hand from the water but not wiping it off. "You have grown more competent with water and earth, but there is much you can learn. I have waited for a bond to form to both. The nymid made the most sense; you knew them first."

"I don't know that it works quite like that. I can speak to the udilm as well, but haven't bonded there. I can reach golud, but the earth elemental has never answered me directly. I can ask of it, but am never certain if it responds."

Amia stood and studied the walls. Golud infused the bedrock throughout the city, the earth elemental giving strength to the archives above, to the palace, and creating the tunnels here. "What if golud is not the elemental you would bond? You control saa, yet are bonded to the draasin. You didn't bond to ara, though you can speak to it. You have spoken to udilm, but it's the nymid you know best. What if it's the same with golud?"

Tan wondered what other earth elemental there would be. He only knew of golud, not of any others. If the nymid were anything like Asboel, they wouldn't share what they knew of the other elementals.

Tan focused on the water, reaching toward the nymid swirling there. *Will you tell me when the Child of Water is found?*

You will know, He Who is Tan.

Tan sighed and pulled himself away. Amia followed him as they made their way back through the tunnel, back to the archives, when a sudden gust of cool air made him pause. Amia pulled on his sleeve and motioned toward the wind. She felt it too.

Honl? Tan asked.

The wind elemental that appeared was not the one Tan expected. Honl could become something like a translucent figure, and he grew more distinct each time he attempted it, but this was something different. Ara appeared before him, not as an indistinct sense of the cooler wind elemental. This appeared with definite features that Tan recognized.

Aric, Tan said. He knew his mother's elemental but would not have expected to see him removed from his mother. The wind elemental had been particularly protective of her since they had nearly been separated in Par-shon.

Zephra summons, Tan.

Tan frowned at the wind elemental. *She summons?*

He hadn't seen her in days. She hadn't known that Cora was healed. She wouldn't have known that the First Mother had died. Or even that Tan had risked traveling into Doma. She had been gone, supposedly scouting along the border and beyond, into Incendin itself, bringing word of Incendin's movements. After what he'd learned of the barrier, Tan wondered if she weren't tasked with trying to raise it again as well.

She summons. There is something she wishes you to see.

Where? Not in the city?

Not the city, Aric said. *Come. I will lead.*

CHAPTER 16

When Fire Attacks

TAN RODE A SHAPING OF WIND. Honl aided the shaping, granting him strength as they chased Aric across the kingdoms. The wind elemental moved quickly, almost more quickly than Tan could manage. He added a touch of fire shaping to the wind, propelling them across the countryside. Had he known where Aric led him, he might have been able to use a traveling shaping. It would have been fastest.

Amia clung to him, saying nothing after learning that Zephra summoned. Tan began to suspect what she had found and why she called him, and the fact that they made their way ever faster to the south did nothing to dissuade him. His mother had found something of Incendin she wished him to see.

They crossed into Nara. With the falling sunlight skimming across the barren rock, it looked actually quite beautiful. Heat shimmered from the sand, giving a soft sheen to the land. The twisted plants managing to grow in the heat caught shadows, leaving them stretching across the land. Had the draasin changed him so much that he now found a place like Nara beautiful?

But he saw beauty in all parts of the kingdoms. Galen still held a certain place for him, the forested mountains where he had first learned to sense, climbing along the slopes with his father teaching him to ignore every other distraction and remain focused on everything around him while keeping his mind open, letting awareness of earth and life flood through him. It was a difficult balance and one he had not yet mastered nearly so well as his father. Ter held the beauty of Ethea, and the surrounding lands around the city covered with farms. Tan had rarely visited Vatten, but the sea washing along their shores would rival any other place in the kingdoms.

Aric began to slow as they reached the far edge of Nara. Tan didn't so much recognize it as he felt the flickering effects of the barrier pushing on his awareness. Zephra was there, facing the border of Nara and on into Incendin as if something important demanded her attention. She wore a thin gray dress that swirled around her. Black hair streaked with gray hung loose about her shoulders, nothing like her usual stern bun. She turned as they approached.

"Tannen. Aric found you more quickly than I expected."

"You didn't want to use the summoning coin?" he asked.

She shook her head. "I could not have risked others coming."

"What do you mean?"

"Come. Where we go will be dangerous." She glanced at Amia, her lips pressed into a tight line. "You may want to consider returning to the city."

"I will stay with Tan."

Zephra's hands clenched briefly. "I would have said the same about Grethan once."

Tan and Zephra created matching wind shapings that took them across the barrier. Tan's skin tingled, surging with a growing strength. With enough time, shapers would return the barrier to what it once was.

Zephra pointed toward the south, and they continued into Incendin. The ground beneath them was scarred and cracked, wide fissures splitting open and dropping off to darkness far below. The stunted and twisted plants pushed against his earth senses, as if the fire that tormented the plants tried to push away his earth sensing. On one tree, a single white flower bloomed, almost as if the tree wished for a different time, a time when Incendin had been more like Nara, before the Rens split.

Tan stretched out with his earth sensing as they floated above Incendin. Nothing moved, nothing that would explain the reason that his mother had brought him here.

A low howl startled him, almost leading him to lose control of the shaping. Hounds. Tan turned toward the sound, but it was distant, far enough away that they wouldn't be in any immediate danger. The last time he'd faced hounds, he had been nothing more than an earth senser. He had grown considerably since then and could probably handle hounds, but their sounds still left an anxious and worried sensation deep within him.

"What do you want to show me, Mother?" Tan asked.

"It's not far from here now," she said and turned toward a tower of rock that rose off to the west.

As they approached, the rock took on shape. It was not a single finger, but stones stacked atop each other. Given the size, they were likely shaped.

"What is this place, Mother?" Tan asked when the landed and Zephra still said nothing.

"You know that I traveled with the Aeta for a time?" she asked. When he nodded, she pointed to the rock. "This is where it first began. I had been sent on a passing, an attempt to help me catch the wind." She studied the rock. "I had begun crossing Incendin. This was before I could shape with any consistency, and well before I first spoke to the wind. I was to reach my home, where it was thought I would be able to catch the wind."

"Mother?"

"This is where I found the Aeta. There was a young woman there, barely more than a girl. She was strapped to a rock," she motioned toward a flat rock, faded by the sun. "That was when I saw the fire shaper. He forced a shaping, twisting it onto the Aeta. It was when I truly began to understand how far Incendin would go for the power they sought."

Her jaw clenched and she took a shaking breath. "You understand what I saw, don't you?" she asked. "I did not, not at the time. A fire shaper, and one determined to harm one of the Aeta. I did they only thing I could think of doing. I saved her."

Tan hadn't heard this story before. He knew that his mother had traveled with the Aeta, that she had been granted more access than any shaper had ever been allowed. Likely she had known that the Aeta had spirit shapers long before any others in the kingdoms but had kept their secret for reasons of her own.

"Who was she?" Amia asked.

Zephra inhaled deeply of the hot Incendin air. Ashi swirled through, though hints of his mother's elemental gave occasional cooler gusts to it. "The girl? She was named Lia."

"I hadn't known you were the one to save her," Amia said.

"Yes. I knew her before then, when she went from Daughter to Mother."

"Why did you bring me here?" Tan asked.

In answer, she lifted onto another shaping of wind that took her around the pillar of rock. Tan followed, landing on a soft cushion next to her.

He didn't need to see the broken wagons or the bodies splayed across the ground, and didn't need earth sensing to guide him either. His nose told him all that he needed to know. The stink of charred flesh and rot burned in the air. The fragments of color mixed in with the wagons made it clear that these were Aeta wagons and Aeta dead.

"Theondar asked me to scout," Zephra said softly. "I have searched throughout Incendin. Why should this place be such a place of death? What is it about this rock that demands blood?" she asked. "And why must the Aeta continue to suffer?"

Amia had turned away, unable to look. "They were traveling for the Gathering, drawn for the time of mourning," she whispered. "This would have been the fastest way for those traveling on the edges of Incendin."

"The Gathering is over," Zephra said, fixing Amia with a hard expression.

"The First Mother summoned another," Tan said.

"Why would she summon a Gathering?" Zephra asked. "She's confined within Ethea. Did she really think Theondar would allow her to meet with the Aeta?"

Tan glanced at Amia before answering. How much should he share? His mother cared about the Aeta, but with everything that had happened since Amia first showed up in Nor, Zephra had changed. "She's gone, Mother. Before she died, she called the Gathering."

His mother closed her eyes and turned slowly in place. "Gone. You are certain?"

"I'm certain. Her body has been returned to the Aeta."

Zephra sighed as she stood on the edge of the rock, looking down on the wagons. "A great shaper has passed," she said softly.

"What did this?" Tan asked.

"When I found this place, I had the same question. This could be Incendin."

"You don't think this was?" Tan had caught the emphasis she put on *could* and now he studied the bodies, the way they and the wagons had burned. He had the answer without needing prompting. He had seen it before within Ethea. This was the reason that his mother wouldn't risk the summoning rune.

"You think this the work of the draasin," Tan said.

Tan focused on his connection to Amia. *This could not have been the draasin.*

Not Asboel or Sashari, Amia agreed, *but what of Enya? We don't even know where she is.*

Tan grimaced. It couldn't have been Enya, could it?

His mother nodded solemnly. "You understand why I wanted you to see this first."

"Mother," Tan began, "this isn't the draasin. I've bonded to one and know it wasn't him. And now Cianna has bonded another."

"Cianna?" she asked thoughtfully. "She would serve well. But there are three adult draasin, Tannen. Can you tell me that the draasin had nothing to do with this?"

He couldn't. Not with real certainty. Tan didn't know where Enya had been since Asboel had stopped her from withdrawing fire. He hated to admit that it was possible that she had been here.

"You wanted to show me this to prove something to me?" he asked. "Is that what you thought?"

"Not prove. You are bonded to the draasin. You understand them better than anyone alive. You should be the one to hold the draasin accountable."

"What of you?" he asked.

"Theondar will need to know what I've seen," she answered. "He is our king now."

"That's not what I'm asking."

"I continue to search," she said. "That is my task. And Incendin moves. You think we only need to fear Par-shon, but the Incendin threat is not gone. They are a greater threat than any shapers across the sea. I will see that we are ready when Incendin comes again."

She lifted to the air on a wind shaping and disappeared from view.

Asboel, Tan sent, not wanting to wait to reach the draasin. *You are needed.*

"Do you think this could have been Enya?" Amia asked.

"I don't know," Tan admitted.

"Why would she have done this?"

He could think of several reasons. She'd been shaped by the Aeta once before, though that had been by the archivists. The archivists had scattered, but now they seemed to be returning to their families. What if Enya tracked the archivists for vengeance?

Amia still didn't look at the remains of the wagons. It reminded Tan of what he'd seen when he first found Amia's wagons, when he had thought the lisincend had destroyed her. Incendin had attacked with fire and explosions and death.

Tan was crouching near the broken wagons when Asboel settled to the ground near him.

Was this Enya? he asked without looking up. *Fire destroyed these people, Asboel. The attack is similar to what I saw when Enya attacked Ethea. I can't tell if this was her, and I pray to the Mother this was not.*

If it was, it would make everything that much more difficult. If the draasin were feared again, if hunters of draasin returned, nothing would have changed. The bonds to the draasin were to help that.

Asboel stretched his long neck over the wreckage, inhaling deeply. *This was fire.*

Fire. Not draasin. *Not Enya?*

You should not need me to tell you that.

Tan reached with a fire sensing and stretched it out and away from him. It touched on the bodies, on the charred remains of the wagons, and he felt the residual effect of the shaping that had happened here. It wasn't draasin.

I should have sensed this myself first.

Yes.

This wasn't twisted fire either, Tan realized.

He had thought it either Incendin or draasin, but what if it was neither? What fire shapers would attack the Aeta?

This was fire, Asboel agreed.

"The draasin didn't do this," he said to Amia. His shoulders relaxed and he lifted his head in relief.

"He's certain?"

"*I'm* certain. I shouldn't have needed Asboel to tell me, either. Enya wouldn't have done this. I don't know if she *could* have done this with the shaping you placed on her."

"If she's bonded—"

Tan frowned. "The bond removes the shaping?"

"I don't know. When Cianna bonded, I could no longer sense the shaping over Sashari. I'm not certain why."

Tan wondered the same thing. What about forming the bond changed the shaping Amia had placed, and why had it not changed the shaping on Asboel?

"If it's not the draasin, you know what that leaves," Amia went on.

"Why would Incendin do this? They have no reason to attack."

"Are you sure of that? Your mother and Roine are right, Tan. We still don't know anything about Incendin. They have attacked the kingdoms for years. That won't change simply because we've learned of Par-shon," Amia said.

What did Tan know? Only what Cora had shared and what he'd seen. And hadn't he seen Aeta attacked and killed by Incendin? "It wasn't the lisincend. This wasn't twisted fire," Tan said. "It could still be Incendin fire shapers, but why would they have destroyed the Aeta wagon?"

He didn't expect any answers, and Amia provided none.

Tan turned to Asboel. *Will you hunt with me?*

You will find who did this?

There's something I'm missing. I would know what it is.

Then I will hunt, Asboel said.

Tan pulled Amia with him onto the draasin's back. He could shape them, but riding Asboel gave him an advantage that shaping did not. He could use Asboel's sight, could reach through the draasin and see the world in the shades of orange and red that he could not access when he traveled by shaping. To find fire, the draasin would be quickest.

He settled into his usual spot on Asboel's back. Amia followed him, fitting between the heated spines, careful not to hold too tightly.

Where do we hunt, Maelen?

The Sunlands, Tan answered. In some ways, Cora's name for these lands felt fitting.

They curled around to the north, flying high above Incendin. Asboel trained his eyes on the ground, his amazing draasin vision searching for movement or anything that would explain the fire. As they flew, Tan felt a growing unease. For them to face Par-shon and survive, they would need the draasins' help. They might need Incendin's help. Now he was spending time searching for fire when he should be searching for Elle.

Water searches on your behalf, Maelen. You needn't worry.

Tan sighed. He would have to let the nymid search and be content that it would be enough. It was hard for him to let go, especially when someone he cared about was in danger, but there was too much for him to do alone.

Now you begin to understand. You will gain wisdom yet. Asboel made a clucking sound much like a laugh.

Tan gave Asboel a stern kick. That hadn't been funny.

Asboel dropped his nose and dove.

Through the draasin sight, he expected to see one of the lisincend, or perhaps fire shapers, but instead he saw something else entirely.

Aeta.

You will frighten them, Tan warned.

Fire burns already, Maelen. Do you not sense it?

Now that Asboel mentioned it, he did. It burned slowly, steadily, but the intensity of the flames increased.

If he did nothing, fire would destroy these people the same as the others and he couldn't wait for Asboel to reach the ground.

Tan stood and jumped from the draasin's back, streaking down on a shaping of lightning, exploding near the wagons.

Tan didn't give the people time to react to his arrival. He focused on the fire shaper among the hundred or so Aeta huddled in their wagons. With a spirit shaping pressed through his sword, he cut off the fire shaper's ability.

The fire faded.

Tan jumped into the wind, landing on the other side of the wagons. *Where is he?* he asked of Asboel. He sent a shaping of spirit and earth searching for where he'd sensed the shaper.

Asboel showed him a vision of the wagons through his eyes. A flash of brighter orange moved near the back one.

Tan leaped forward on the wind. The shaper was dressed in black leather and his head was shaved. He crawled forward with wide eyes staring toward the sun, and his breathing was erratic.

An Incendin fire shaper, but why?

"Who are you?" he demanded.

The fire shaper didn't answer.

Tan prepared another shaping, this one building with his anger at what the fire shaper had nearly done. He had thought they could work with Incendin, that they could find common ground, but what if he'd been wrong? Could Incendin really want nothing more than power? Was that why they had attacked the kingdoms for decades?

Maybe they wouldn't be able to use Incendin with Par-shon.

Movement behind him caused him to spin. A thin man in a black robe stepped out of the nearest wagon. Tan shielded his mind before realizing he probably didn't need to. Now that he shaped spirit, he was protected. At least, he thought he had been, but now that he knew one of the archivists was here, he recognized the subtle effect of his shaping, the way it slithered across his mind, only enough to add to his doubts.

"Impressive work," the man said. "Made all the more impressive when it's learned that you killed all these people."

"You're mistaken if you think you can shape me," Tan said.

"I've shaped other warriors before. You will not be the first."

Tan raised his sword and pulled angrily on a shaping of all the elements, surging it through the sword. "You haven't shaped anyone like me."

"You are all the same. Weak minded."

Tan laughed darkly. "And you are predictably blind."

Asboel's dark shadow began to descend. The man looked up, and as he did, Tan pressed a shaping through his sword, using the combined elements to wrap the archivist's mind and bind it with power.

As the shaping took hold, the archivist tore his eyes away from Asboel and stared wide-eyed at Tan. "That's not—"

"You know nothing of what is possible."

Tan twisted his shaping, and the archivist collapsed.

Chapter 17

Spirit Shapings

TAN STARTED TOWARD THE FALLEN archivist as he rested against the wagon, his back arched uncomfortably, with one foot bent behind him. One hand reached toward a prickly bush, his fingers spasming. Tan checked the archivist's injuries and found that he still breathed.

He hadn't killed him, but what *should* happen to him?

The archivist had wanted the Aeta dead. He had known about the fire shaper. "Can you see if there's a shaping on him?" he asked Amia as she approached, motioning to the fallen fire shaper.

Amia made her way toward the man.

Tan reached out with earth and spirit, layering the sensing over the Aeta within the wagons. None were dead, only stunned—*shaped*—though the shaping was a simple one. He sent a shaping through the sword and reversed the hold on the Aeta.

Thank you, he sent to Asboel.

I will hunt. You will join when you are finished here.

Call Sashari and Cianna, Tan said. *This will need more than only us.*

Asboel huffed in agreement.

Hunt well, Tan sent.

Asboel leaped to the sky and quickly became nothing more than a shadow. Tan turned back to Amia.

"He was shaped with spirit," Amia noted.

"That is my fault," Tan said. "I needed to stop him from shaping quickly."

"No," she started, looking back at him. "Not yours. This is another. Different and complex. He was compelled." She turned to the fallen fire shaper. "It's much like what Althem used, but less complex. I think I can remove it, but it will take time."

"See what you can do."

Tan didn't know what to do about the archivist. If he left him here, he ran the risk of the same thing happening again when he recovered. The shaping holding him should work, but what if he managed to escape from it? Could Tan risk that with the Aeta?

He started down the line of wagons, checking inside. There would be the Mother, a Daughter, and the leaders of the wagons. Searching wagon by wagon, though, would be much too slow.

He focused on a shaping of spirit and earth. If another among the Aeta could shape spirit, he might be able to sense them. Not all Aeta were led by someone with the ability to shape, but Tan suspected enough were, a secret the First Mother had hidden from even the rest of her people, leaving most thinking the ability much rarer than it really was.

He didn't really expect another spirit shaper among the wagons. For the archivist to be successful, he needed to be the only one able to shape. Tan sensed the hint of a void, but nothing as he had with the Aeta they'd met with Roine outside Ethea.

He went back to searching the wagons one at a time. He paused at the innermost wagon, set in the middle of the line, and pulled the door open. A young girl, barely older than his friend Bal had been when he last saw her, stirred on the ground. A band of narrow silver encircled her neck.

"Daughter," Tan said as he approached her.

She cocked her head and blinked sluggishly. He detected her weak attempt at shaping and blocked it. She started struggling, kicking.

"Shh," Tan soothed, holding his hands out to her. "I'm not going to hurt you."

"You're Incendin! They attacked—"

"Not Incendin," Tan said. "I'm from the kingdoms. And it was not Incendin who attacked you anyway."

"I saw them… I sensed them," she said.

"You were shaped into sensing them," Tan said, extending his hand to her. "Come. Let me show you."

She eyed his hand for a moment before taking it and letting him lead her outside. Some of the others had begun to recover enough to come outside on their own. They stood around, dazed expressions on most of their faces, confusion on the others.

Tan braced himself as a younger man with more mental clarity than the others threw himself in front of the girl. "What is this?" he demanded.

He couldn't be more than sixteen or seventeen. The jacket he wore was tattered and stitched in dozens of places. His pants were loose. Tan had once thought all the Aeta families were successful traders, but this one appeared to have fallen on hard times.

"This is us saving you," Tan answered, trying to push past him. He wanted to show the Daughter the archivist. She needed to know what had happened.

"By abducting the Daughter?"

Tan suppressed the frustration he felt. It wasn't this boy's fault that he'd been shaped. "Had I wanted to abduct the Daughter, I would already be gone."

The Daughter rested a hand on the boy. "Easy, Kayl," she said. She shaped spirit, using a faltering attempt to soothe him. She might be young, but she had grown accustomed to leading.

"Where is the Mother?" Tan asked her.

"She fell sick. We were nearly to…" She trailed off and shook her head. "It doesn't matter now. We had to turn back. Search for healers."

They had been heading to the Gathering in Doma, Tan suspected, the Gathering disrupted by Incendin. "Incendin attacked. You would not have wanted to be at the Gathering."

Her eyes widened.

"How is it you know of the Gathering?" the boy demanded.

He stepped in front of Tan again, his hands outstretched to stop further movement. He wasn't particularly tall, or even threatening, but Tan appreciated the show of loyalty.

Tan glanced from Kayl to the Daughter. There was more to this than he understood. With a quick sensing of spirit, he recognized she was more than the Daughter to him; she was his sister. "I won't harm your sister," Tan said softly, leaning toward him. "I'm here to help."

Kayl's gaze slipped from Tan to the Daughter and then back.

"Kayl," the Daughter said soothingly.

Kayl frowned but stepped aside, hanging on her arm and making it clear that she wasn't going anywhere without him. He motioned toward the other Aeta, now coming out of the wagons.

Tan shaped soothing spirit, much like he had when shaping all of

Ethea, using what he'd learned from the First Mother. He didn't need a battle here. What he needed was to understand where the Aeta were headed and how the archivist had come to join them.

Tan stopped in front of the archivist. He lay unmoving, though his eyes were now open. Tan sensed the other man's tension, like a coiled snake waiting for an opportunity to strike. He sensed the intent hanging within the archivist as well.

"Use the knife or don't," Tan said. "You will find that you won't reach me if you try."

The archivist jerked his head around so that he could meet the Daughter's eyes. "Do not trust him. He is of Incendin. My family's caravan was attacked by one like him," he said.

The Daughter clutched her dress in her hands and her neck drooped. "You would do this?" she asked Tan

Tan restrained the urge to kick the archivist but allowed himself the small pleasure of a shaping of earth so the man couldn't move. "I've seen too many Aeta die already. This man is one of the archivists, sent to Ethea because of his ability to shape spirit. His kind have caused more destruction than any deserve. Where did you come across him?"

"Archivist?" she asked, blinking.

"He joined us in Doma." An elderly woman stood leaning on a twisted cane of oak. She had hair so gray as to be nearly white, and a sickly sheen left her skin glistening. A wide band of silver circled her neck. "His family was lost, he said. He is one of the People so we provided shelter."

"Mother," Tan said bowing to her. "The wagons are safe now." He glanced at the archivist, still wondering what to do with him. Leaving him with the Aeta was risky, especially if he escaped, but it seemed particularly cruel to release him to Incendin. "I'm sorry for your illness."

She swallowed and licked a dry tongue across her lips. Her voice came out weak and wavering. "You are from the kingdoms?"

"I am Tannen Minden, Athan to the king regent."

"You are young to be named Athan," she said and coughed. A thick bubble of blood-tinged phlegm came to her lips.

Tan used a soft shaping of spirit and water. She would need healing, but the illness he sensed was beyond him. He wondered if a water shaper skilled in healing would be able to help her or if she'd gone beyond the point where anything would help.

"Perhaps I am undeserving of the title," he said.

When the coughing fit passed, the mother regained her composure and took in the scene: Tan before her and Amia kneeling over the fire shaper. "You're a shaper, are you not?" the Mother asked.

"I am."

"What can you shape?"

"I am a warrior shaper," Tan answered simply

"And the Daughter?" she asked.

"You recognized her?" Tan asked.

The Mother pushed herself forward, using the cane for leverage. She coughed as she approached, then wiped her hand across her mouth. "You really think I should not have?"

He suspected that she sensed Amia working with spirit. Would she know when he did the same, or had she thought it only Amia? "She chose to leave the People," Tan answered.

The Mother stared at Amia. "A loss, then."

"You knew her?"

"Not her. I knew her Mother, and knew how proud she was of the blessing the Great Mother had bestowed upon her. Tell me, what happened to separate her from the People?"

"This is a long tale. Let's sit and we can talk," Tan said, taking her arm. She was frail and sickly and he feared her falling and injuring herself. Tan hadn't learned enough of water shaping to help her if she were to collapse.

When they reached the shadows near the wagons, the Mother took a seat on the nearest steps. The Daughter stood near her shoulder, and Kayl stayed near them both. Others of this group had managed to fully shake off the shaping the archivist had placed upon them. Some studied Tan discretely, or at least they tried to, while the remainder set about to going through the wagons.

"The lisincend attacked them," Tan said when the Mother was settled. He felt Amia's work on the fallen fire shaper as she steadily layered spirit over and over in an attempt to release him from the archivist's work. "They were captured. Most killed."

The Daughter cupped her hands to her mouth and gasped. "They would do that, Mother?"

The way the Mother watched Amia told him that *she* believed. "Did you know that he could shape?" he asked.

"He had some talent. Most sent to the university have some talent," the Mother answered.

"He was going to let the fire shaper destroy the wagons."

The Mother snapped her head toward him. Her hand quivered on the cane. "He is one of the People. He would not—"

He nodded to the daughter. "She has some skill, doesn't she?" he asked.

The Mother's mouth tightened.

"I am bound to a woman once Aeta. I've attended the Gathering. And I've learned from the First Mother. There may be secrets of the Aeta I don't know, but that isn't one of them," Tan said.

"You… you learned from the First Mother?" the Daughter asked, her voice dropping in reverence and her eyes widened.

Tan thought he understood: they traveled for the Daughter to learn. How would they react when they discovered that the First Mother was gone?

"I think he feared you reaching the Gathering with someone able to shape," he said.

"We answer the summons," the Mother said. "We've been called. The Gathering has been called. It is rare for the People to convene so often. Tell me, Athan, why are *you* here?"

"There was another caravan destroyed near the border," he said. "Made to look like Incendin or the draasin did it."

The Mother coughed into her hand. "Then the stories are true."

How far had word of the draasin's return spread? Far enough for the Aeta to have word. Far enough that Par-shon knew to send bonded shapers here after them. "They are. The draasin have returned. But they did not do this. For whatever reason, the archivist intended to destroy your wagon in a similar manner. Had we not arrived, you would all have been killed."

"You have prevented him from shaping us?" the Mother asked.

"He is bound. He cannot shape you now."

"Good," she said and then sighed slowly. "You have given me much to consider. When we reach the Gathering, we will seek guidance from the First Mother. She will help decide what must be done with him."

"I am not certain that it's safe for him to remain with you," Tan said.

"You are not of the People. *He* is. We will see that he's confined."

Amia came over to him then, wiping sweat from her brow as she walked. She shook her head slowly. "The shaping is complex," she said softly. "I can remove it, but it will take the better part of a day. Maybe more."

Tan considered their environment. They couldn't remain beneath the heat of the sun, and he didn't want the caravan delayed further.

They deserved to reach the mourning ceremony for the First Mother in time. “Taking him to the kingdoms will make him a prisoner, and he hasn’t done anything to warrant that.”

The Mother’s forehead wrinkled. “You attempt to heal the Incendin shaper?”

“He wasn’t complicit in this,” Tan said. “Anything that happened was shaped on him.”

The Mother’s mouth turned in a confused expression. “You seem almost… angry.”

“This isn’t the first time we have experience with spirit shaping,” Tan answered. “Think of how you’ve hidden this ability from the world. Think of all the things the Aeta were once accused of doing. And now think of how the archivists were willing to use this ability.” His voice rose as he spoke, but he didn’t care. The Aeta needed to know. Tan glared at the archivist and made a point of speaking loud enough for him to hear. “The kingdoms’ shapers have all learned how to protect their minds from spirit now. And a warrior shaper able to shape spirit has emerged.”

Amia sent a soothing shaping through their shared connection. “I could stay—”

“I’m not leaving you alone in Incendin,” Tan said.

“Let her travel with us,” the Mother said. Her gaze went from Amia to the Daughter, and Tan could see the wheels turning within her mind. “We make our way toward the Gathering. The First Mother said we would be welcomed in the kingdoms, that we could hold the Gathering openly.”

“Theondar has given you free passage,” Tan agreed.

At Theondar’s name, the Mother’s eyes widened slightly and she ran her hands across her dress. “It has been many years since the People did not have to hide the Gathering,” she said.

Amia touched his arm, pulling his attention to her. "I can do this before they reach the border with Incendin. Then we can release him to return to his people," Amia said.

"Are you certain?"

She studied the fire shaper, and he knew the thoughts going through her mind. He felt many of the same. Helping the fire shaper meant helping Incendin. Tan had intended to use Incendin, not necessarily help them, but something had to change if they were going to hold back Par-shon. Change had to start somewhere.

"I will do this," she said.

"Then I will stay—" Tan began.

Maelen!

Asboel's voice cut into his thoughts with a violent urgency. Tan turned to the sky, half-expecting to locate the draasin flying overhead, but there was nothing.

What is it?

Fire attacks like before. Come. There is not much time.

"Amia…" he started.

"Go. I will stay here and do what I can."

"I'll find you when this is finished," he said.

She smiled and touched his lips. "Go."

Tan pulled the warrior shaping down, the flash of white lightning catching him and lifting him to the sky as he focused on Asboel's location.

CHAPTER 18

Attack on Incendin

ASBOEL FLEW NEAR THE BORDER of Incendin and Galen. The mountains began sloping to the west, rising toward white-capped peaks, and Asboel soared above rock and a deep ravine that dropped to a thin stream far below.

Tan's shaping took him to the draasin's back and he stood for a moment, balanced atop Asboel. Without a word, he reached through the connection and saw through the draasin's sight. Far below, another caravan of Aeta wagons was stopped near the ridgeline. A bloom of light showed Tan the fire that already burned through the wagons, racing through like dried firewood, fed by the strength of the shaping. Tan could feel the way the shaper used fire, so different than anything he'd ever seen from Cianna.

Can you withdraw the fire from the wagons? he asked Asboel.

You still question the draasin with fire?

Well, if you can't, then I'll see if Honl can help.

Asboel roared and Tan smiled grimly as he leapt toward the ground on a shaping of lighting, using wind and earth to soften his landing.

Spirit assaulted him, more powerful than what the other archivist had attempted. Tan used what he knew of shapings to protect his mind, water and air combining to keep his thoughts safe. He unsheathed his sword and drew upon its strength, funneling a shaping of spirit and mixing each of the elementals within it. White light exploded from it.

Tan jumped to the wind, Honl aiding him, and hovered over the wagons. The flames raged, and already the wagons were too damaged to be functional. *Help Asboel,* Tan directed Honl. *Fire must be quenched here.*

The wind elemental slipped away, drifting down to smother the flames. At the same time, Asboel pulled on the fire, forcing it down and away from the wood and sending it deep into the earth.

Help the draasin, Tan demanded of the earth. It came as a booming, rolling command, and he wasn't certain that he'd even find an elemental of earth here.

The ground trembled in response. A deep, echoing sound drifted through his mind and was gone. Tan nearly lost control of his shaping.

Had he finally heard golud?

Another shaping struck at him, this coming from the fire shaper. Tan used the sword and caught the shaping, sending it off and into the ground.

A third shaper appeared, this one using wind. A cool breeze blew against his face, gusting out of Galen and toward him.

The archivist must have found a Doman shaper to twist as well.

Honl, Tan sent. *Help with this.*

The hot Incendin wind was strong here and Honl, one of the ashi elementals found throughout Incendin, smothered the wind shaping.

What were the chances that the archivists would attack these caravans at the same time?

They must have connected to each other somehow, warning the others. He had to end this now. Other caravans might be in danger.

Tan pulled on spirit, drawing as much as he could through the sword, mixing it with the other elementals much like he had when trying to reach Elle. Then he sent it sweeping it out and away from him in an angry rush.

Everything stopped.

The flames were extinguished, squelched by the combined effort of Asboel and Honl. With earth and spirit, Tan sensed the Aeta within the wagon. One wagon was too badly burned, the two Aeta within already dead. In other wagons, most lived, though they would need help.

Tan found the wind shaper. He lay against the middle of the caravan, the blackened sides of the wagon smearing against his dark leathers. Tan blocked his abilities in a shaping of spirit and left him there for the time being. Near the edge of the ridge, he found the fire shaper. She was younger, and dressed much like the wind shaper. He sensed the spirit shaping woven deep into her mind. Tan bound a quick shaping of spirit atop what the archivist had done, blocking her from reaching fire. Then he went searching for the archivist.

He was running from the wagons when Tan found him. He was flabby and older, a crop of gray hair thinning atop his head, his brown eyes sunken into the folds of his cheeks. Like the other archivist, he was dressed in a black robe.

"You will not shape spirit again," Tan whispered. Anger surged through him.

The archivist shook his head. "You can't do this—"

Tan didn't give him the chance to finish. He used a shaping of all the elements under his control and wrapped it around the archivist's mind, slicing it into place so sharply that it cut him off completely. Tan sealed the shaping, tying it in place. Even Amia might not be ale to remove it.

"What did you do?" the archivist asked in a panicked voice.

"Less than you deserved." He gave his prisoner a push toward the other two.

The archivist turned to face Tan, backing away from him. "You don't understand what you've done. You don't understand the danger you've placed—"

Tan shoved him again. "How many others?" he demanded.

"I don't know what you mean." He tried pulling away, but the shaping of wind held him in place.

"If you don't tell me what I want to know, I will feed you to my friend," Tan said. He jerked the archivist's head around so that he could see Asboel flying overhead.

The man's mouth dropped open and he started trembling. "The draasin," he breathed.

"How many more?" Tan demanded.

The archivist shook his head, unable to take his eyes off Asboel. "Most have already reached the Gathering. The First Mother sent that a successor would be chosen. We were to use the Gathering to take control," he blubbered. "You don't understand! We did it to protect the People—"

"Protect?" Tan repeated, stepping toward him. He almost unsheathed his sword in his anger. "By destroying them? You think that protects the People?"

The archivist sobbed and didn't answer.

"How many haven't reached the Gathering? How many were you going to destroy?"

The man didn't look up as he clutched his head between his hands. "We had to make it look like we were attacked."

With a hard jerk on the man's robe, Tan reclaimed his attention. Fire surged from Tan's skin, and he breathed out a puff of smoke. "Tell me!"

"I don't know! Five families crossed Incendin out of Doma, but we couldn't have any blessed by the Great Mother claimed by—"

Tan slammed his sword against the man's head, knocking him unconscious.

Five families. Counting the three they had found, that left two remaining.

Sashari. Is she here? he asked Asboel.

She is coming, Maelen.

She must take these people to join the others. Show her where.

It is done. What of you, Maelen?

I must hunt, Tan said.

They reached the next caravan not far from the last as it wound along the river valley. Like before, Tan had to use spirit to incapacitate the archivist and the Incendin shaper attacking, but they stopped the flames before they consumed the entire caravan. Three Aeta and all but one of the wagons were lost. Tan mourned them, but did not have time for more than that, pausing only long enough to soothe the survivors with a spirit shaping.

By the time they found the last caravan, they were too late. Fire raged through the wagons, consuming them completely. Nothing moved inside. The fire shaper responsible burned near the last wagon, as if he had thrown himself into the flames, immolating much like the lisincend Tan had once thought to heal. Only the archivist survived, hurrying alone across the Incendin waste. Tan chose no mercy and struck him with the full might of a combined shaping through his sword, destroying him completely.

He leaned against Asboel, numb.

You did all that you could, Maelen.

Did I? I knew the archivists were still out there. I should have hunted them before.

You cannot hunt everything. You cannot save everyone. This will have to be enough.

Tan said nothing as Asboel turned back toward the previous caravan. Cianna and Sashari were there. The slender draasin was perched away from the wagons, sitting as if ready to attack at any moment. She flickered her tail when she saw Asboel and breathed out a streamer of smoke. Asboel landed next to her and they nuzzled for a moment.

Tan dropped near the remains of the caravan to find Cianna dragging the surviving Aeta to a single wagon. Ash covered Cianna's skin, and the lines on her face left her looking weary. She took one look at Tan's face and nodded grimly.

"I will help," he said. Cianna stepped aside without saying anything.

Tan used spirit to keep the Aeta unaware as they rescued them. They would have time to mourn, but they would get them to safety first.

Tan breathed out, struggling with the emotion threatening to overcome him. He had been so focused on Par-shon, on Elle, that he hadn't paid attention to the other threat he knew still existed. How much of this could have been prevented? How had he have forgotten about the archivists?

Asboel watched him, but there was no sense through their bond of what he was thinking. *Can you carry this?* Tan asked, indicating the wagon.

Do you think I could not?

I think these people should be with the others, Tan said.

Asboel lowered his head, sensing Tan's mood. *Maelen, I will carry this. Sashari has already seen to the other wagons.*

Thank you.

All this time, he'd been struggling to convince Roine that Par-shon was the real threat, and all this time he had been overlooking another threat, equally real.

A tired sob worked through him. What would make the archivists attack their own people? How could they attack the Aeta, knowing how the People had already suffered?

Althem had been the same way, willing to harm the people of the kingdoms, and for what? Power? Some other reason?

And Tan thought he could use Incendin to help stop Par-shon? He couldn't even convince the shapers within the kingdoms to help him save Elle. What if Roine was right, that they should let Incendin and Par-shon bloody themselves?

But too many would suffer. Many already had suffered, including the elementals.

Tan tried to let go of the emotion washing over him, letting the cloud shaping carry him where it would.

Would he ever be strong enough to save everyone he cared about, or was that not what the Great Mother intended of him?

A bright light flashed to the east, deeper into Incendin. Tan let curiosity lead his travel. He felt no fear, nothing but a numb sense that had come over him after he'd been forced to destroy the archivist. Only, he hadn't been forced. That had been his choice, one made out of anger at what they had done to their own. Maybe that was the reason he felt so numb.

The farther he drifted, the better sense he had. He remained high overhead, hiding among the clouds. Far below him, he saw a city, somewhat larger than Velminth, spread across the land. The bright flashes came regularly and he realized what it was that he saw: fire shaping.

Tan changed his focus, stretching toward the ground with spirit and earth, wanting to gain understanding of the fire shaping. Maybe Incendin shapers really did attack their own people. Earth sensing gave him awareness of the fire. It streaked away from the village, but also toward it. Not just fire, but earth and wind came at the city in a steady torrent.

This was an attack.

Tan knew that he should return to Amia, that he should return to ensure the Aeta made it to safety, but he needed to know what this was.

His travel shaping brought him closer to the ground. The buildings here were different than any he'd ever seen, with rounded roofs covered with thick tiles. A stacked wall marked the city border. Unlike in other parts of Incendin, there were dozens of stunted and twisted trees growing throughout the city. The people he could see all ran from the shapings, their terror clear to his spirit sense.

A line of fire streaked across the ground, forming a complicated shape. A rune, and one that he'd seen in Par-shon. Tan frowned at it, reaching toward it with a sensing of fire and earth.

A trap. Par-shon used this rune to trap elementals.

More than anything else that he'd seen, seeing the trap angered him. That they would force what should be freely given, that they would attack the elementals…he could not allow it to continue.

Tan used a shaping of fire, mixing it with earth, attempting to draw the rune away from the ground. The rune pushed at him, as if trying to force him away, and the shaping failed. He added spirit and earth, blending water with it as well, and surged this toward the shaping. This failed as well.

Fire surged toward him, like a thing alive and suddenly aware he was there. Tan used the warrior sword and turned it away, unable to take his eyes off the trapped elementals. When another attack stretched toward him, he started into the air.

He nearly collided with a wind shaper who hung on a foreign shaping of wind. Between the man's clothes and the wrong feel of the shaping, Tan knew he faced someone from Par-shon.

Both were startled, but Tan recovered first, pulling on spirit and wind and forcing them into the rune he sensed on the bonded shaper. He had used this before, but this time, it failed. The Par-shon shaper, who was using a funnel of wind to force Tan to the ground, had been bound to his element differently. What Tan had done before wasn't going to work this time.

Tan pulled with increased strength on the sword. His feet touched the ground as wind swirled around him, attempting to suffocate him. Then, with another push, the bond exploded and the shaper fell. Tan couldn't react in time to save the Par-shon shaper, and he dropped to the ground and landed in a limp pile.

Tan jumped to the air again. Honl reached him and supported him, aiding his shaping.

Dangerous, Tan. You should have Fire with you.

Fire is needed elsewhere, Tan answered. *Keep me in the air. We will help these people.*

Earth sensing told him there were at least two other shapers outside the city, one of fire and one of earth. Tan focused on them and found the fire shaper first.

He was near the outer edge of the city, using his elemental bond to hold him aloft. He readied a shaping of spirit and fire, and mixed earth within it. The shaper spun and twisted, streaking toward him.

Tan used Honl to help him slide to the side and avoid the shaper, but earth reached for him and pulled him from the air.

Too late, he realized this shaper had bonded two elementals.

Honl!

Honl could do nothing to free him from an earth elemental bound to a Par-shon shaper. The shaping was powerful and gripped him, holding him in place.

The arm holding his sword was trapped. With his free hand, he jerked on the other while sending an earth shaping through the ground, but the bonded elemental overpowered him.

The fire shaper spun into place overhead. He smiled darkly.

Using a mixture of all the elements, with spirit binding them, Tan breathed out a shaping.

It took nearly all the energy he had remaining. Without his sword, it was unfocused, but caught the fire shaper in a flash of white light.

Still holding the shaping—or what remained of it—Tan jerked his arm free and shifted his focus to draw through the sword, at the same time pulling on Honl, on Asboel, on the other unnamed elementals all around him, drawing strength from them. He jumped to the air to figure out what else he could do. The fire trap burning on the edge of Incendin seemed to have faded, but it still held the elementals within.

There must be another holding it in place.

Tan found another earth shaper destroying the wall to the village, burying a shaper beneath the earth. Earth sensing told Tan that the Incendin shaper still lived, but barely. The Par-shon shaper was a solid man, his head shaven, with a patch of beard growing from his chin. His black eyes widened when he saw Tan.

Tan used an earth and spirit shaping to dissolve the Par-shon shaper's bond. His shaping failed and he crumpled.

The Incendin shaper was still trapped beneath the earth. Tan's strength was fading, and he feared lingering much longer. He needed to leave, but knowing that someone—even an Incendin shaper—was trapped by earth made him pause.

Could he really help Incendin? Hadn't he already by allowing Amia to remove the spirit shapings from the Incendin shapers the archivists had used?

He felt the pressure from the shaper attempting to wrest free from the earth.

Whatever else happened, he wouldn't let the shaper die.

He sent a demand to the earth elemental. *Release him!*

He wasn't sure if the earth would answer or if he was still strong enough to send, but the earth rumbled and a faint sound rolled through the back of his mind. The ground parted and the Incendin shaper crawled free. She was thin and covered with dust. Black hair was tied in a thick braid and her sharp eyes scanned the city first before catching the Par-shon shaper lying unmoving.

Tan took a moment to press out with spirit and earth. No other shapers were there.

"Who are you?" she asked, taking in his clothing and the warrior sword gripped in his hand. A fire shaping built from her, and she kept it readied and unused.

Tan considered answering, but was too tired to think of the right thing to say. Would Incendin think a kingdoms' shaper had attacked or would they realize that he'd done what he could to help?

"An ally," Tan said.

His strength sagged. If he waited, he might not be strong enough to return to Amia.

He pulled the travel shaping down on him and disappeared in a bolt of lightning. As he did, he briefly glimpsed the Incendin shaper watching him.

CHAPTER 19

The Gathering and a Choice

NIGHT HAD FALLEN BY THE TIME TAN returned to the Aeta. Amia was waiting for him, the worry on her face reflected strongly through their bond. She half-carried him to the caravan, pulling him between two wagons. She said nothing until she had him settled comfortably. The dark rings around her worried eyes said plenty.

The fire shaper he'd first rescued sat nearby. Amia's shaping had already helped him. How much longer until he was fully restored?

"What happened?" she asked him, drawing his attention away from the fire shaper.

"I… I killed one of the archivists," he said, making a point of keeping his voice lowered.

Since leaving here only hours before, so much had changed. The camp had nearly tripled as Aeta had been brought from the other two caravans to join this family. The wagons had been set into a tight circle, and a single fire pit glowed warmly in the middle. The sounds of a soft lute mixed with the strumming of a mandolin, almost as if unmindful of the fact that they camped in the midst of Incendin and might be discovered. Singers added their voices. Some people danced while others sat around the fire, speaking softly to one another.

"Cianna told me," she said.

"Where is she?"

Amia inclined her head toward the fire. Tan caught sight of the fire shaper's red hair. She chewed on a lump of bread and laughed as one of the Aeta spoke to her.

"And her draasin?" he asked.

He sensed Asboel, but he was faint. Tan suspected he had returned to the den beneath the city. Cianna would know where Sashari was.

"Ethea, I think. There were a few surprised faces when Sashari carried the first wagon and set it near the others. There were a few more surprised when Asboel came with his wagon."

Tan allowed himself to smile.

"I've been working with the Incendin shapers." She motioned to the one sitting nearby. "There isn't much more that I can do for him. Some healing requires him to choose."

"And the archivists?"

"The Mother saw them bound and separated. Tan," Amia started, hesitating as she peered around the camped wagons. "I worry what will happen when they reach the Gathering. What would make them rejoin the caravans?"

Tan shared the same concern. If the archivists were openly attacking, what would they do when all of the Aeta gathered? Was there anything he could do, or would it have to come from the Aeta? And *why* had they chosen to attack?

"I'm sorry I took so long to return," he said.

"Are you?"

"If the archivists can do this to their people, if they could attack..." He couldn't finish. The archivists had attacked their people, but he had destroyed the archivist in anger. Was that who he had become?

"You've only done what's been needed," Amia said.

"That wasn't needed."

Tan stared at the fire, watching the flames dance within it, swaying to the sounds of the Aeta music. Even here, saa was drawn to the fire.

"Par-shon attacks Incendin," he said after a while. "And they trap elementals."

Amia's breath caught. "You saw it?"

The longer he sat here, the better he felt. Not that he felt good, only that his strength had returned. With the help of the elementals, he was refreshed more quickly these days.

"I saw it," he admitted. Amia might have known anyway. The bond between them would have given her insight about what he saw, but she'd also been distracted trying to heal the Incendin shaper. "There were three Par-shon shapers attacking a city. Incendin had only one fire shaper for protection."

A soft voice spoke with a harsh whisper in the dark shadows near the wagon. "Where was the attack?" The fire shaper stared at the dancing flames but didn't move as he spoke. No shaping built from him. There was no fight in him.

"I don't know. A city to the north and east. A stone wall surrounded it. There were trees." Tan said the last as if it was somehow important. He knew so little of Incendin, not enough to know how common copses of trees like he'd seen were found.

"Lashasn."

Amia nodded, touching the gold band around her neck as she did.

"I have been there once before. The people were welcoming. Happy traders."

"They were attacked?" the fire shaper asked. "What happened?"

"I stopped Par-shon. Your shaper lives."

The fire shaper stared at Tan with hollowed eyes. "But you are of the kingdoms. Why would you let them live?"

"She did nothing but protect her home. I did what I could to help."

The man studied Tan for a moment and then turned his attention back to the fire, the light sending shadows shifting across his features.

"There were two from the other caravans," Tan said. "What happened to them?"

Amia pointed toward a wagon to his left. "They are within that one. The Mother set men to watch, but you left them restrained."

He sighed. What he needed from Incendin started now. If they were to use Incendin—no, if they were to work *with* Incendin—he would have to see them fully healed. Amia would have to help. "If they were shaped, I wanted to give you a chance to remove it." From the way the fire shaper stiffened, Tan could tell the he was listening. "All will be needed to face Par-shon."

"I will do what I can." Amia took his hand and squeezed. "These families…" she started.

"They must reach the Gathering. They will mourn the First Mother, as they should, but these families must reach the Gathering." He looked into her eyes, not certain how she would react to what he needed to say next. "You will need to be there, Amia. If the archivists attempt something more…"

Amia nodded slowly. "I will do what I can," she whispered.

For the trip to the final Gathering summoned by the First Mother, Tan shaped earth and wind to carry all the wagons, horses, and Aeta across the lands.

Amia spent her time working with the Incendin shapers. The Daughter stayed with her, watching her work, and Amia didn't seem bothered by the company. On the contrary, she began teaching the young Aeta, allowing her to assist where she could.

The Mother came to him as they camped their second night. The landscape of Incendin had changed little in spite of the speed they traveled. The waste was barren and bleak, and the hot sun burned constantly.

Tan sat alone, off to the side of the fire. Cianna had remained with them as they traveled, more for curiosity, he suspected, than any need for protection. Tan was happy to have her with them just the same. If they were attacked, it would be good to have another shaper to help.

"This is you, is it not?" she began. "You're helping us reach the Gathering." A coughing fit overcame her and she covered her mouth, hiding the thick phlegm that she coughed up.

"I'm doing what I can to help," Tan said. "There's only so much that I can do, but you need to reach the Gathering."

She studied him. "I cannot sense you, or the Daughter, but I've grown skilled at reading people in other ways. There is something you do not wish to tell me."

"It is not mine to share. I am not of the People."

The Mother snorted. "You have saved three caravans from attack."

"And what of the caravans that were lost?" he asked.

"What of them? What would have become of the caravans had you done nothing? You deserve no blame for what happened." She coughed again as Tan watched her, but her eyes were bright, still vibrant and filled with strength. "Now, tell me what you think I should not hear."

He sighed inwardly. The Mother deserved to know, but should he really be the one? "You remind me of Amia's mother. I didn't know her long, barely a few days, but she had the same strength." Tan smiled at her memory, and of the way she had stood up to Zephra. "Amia is much like her. She pushes me the same way." He inhaled deeply, and met the Mother's eyes. "She is gone, Mother. That is why she called the Gathering. I suspect that she knew her time was short."

The Mother's breath caught and she began to nod her head slowly. "Perhaps she did. She has served for many years. She has guided the People through many difficult years. Her wisdom and leadership will be missed." She coughed again and abandoned an effort to stand. "I will need to share with the others."

The Aeta didn't know what else the First Mother had done, or how Theondar had held her at the end. What purpose would that serve, other than to stain her memory? It was best that only those who knew what she'd done were tainted by those memories.

"The Gathering will choose a new First Mother?" Tan asked.

"Normally, a successor has already been chosen, but only when the families are all gathered will she be revealed."

"The Mothers have some idea," Tan said.

"Some," she agreed.

"The last Gathering was interrupted. Do you think she has chosen a successor?"

The Mother stared at the Daughter, shaping spirit with Amia as they worked to heal the wind shaper. Tan still suspected the wind shaper to be one of the Doman shapers, stolen by Incendin.

Another coughing fit overwhelmed the Mother. Then she smiled at Tan. "I don't know what plans she had in place. So many families have been lost. Perhaps her choice was among them. That is what *they* hope," she said, motioning toward the remaining archivists, who sat in a ring near the fire.

"They want to influence the choice?" Tan asked.

"They are afraid," she began. "That one," she pointed to the sharp-faced man who had attacked her wagon, "was in Doma when the attacks began. I think he fears them."

Tan studied the archivist, wondering if there was a connection to what Par-shon did and the archivists' return. The man seemed to sense Tan's eyes on him and turned and met Tan's gaze. "We should all fear them," Tan said.

"We have nothing to fear if we choose to honor the Great Mother," she said. "Her hand guides us all."

She smiled and then the Mother stood, taking a moment to compose herself, and made her way to the fire, touching her people lightly as she greeted them. Occasionally, she stopped and joined in a song, but only until she began to cough. Her way of touching her people reminded Tan of the First Mother.

The Incendin shapers remained behind when the caravan crossed the border into the kingdoms. Even the wind shaper wanted to remain behind. Amia wasn't able to tell whether he had been shaped by the First Mother or not, but said that all signs of shapings had been removed from him.

Now that they were closer to Ethea, Tan risked even more of his strength to power the wagons, and they moved even faster toward the Gathering. He wanted to get the Aeta to the others as quickly as possible, not only so they could reunite with their people and find their strength again but because this journey had cost him two days in his search for Elle, two days that he'd begun to see how far Par-shon had already pushed.

Did he dare wait until Roine was ready to face the threat, or did he need to do something on his own?

Answers didn't come, at least none that were easy.

By the evening of that third day, the wagons reached the Gathering.

Tan had grown increasingly tense the closer they came and the Aeta grew increasingly somber. Word had spread about the First Mother, and a mournful sense had come over everyone. Amia sat next to him atop the lead wagon, silently staring at the gathered families.

He let the wagons slow, conserving some of his energy as he prepared for the possibility that he would need to shape spirit if any archivists remained. There was at least one more, the one who had summoned when he and Roine had answered. What would happen when these three archivists joined the other?

Without needing to say a word, the wagons already gathered parted, splitting and widening the circle. Their caravan rolled into place, filling the gap. Tan didn't feel that he should be a part of this, but didn't move away from the circle. The Aeta were in the kingdoms and as Athan, it was his responsibility to ensure their safety.

When the wagons came to a stop, the Mothers joined the other gathered Mothers.

"What will happen now?" Tan asked.

"They would have been mourning this entire time. They waited for the remaining families to arrive."

"Will there be others?" he asked.

"I sense that this is it."

"What of the archivists?" Tan asked. He scanned the Aeta, looking for signs them, but couldn't see them. Using a shaping of earth and spirit, he quested for them, searching in the wagons. Anyone standing in the middle of the circle able to shape would be one of the Mothers, or possibly the Daughters.

"It depends upon the Mothers," Amia said, "though it really depends on who is chosen to follow the First Mother. She will decide."

The sickly Mother motioned to Tan and Amia. The others stared, watching them, as the Mother spoke.

"Is that our sign to go?" Tan asked.

"Not yet," Amia said.

There was tension in her voice, though he didn't feel it through their bond. Instead, he sensed a hint of apprehension—and also a sense of reluctant acceptance.

What did Amia know?

The Mothers started toward them, moving together. As they did, three men emerged from wagons on the far side of the circle. All wore the black robe signifying the archivists. Tan felt their shaping build simultaneously, with more power than he thought he'd be able to contain.

Amia stood casually, as if expecting this. The shaping she crafted was more immense than anything he'd seen her perform outside of working with the First Mother while attempting to heal Cora. This was nothing like that shaping. This was elegant and complex, but powerful as well.

As she shaped, Tan realized she drew *through* him, borrowing from his stores, and used this to lash out at the archivists.

They didn't have a chance to struggle. There was strength to their combined shaping, but it was nothing compared to what Amia managed. She overpowered them easily.

They stopped near the fire as if to run. Tan held them with earth.

Amia touched the band at her neck as the Mothers approached. The sense of apprehension from her intensified.

"Daughter," the Mother from their wagon said.

Amia tipped her head. "I no longer have right to that title. I renounced my claim to the People."

The Mother smiled at her. "You may have renounced it, but the People have not renounced you. It became clear to me as we traveled that the First Mother *had* prepared for her passing." She tottered forward another step, leaning fully on her cane. Tan sensed the effort she exerted to remain upright. "I do not know what transpired to convince you to renounce the People, and the Great Mother knows I may not need to know. If it is because of Tan, then the choice was a folly. He has proved himself many times to serve the People." She caught Amia's eyes, holding them with a commanding strength. "Will you follow his example? Will you serve the People?"

Amia remained silent. He sensed the conflicted emotions running through her, but underneath was a sense of purpose that had been missing from her for so long.

Do what you must, he sent through the connection.

Amia tensed as she took a deep breath, facing the Mothers. Then a serene sense of peace worked over her and passed through the bond to Tan.

"For now, I will serve," she said.

CHAPTER 20

A Decision Made

WHEN TAN RETURNED TO THE HOUSE that night, the small room felt empty and cold without Amia. Now that she'd agreed to serve as First Mother, Amia remained behind with the Aeta, and had needed to meet with the other Mothers to decide the fate of the People, and the archivists. Since returning, Tan hadn't bothered to start a fire in the hearth, even though it would not take much of a shaping. The chill flowing through him was not something fire would remove.

He had pulled the window open, letting the combination of ashi and ara swirl through the room, carrying the sounds of the street below him. Voices carried from dozens of people still out at night. Music drifted distantly from a tavern somewhere, the first time he'd heard a sense of merriment coming from within the city since the attack months ago.

He stood at the window, focusing on his connections. Asboel circled the distant countryside—probably Vatten, from what Tan could see through his shared sight—hunting with Sashari. Honl remained near Tan though was mostly silent, content to remain near his bond.

Then there was Amia. That was the bond he most feared losing. He sensed her distantly, where she remained with the Gathering. For the first time in months, she exuded a sense of purpose. She was content.

How would serving as First Mother change things between them? Not their bond; that would not change. But the physical sense of her was missing. He had become accustomed to having her with him and now she would not be. He could travel to her, but he couldn't stay with her, not if he intended to serve as Athan. Responsibilities pulled them in different directions, drawn by the demands of their people. Would they ever be able to simply remain content, together?

Now that they'd returned to Ethea, Tan couldn't shake the thought that he needed to do more. Incendin couldn't face Par-shon alone, and Doma couldn't be left to suffer. As a shaper bound to the elementals, Tan could help. Wasn't that the reason he'd been given the ability to speak to the elementals?

A knock at the door pulled his attention away from his thoughts. They were troubled thoughts anyway, and he was thankful for the distraction.

On the other side of the door, he found Zephra. She wore a heavy brown cloak and her graying hair was pulled into a braid. "Mother," he said.

"You've been gone. I expected you to return to the city after I showed you the draasin attack. Theondar expected you—"

"Theondar expects me to do what is needed," Tan said, gently reminding her that he was Athan. "It was not the draasin. They had not attacked the Aeta. This was something worse. The archivists, making it appear that it was the draasin or Incendin, for some reason I have yet to learn." He wished he understood what would make them return to the Aeta. Could they have learned of Par-shon? Did they return for safety?

"You're certain?"

"We found four more caravans. We were able to save three."

Her eyes narrowed and she tapped a finger on pursed lips. "That is where you've been. You've been saving the Aeta when Incendin continues to move and attack? You are Athan now, Tannen, you have greater responsibilities than—"

"I do not need you to tell me what my responsibilities are, Mother. *I* am the Athan."

She hesitated before saying anything. "What of the Aeta, then?"

"They are Gathering. The First Mother is gone and they have selected another."

Zephra frowned, glancing around the room and noting that Amia was missing. "I thought that she abandoned them."

"Only because she thought they abandoned her. I don't think Amia ever really could leave the People. They are a part of who she is."

"She was selected?" Zephra asked.

Tan's voice caught as he answered. "She was. She agreed to serve."

Without saying anything, his mother wrapped her arms around him in a tight hug. For a moment, Tan was a child again, living in the mountains of Nor. For a moment, he was reminded of the closeness he'd once shared with his mother. Then she released the hug and pushed away from him.

Tan forced confidence into his voice that he still didn't completely feel. "She needed to do this. The Aeta needed her to serve." He took a breath and pushed away. Much like Amia needed to serve, Tan was beginning to realize that he needed to do more than he had. Seeing

Par-shon attacking had made that clear. If they left Doma helpless, what would happen by the time Par-shon reached the kingdoms? "What of you? What did you learn in Incendin?"

"Their shapers are amassing. I've seen movement but have been unwilling to venture too close. I don't know what it means."

"It means Par-shon attacks Incendin directly," Tan said. Would Roine understand if he shared how he'd helped Incendin? Would any of the kingdoms' shapers understand?

Tan still wasn't certain how he felt about helping Incendin. It was one thing to use them, but another to actively help. Incendin had destroyed his home, had taken his father, and everyone he'd ever known at the time, away from him. But had he not helped, Par-shon would have destroyed the city.

"Good," she said. "Let Incendin and Par-shon destroy each other. They will weaken each other, and the kingdoms will be safer for it."

Tan was not surprised that Zephra shared the same thought as Roine. They had lived through Incendin wars. "The kingdoms are not safer with Par-shon on our shores."

"But they aren't on our shores, Tannen. They have come to Doma, and now to Incendin. I know you fear Par-shon, and I fear, too, what would happen were they to reach the kingdoms, but this is for the best. Theondar has us working to rebuild the barrier. In another month, we will have it reformed, strengthened again, and we will no longer have to fear Incendin crossing our borders."

"The barrier never really kept their shapers out," Tan said. "Even the lisincend managed to cross. It will not keep Par-shon from us, either."

"They only crossed at great cost to themselves. We have learned since then. When complete, the barrier will seal out Par-shon and Incendin alike."

"Which means we seal ourselves inside?" Tan asked. That felt like cowardice, and worse: it abandoned the elementals beyond the barrier.

His mother's eyes narrowed. "I thought this would please you. You've seen what Incendin and Par-shon can do more closely than most. This will bring our people peace."

Whatever it did, building the barrier only delayed what was coming. He'd seen how Par-shon had attacked the village of Lashasn. What was next? Would Chenir suffer the same fate? How many would fall? How many elementals would be trapped and forced to bond in that time?

Too many would suffer if he did nothing.

"Has there been any additional word from Elle?" she asked.

"None. Doma is silent."

Either she had died, or Par-shon had separated her from her bond, assuming that she had managed to form a bond to the udilm. Either way meant that she was lost. Yet there was something he could do, something that he began to suspect he *had* to do, especially now that he'd seen the way Par-shon attacked. If he waited much longer, the kingdoms would be in real danger.

When he hesitated too long, Zephra studied him. "What do you intend, Athan?"

He couldn't tell if she used the title as a slight or if there was pride in her voice. Regardless, he didn't know what he would do. There was what he wanted, different even than what others wanted of him, and then there was what was needed.

None answered his mother's question.

"I will do what is best for the kingdoms," he said.

His mother let out a deep, gratified sigh. "I know you will. At least the Aeta have gathered within the kingdoms. You do not have to fear losing Amia."

Then she departed, leaving him staring after her, wishing that she could understand that though he might not have Amia with him, he would never really lose her.

The lower level of the archives was cool, no evidence of ashi blowing through, nothing but the damp walls suffused with the nymid and golud. Tan trailed his fingers along the stone as he made his way through the tunnels. Asboel was here and he needed to speak to him about his plan.

He paused at the pool where he'd bonded the nymid. Green water swirled within, moving slowly. Tan touched it and found it cooler than before. *Nymid*, he sent. *Is there word from the Child of Water?*

The nymid swirled with increased agitation, before settling. A streamer of green crawled up Tan's arm, settling around his neck. *He Who is Tan. You asked for word on the Child. Water still searches.*

Does she live?

That was what he feared more than anything. Elle could be dead, and then what? Because he'd acted too slow? It was the same as what had happened to the Aeta. He had acted too slowly to be of any real help.

He couldn't do that with Par-shon, not and risk the entirety of the kingdoms. But acting as he suspected he needed meant more than risking his life facing Par-shon, it meant going against what Theondar wanted. If he did, the kingdoms' shapers would not come to help. He would be isolated, but hopefully not alone.

You will try to help the Child? the nymid asked.

I think I have to, Tan said, coming to a decision. *I've been given the ability to help the elementals, to keep them safe. If I do nothing, I have already failed.*

The nymid swirled up and around his neck, leaving him with a vague sensation, not at all unpleasant. *The Mother chose well.*

Tan started toward the draasin den. He let his hand trail along the wall as he did, wishing he could somehow figure out the secret to reaching golud more easily. The elemental was there, he *felt* it, and he'd heard the distant sound of golud deep in his mind, but it was not consistent. He sighed; maybe it didn't matter. Maybe all that mattered was that golud listened.

Asboel waited for him inside the draasin den, his yellow eyes glowing with a keen intensity. The hatchlings weren't in this part of the cavern. *Maelen. You have made a choice, but you are uncertain.*

It's what I must ask of you that makes me uncertain.

Asboel made that strange chuckling sound that he did. *Do not fear for the draasin, Maelen. There is a reason we have survived the longest.*

Because you were frozen?

Asboel snorted fire at him. *You have grown confident. You will need confidence with what you intend.*

This must stop, he started, thinking of the way Par-shon attempted to trap the elementals in Incendin, *and it will start by clearing Doma. Only, I'm not certain whether it's confidence or foolishness.*

Fools are confident without reason. You are no fool, Maelen.

Tan wished he knew whether that was true. He turned in place, studying the rocks piled behind Asboel. *Where are the hatchlings?*

They learn the hunt.

I'm sorry I keep you from it, Tan said.

It was Sashari's turn for the lesson. You have a different hunt in mind.

I do, but what I must ask puts you in danger. If Par-shon manages to capture you, there might be little I can do.

You will know. You would come, Maelen. That is enough. Asboel stretched his neck forward to peer more closely at Tan.

You will hunt with me? Tan asked.

Asboel sniffed a streamer of fire at Tan. The fire melted away from him. *I have already said that you will never hunt alone.*

Then we will go soon, but there are a few others I must ask.

Sashari will come.

And if you're injured? Tan feared what would happen to the hatchlings were he to fail. They had nearly been lost once; he didn't want to be the reason they were lost again.

The hatchlings will be safe if we fail in the hunt. They grow strong. Soon, they will be strong enough to take on a name. Do not fear for them, Maelen. Asboel crawled forward in the den and pressed his face close to Tan. *This is what the Mother means for you to do. This is why the Mother aided our bond.*

I intend to return, Tan said.

Asboel sniffed and made a soft grunting sound. *All intend to return from the hunt. Not all can.*

The bonded cannot be allowed to force any more of the elementals. The others don't see it, but if they reach these lands, in this place of convergence, there will be nothing to stop them.

That is why we will stop them, Asboel agreed. *That is a reason to hunt.*

CHAPTER 21

Price of Freedom

AS TAN ENTERED THE ROOM where Cora was held, he found her with her hands folded in her lap flipping absently through a book lying open in front of her. Light from a shapers lantern lit her page, and a cracking fire raged in the hearth. The air smelled of cut flowers and the mint tea steaming from the cup set onto the table next to her.

"You have been gone many days. There are some who worry about you," she said.

"I'm sorry. I should have warned you that I'd be gone."

"You owe me nothing," she said, but he heard the sense of frustration in her voice at his silence. She'd agreed to the barrier formed by Amia's shaping, but leaving her like that indefinitely—especially alone after what she'd gone through—seemed a cruel torment.

"I owe you an explanation. And an opportunity."

Cora waited for him.

"Par-shon has moved beyond Doma. They have begun attacking in Incendin."

Cora gripped her skirt, squeezing it in her fist. "You have heard this?"

"I have seen. Three bonded shapers attacked a city on the northeastern edge. There was a single shaper there, not enough to stop them."

Her eyes fell closed. "What city was lost?"

"None. At least not when I last saw." Cora studied him, searching for answers. "I did what I could. There were three Par-shon shapers there."

"You?"

"You think I would not?"

"You have described how the Sunlands have hurt your people. I did not think that—"

"And I have seen what happens when Par-shon is left to attack unchecked. I can't say that I agree with how Incendin has striven for power, or how they've used that power once they achieved it," he took a deep breath before going on, "but I don't blame their people for wanting anything more than peace."

It was the only thing he wanted, and now he might not have a chance at it until Par-shon was stopped. Even then, what would peace be like? Would he be able to settle with Amia, to have the home that both of them wanted? Or would there always be a new threat, new archivists or Incendin or Par-shon, always wanting to tear them apart?

Cora placed her hands flat on her lap. "What would you have me do? You claimed there was an opportunity."

"I would ask for your help," Tan said. "You're a shaper, trained by Lacertin. I don't expect much help from the kingdoms, but Incendin needs help. Doma must be freed. We must stop Par-shon."

"You would free me and release me to the Sunlands?"

"Par-shon bonded aren't the only ones who take shapers and try to use them against their will. There are others, nearly as bad, and they call themselves archivists. You would have been gone when they attacked, or maybe you were a part of their plan." Tan didn't want to know if that was true. It would make him asking Cora for her help even more difficult. "But they are spirit shapers controlled by our king. They thought to use our shapers in plans of their own. They have returned, and now they attempt to use Incendin shapers. Amia has freed those we've found, and we left them in Incendin."

"You healed them?" Tan nodded. Cora leaned toward him. "That is not the response I would expect from the kingdoms. Perhaps one of these days, I will understand."

It wasn't the reaction he expected, though Tan didn't know what he expected from her. "You haven't answered me yet. Will you help?"

"A chance to return to the Sunlands. To help my people and avenge what Par-shon has done?" She stood and crossed her arms over her chest. "Of course I will help."

Tan allowed himself a moment of relief. He had expected that Cora would help, but hadn't been entirely certain. He needed her for any hope for his plan to work. If she was the shaper Cianna claimed, then she could go to Incendin and convince them to stop attacking the kingdoms. Maybe then they could begin to work together.

"When do we do this?" Cora asked.

"How about now? Are you ready to return home?"

"Ready? I was prisoner in Par-shon and now the kingdoms. Each time I've been held by shapers with more power than anyone I've ever faced." She fixed him with a curious glance. "What would you ask of me?"

"Ask?"

"Demands. What is the price of my freedom?"

"Only that you do what you can to oppose Par-shon."

"And you? What is it that you intend?"

"I will go to Doma. I intend to push Par-shon from Falsheim and find my cousin if she lives. It needs to stop now, before they move further inland. I think the first attack was only to determine the defenses within the border cities. When this comes, your shapers must be ready. If I fail, you will be needed. The Sunlands must be ready."

Cora actually smiled. "You don't even know how many Par-shon are in Doma," she said.

"No."

"And you think you can do this thing on your own?"

Thinking that he had to be the only one to help had been his mistake in the past. When he went to Doma, he did so on behalf of the elementals and the people of this land. Tan did not expect to be alone. Asboel would be with him. Sashari with Cianna. Honl. And there would be other elementals, not bonded, who Par-shon had not yet been able to force into their service. The Great Mother had given him the ability to speak to the elementals for a reason. This was part of that reason.

"What makes you think I'll be alone?" he asked. He went to the door and waved her forward. "Come, Cora, it's time you return to your homeland."

Cora trailed behind, her eyes scanning all around as if half-expecting her sudden freedom to be a trap. When they stopped in the middle of the university courtyard, Tan saw hope filling her eyes. Tan remembered the first time he'd seen her, when *nothing* had been there. It was good that she had been healed, just as it was good that Amia had healed the Incendin shapers twisted by the archivists.

Without waiting, Tan reached toward the shaping surrounding her mind and quickly unraveled it. Cora gasped. Wind and fire shaped softly from her, and the earth rumbled faintly.

"If this fails and Par-shon attacks from more than only Doma," Tan started, not certain how to continue. That was a real possibility, but he counted on the strength of the Fire Fortress to still serve as some sort of deterrent. It had to be the reason Doma had been targeted. It was the reason he feared for a place like Chenir, mostly hidden from the kingdoms. Either would be ideal launching points for an attack without worrying about the Fire Fortress and the strength found there.

Cora raised a hand. "You have done more than any would ever have expected, Tan."

With that, she pulled a traveling shaping and disappeared in a flash of light.

As Tan stared after her, he sensed Ferran approach. "Will you report me to Roine?" he asked the earth shaper.

Ferran removed the shaping that partially obscured him. "You released her to return to Incendin?" He sat on one of the remaining piles of rock, his lean face hidden in shadows. He wore loose breeches and a plain shirt. His face was unshaven, making him appear older than when Tan had first met him.

"Cora is not our enemy," Tan said.

Ferran stood, and stepped out of the shadows. "Perhaps she is not, but Incendin remains our enemy. One shaper does not change that."

"It's more than one shaper," Tan said, mostly to himself. He hoped that were true. Would releasing the spirit shaped Incendin make a difference? "It's late for you to be here," Tan said.

Ferran nodded toward the university building. "The stone calls to me."

"You're an earth shaper," Tan answered. "Of course it would call to you."

Ferran met his eyes. "That is not it. This is different."

Tan went to the pile of fallen rock, noting the progress that had been made with the university in such a short time, and understood. "You hear them, don't you?" he asked.

"I have lived my life knowing the earth elementals exist, but never expected to hear them. No one hears them, not for many years. And then I met you. You are able to speak to golud. The first since the ancient scholars. And now?" His voice grew more incredulous. "How is it this is possible? How is it that I now hear them?"

It was more than Tan had managed with golud, but it seemed fitting that it should be Ferran who would reach golud. He was a Master earth shaper, as skilled as any Tan had ever seen, and able to use earth in ways that Tan could not, not yet, and not without asking it of the elementals.

"Has one named itself?" Tan asked. He didn't want to know the name, only whether a bond had formed.

"I… I am too frightened to answer. The voices are there, like the steady rolling of thunder after a storm. I feel them within me."

"Ferran," Tan said, "you must answer them."

"Why is this, Tan? Why should I suddenly gain this?"

Tan didn't know. Maybe it was the same reason Sashari chose the bond. Maybe something was changing, the elementals choosing sides, knowing that it would be needed as the fight with Par-shon became inevitable. Or maybe it was none of that. Why wouldn't Ferran be worthy?

"There are many reasons you would have been chosen," Tan answered. "Any one of them a valid reason for golud to wish to speak to you. The thing is," he went on, trying to make Ferran understood how important what he said next would be, "is that the elementals need the connection to shapers, whether they know it or not. When the draasin and I first bonded, he didn't think there was anything for him to gain from the bond. Maybe that was true at first, but it isn't now.

With what is coming, all of us are in danger, including the elementals. So please listen to golud. Answer if you can. The kingdoms will need your connection to the golud, and the elemental will benefit as well."

Ferran focused on the ground. "I trust that you've made the decision necessary, Athan. May the Great Mother watch over you."

Ferran returned to the stone pile and took a seat in the shadows. Tan hoped he opened himself to golud.

For the first time in a long time, when thinking about what they might face, he felt hope. If the kingdoms' shapers could regain a connection to the elementals, then they might be able to withstand an attack even if Tan failed. They might be able to protect the elementals in his absence. And there was a real possibility that the shaping he intended, where he needed to go, would fail.

You understand what I must do, he sent to Amia.

Her answer came slowly, as if reluctantly. *I understand. I could come with you.*

You have a different task now.

I do, but I will have you return to me, she said.

The elementals will see that I return.

Before departing, there was one more place he needed to go, one more friend he needed to warn. This might be the hardest of all.

Honl, Tan said, *we must go to the palace.*

As Tan shaped himself toward the palace, he pressed a shaping through the summoning rune, calling to Roine. When he arrived, a lone figure stood in the courtyard.

"Theondar," he said, using Roine's given name. Now that he served as king regent, in some ways, Theondar was more fitting. In Tan's mind, he would always be Roine, a man hiding that he was a warrior shaper, that he had abilities that very few elsewhere in the world possessed.

"When you summoned, I thought it might be a mistake. Tannen

has been missing for days, without word of where he traveled." Roine was dressed in a simple ornate robe, each day looking more like a king and less like the warrior he had been.

"The archivists attacked again," Tan said.

"Where?"

"Incendin," Tan said, starting to explain, but Roine waved him off.

"Zephra thinks we should let Incendin and Par-shon battle each other," Roine said. "I take it you do not."

"The archivists weren't attacking Incendin, only attacking *in* Incendin. They attacked the Aeta, who you have granted your protection."

A sly smile spread across Roine's face. "Indeed. Am I to understand that my protection extends into Incendin, then?"

"It does," Tan said.

"What of the Aeta you found?"

"They have joined the others in the Gathering. They have selected a new First Mother."

"Since you are here alone, I presume Amia accepted."

How was it that everyone else seemed unsurprised that Amia would be asked? "She remains with the Aeta," Tan said.

"Will she ask them to wander, or will they remain within the kingdoms?" Roine asked.

Tan hadn't asked. "For now, I suspect they will remain. Traveling has become unsafe."

"You will tell her that she has my support?"

Tan was thankful that Roine would continue to support Amia. Assuming the role of First Mother made her Roine's equal in some ways. The Aeta might be landless, but they were not entirely powerless. And some would begin to fear them once they learned that they could shape spirit.

"I will tell her."

"This is not why you've come to me tonight."

"It's not."

Roine crossed his arms over his chest. "Get on with it then. What are you going to do?" Tan stiffened, his breath catching, and Roine laughed at the reaction. "I was Athan for many years, Tan, and you are more like me than you might want to admit. I know what it's like to think you know what needs to be done when the throne wishes something else. So, tell me what you plan to do and I'll do my best to talk you out of it, knowing that it won't matter since you're a much stronger shaper than me anyway." He grinned. "Don't look at me like that. You became more powerful than me when you learned to bind spirit. I've been trying and think I might have some of the trick of it, but I won't ever have the same type of shaping as you."

The relief at knowing that Roine would know what he planned made everything easier. Not easy, but still better. "I'm returning to Doma. I intend to drive Par-shon out of Doma. The people there must be freed." He paused and considered his king regent, his friend. "I've seen what it's like when Par-shon attacks. I know what it's like. If that's why Elle summoned, I *need* to do something, even if it fails. More than that, Incendin suffers as well, and they will do what they can to oppose Par-shon."

Roine studied him. "You think Incendin unable to handle Par-shon?"

"They have already been attacked," Tan said, then told Roine about what happened in Incendin. "Incendin might not be strong enough to stop Par-shon directly, not without help. Which is why," Tan started, taking a deep breath and promising himself it would be okay, "I allowed one of their warriors to return."

Roine's eyes flashed with anger, before he suppressed it. "You should have spoken to me first," he said softly.

"You would only have told me no."

"Tannen, I am the king regent. There are ways things are done!"

"Roine, I'm the reason she was here. She should never have been our prisoner. She wasn't captured attacking the kingdoms; she was *rescued* from Par-shon. Whatever you might think of Incendin, she wasn't the one to fear."

Roine let out a frustrated grunt. "Who else?" he demanded.

"What?"

"Who else will you take with you?" Roine turned away and started pacing across the courtyard. "With the work along the barrier, I can't risk too many going. It is nearly in place. Once it is—"

"I won't take anyone unwilling to go. Cianna will likely come, but only because her bond-pair will be coming."

Roine jerked his head around to stare at Tan. "Cianna has bonded?"

"I wasn't sure it would work, but I knew the draasin would be safer were they bonded. Cianna was the right fit, but I had to convince the draasin of that as well."

Roine squeezed his chin in thought. "There were three draasin. Who could bond to the third, do you think? Seanan might be too hot-headed. Visn is older, but might have a steadying hand. Inasha might work, she's quite skilled, but—"

"I don't think the third will take a bond, Roine. She's the one the archivists twisted. She fears us still. I haven't actually seen her since that attack."

Roine grunted. "Now you go and dash my hopes of a draasin army, using them to push back Incendin—"

"The elementals are not to be used. They are not to be harnessed or forcibly bound," Tan said with more heat than Roine deserved.

"That's not what I was saying."

"No, but I know where you were going. Do you know that the

ancient shapers, the scholars we hold in such high esteem, forced the elementals to bond much like Par-shon? They called it *harnessing*, a word I suspect the draasin would find as offensive as any."

Roine's face fell. "I… I didn't know."

"The bond comes from a place of respect. Ask Ferran. He hears golud now. In time, I suspect he could bond to them."

"Ferran hears golud?" Roine asked, his voice growing soft. "How?"

"I don't know. And he's not bonded, not yet, but speaking to them is the first step. From there, the bond is only a matter of finding the right connection."

"But you haven't bound to earth and you speak to them. And the nymid—"

"In time, I suspect I could bind to the nymid, possibly even one of the earth elementals. It might not be golud. I thought ara the only wind elemental, but I have bound to ashi. The udilm were once thought to be the great water elemental, but now we know the strength of the nymid. What else don't we know? What other elementals of earth might there be?"

Roine scrubbed his hands across his face. "I've always thought the ancient scholars were what I aspired toward."

"As did I, but learning how they abused the elementals, I think there was much they didn't know. At least, there was much some of them didn't know." It seemed unlikely that none of the ancient shapers understood the nature of the elementals. Or maybe the elementals didn't understand how some were used at the time. Maybe that was why the Great Mother had gifted him with the ability to speak to each of the elementals.

"As the king regent, I must ask that you remain behind to help protect the kingdoms."

Tan had expected nothing less. Roine had an obligation to do what was needed to protect the people of the kingdoms, and Tan was a warrior shaper. He would be needed to help protect the kingdoms.

"But as a shaper, and a warrior shaper who has now seen all that the elementals can do, all that they have done to help, I feel you must do what you can to help Doma. Save them if you can." His tone told Tan how unlikely he thought that would be. "And prevent Par-shon from abusing the elementals. Even in that, you protect the kingdoms."

Roine took a step forward and grabbed Tan's shoulders in an intense grip. "Do what you can, Tannen. Help Doma. We will keep the kingdoms safe."

CHAPTER 22

Return to Doma

ASBOEL FLEW WITH FURIOUS STRENGTH as they streaked across the kingdoms. With dawn approaching, the sun barely creeping over the horizon as a bright streak of orange, Tan relied upon the draasin sight to see. Everything below him flashed in hues of red, yellow, and orange, all shades of fire. Life moved throughout the kingdoms, and Tan sensed elemental power mixed within, the elementals that he was meant to protect.

Sashari raced alongside, Cianna sitting atop her back. It had not taken much to convince the fire shaper to assist. Tan had not expected it to.

"The two of us?" she had asked when he approached her.

"Theondar cannot send any others to help Doma," Tan said. "He rebuilds the barrier."

"I should be there," Cianna began. "You disagree, but the barrier kept the kingdoms safe for many years."

Tan didn't know what to think about the barrier yet. He remained unconvinced that it would do anything to stop the Par-shon bonded, much like it had done little to stop Incendin at the end.

"Do you really think the two of us will be enough to push back Par-shon?" Cianna went on.

"As I told Cora, it won't be the two of us. We will have all of the free elementals to aid us."

Cianna had grinned and slapped her hands together. "You think the elementals and two shapers enough? You might be as stupid as I once thought, Tan."

"You understand the risk?" he asked. He couldn't have her come otherwise. There was a real possibility that they might not return.

"I understand the bond," Cianna said toward the sky. "And I understand what you must do. I will help."

Vel had come to him as he reached the university and the shaper's circle. "You will take me with you," he said.

Tan hadn't seen him since returning to Ethea. The water shaper had been traveling with Zephra, helping her scout through Incendin. In the time that he'd been returned from Par-shon, he had changed. Not only his clothing, though he was now better dressed, but the wild and agitated expression in his eyes was gone and he carried himself with confidence.

"Are you certain you would do this? I don't have the support of Theondar," Tan said.

"Theondar is not my king. Doma is my home. I heard what you saw when you were there. If there is anything I can do, I will go with you."

"Vel, even with the help of the elementals, we might not survive this."

Vel smiled and that slightly insane twinkle briefly returned to his eyes. "Tan, I was dead once already. Your coming to Par-shon gave me renewed life."

Cianna had looked at Tan and shrugged, so Vel came with them, now sitting behind Cianna. Her orange hair swirled around her, giving her a wild appearance. She had chosen a tight maroon shirt and leggings to match, both similar in color to Sashari.

Where is Enya? Tan asked. The continued absence of the young draasin worried him, especially with Par-shon attacking in Doma and now Incendin. They set traps for the elementals, and if they could reach her, they could force her to bond.

She remains safe.

The draasin were connected by the fire bond, similar to what Tan and Asboel shared, but different in some ways, as well. This was how Asboel knew where Enya would be found. *Are you certain? If Par-shon manages to obtain one of the draasin to bond—*

They will not have Enya, Asboel said. Nearby, Sashari snarled and flames leaped from her mouth, matching Asboel's intensity.

They soared high over the Galen mountains as the sun began to rise over the horizon. Tan stared down at the mountains, wondering when he would next see the place of his birth. How long ago had it been when he thought he would never see anyplace beyond Galen? How long ago had it been when he thought he would never leave the mountains? Now he couldn't imagine any other life. He might never have learned of the elementals or his ability to shape had he not left.

Can you help? Tan asked. *If we need to reach the other elementals, will there be anything that you can do?*

You are the one chosen by the Mother, Asboel said. *There is some connection between the others, but it is not the same. For this to work, you must be the one to do it.*

They were three shapers, two elemental draasin, aided by wind and the free elementals, but it still seemed insignificant, barely enough for a much of an attack, but Tan only intended to drive Par-shon away from Doma. Hopefully they hadn't the time to build any real presence yet. And once Doma was freed, they would find a way to work together with Incendin. They would have to.

Asboel skirted the edge of Incendin, keeping them over the mountains. Tan pressed through the draasin sight and saw the ground below in shades of orange and red, flashes of color that reminded him of what he had seen when nearly transformed into one of the lisincend.

Asboel saw signs of activity, of Incendin cities Tan had no names for. Amia might have known, but he could not have asked her to come, not on this journey. She understood what he needed to do, and that was enough, her last request to him ringing through his mind like a shaping: *Return to me.*

Asboel began to descend toward the ground as the mountains sloped away. Water glistened in the distance as the Doma peninsula stretched away from Incendin, dipping out toward the sea. White capped surges were visible through Asboel's eyes as lighter colors of red.

Do you see anything? Tan asked.

Nothing but land, Asboel said.

That made Tan nervous.

Tan stood on Asboel's back, unsheathed his warrior sword, and formed a traveling shaping as if he was going to jump to the ground. Instead of pulling it to himself, he directed the shaping down, letting it strike near the base of the mountains where they stretched out into the plains of Doma.

A single shaper attacked where Tan would have landed.

Tan pulled a shaping through the sword, using earth and spirit, and targeted the earth shaper. His history with the bow gave him the ability to aim and he wasted no time sending the shaping streaking toward the shaper.

It struck in a burst of white light. The shaper collapsed to the ground.

Asboel roared his pleasure and breathed a streak of fire.

They continued inland and Tan used the shaping again, sending it streaking toward the ground. It struck with a burst of lightning. In that moment, Tan saw two earth shapers.

This time he was ready, at least for one. He shaped earth and spirit, and a sense of relief came from the freed earth elemental.

The other shaper used that moment to attack. He shot into the air, somehow using his earth elemental to travel. Tan aimed an earth and spirit shaping at him, but missed.

The shaper smiled and sped toward Tan, who still stood atop the draasin.

Tan jumped, using a shaping of air and drawing on Honl to keep him from falling. The shaper passed below him, bouncing off Asboel. The draasin snapped at the shaper, catching him with a flash of fangs and releasing him to fall.

Asboel snorted, and Tan landed on his back. As he did, he realized that the earth shapers weren't the only Par-shon bonded shapers hiding. Cianna and Vel battled a pair near them. One, a fire shaper likely bonded to saa, battled Vel. The other seemed to be a wind shaper.

Tan hadn't been certain how Vel would handle a fight. He worked with tight control using a water shaping against a bonded fire shaper who ultimately had more strength. Fire pressed ever closer to him.

Cianna managed better. Connected as she now was to Sashari, she used the bond with the elemental, clinging to her spikes, and sent shaping after shaping after the Par-shon wind shaper. Much longer and she would overwhelm him.

As the fire shaping reached Vel, Tan sent a lancing shot of fire mixed with spirit. It struck the fire shaper and he dropped to the ground. Tan wrapped him in wind, not wanting to be the reason another had to die.

Cianna had no such compunction. Sashari twisted and snapped, catching the wind shaper with her jaws and shaking him.

Sashari banked toward Asboel. "How many others do you think there will be?" Cianna asked across the distance.

Vel sat behind her, water shaped into a buffer that protected him from the heat of the draasin spikes. His face was drawn and the eager expression in his eyes had faded.

"We're only along the border," Tan said. "I suspect we'll find quite a few more as we near Falsheim."

"You think for us to continue to battle them this way?"

"Not if we want to survive," Tan answered. "We need to draw them away from Falsheim." If they could pull Par-shon toward Incendin, they might be able to trap them, to use Incendin to help.

"And you think the Incendin shapers will be ready to help?" Cianna asked.

Tan hoped they would. It would depend on what Cora had managed to do.

"What of your cousin?" Cianna asked. "You have not found her yet?"

"I don't even know if she's still alive," Tan admitted. "She's been silent since for the last few days. When we were here before, I couldn't reach her."

Sashari roared as if understanding what that meant. Cianna stood and stared to the east, toward Falsheim. "Then we will avenge her," she said.

They were further inland, near the village that Tan had covered with sand, when he used the traveling shaping again. The landscape seemed different, bleaker in some ways. The once vibrant colors he'd seen growing from the fields surrounding the sea had faded, almost as if the rock itself faded.

What had Par-shon done here?

As he sent his shaping to the ground, this time there was only a single earth shaper, and Tan managed to separate him from his bond quickly. Once he was gone, other hidden shapers appeared and took to the air to attack.

This land has changed, Asboel said. *They claim too many of the elementals.*

What does it do?

They withdraw too much. It changes the land, Asboel said.

A half-dozen shapers attacked at once. They split, three coming after Tan and Asboel, the other three going after Cianna, Vel, and Sashari. As they attacked, Tan realized that these shapers had more than one bond.

Warn Sashari, he said.

He started a shaping of earth and spirit to strike the nearest shaper, but it would not be fast enough. Asboel was forced to bank, exposing his underbelly to the shapers. He felt the shaping explode from them, more quickly than Asboel would be able to react.

Tan jumped on lightning and air and caught the shaping before it could strike Asboel. He turned it to the ground. Another shaper attacked, and the other. The three of them would be too much to simply incapacitate.

You must hunt, Asboel snarled.

Tan wouldn't be able to separate the bonds, not if he wanted to survive.

Distantly, he saw a shaping strike Sashari. Asboel roared.

The Par-shon shapers shifted their shaping to Asboel again. They feared the draasin, not Tan.

It was time they feared him.

Pulling on all the elements and adding spirit, he shaped through the sword until white light streaked toward the shapers. They each dropped. He readied another shaping, hitting the three shapers attacking Sashari at the same time.

Tan jumped back onto Asboel and they caught up to Sashari. He looked over at Cianna and Vel… but Vel was gone.

"What happened?" he yelled.

"We twisted to avoid the shaping," Cianna explained. "He couldn't hold on."

Tan reached through Asboel's sight and looked for any evidence of Vel. He saw the bodies of the shapers but not Vel.

After everything that he'd been through, it seemed a cruel twist of fate for Vel to return home only to die.

Tan signaled for Asboel to land. Sashari followed him to the rocks overlooking the sea. This too, was different than the last time he'd been here, almost as if udilm rebelled against what the Par-shon had done to Doma.

Do they know? Tan asked Asboel.

Some have been captured, forced to bond. That is all I can tell.

Udilm once bonded regularly to Doman shapers. Was it because of Par-shon that they stopped?

He sensed Asboel's hesitation. *When the bond is taken, they are forced to act in ways that go against the Mother. The udilm can be violent and angry, but they are peaceful as well. I sense they are not offered peace when forced to bond, only violence.*

Asboel looked toward Falsheim. Through his eyes, Tan could see it in the distance. It glowed with bright light, fire coming from the elementals raging along the walls.

Why do they use fire?

It attempts to push away fire. I cannot tell why, Asboel said.

What had Cora told him about how Par-shon trapped the elementals? They required a series of runes, each binding to the other, designed to hold the elementals. Perhaps the flames racing along the wall in Falsheim could be one shaping. What if the shaping he'd found in Incendin was another?

We need to go, he warned Asboel.

You were going to cleanse this place of the those who would force the bond, Asboel said.

And I will. But there is something else at work here.

Yet Tan couldn't leave Vel. They hadn't found his body, which meant he might still be alive.

Tan crept to the edge of the rocky overlook and stared down at the water. Could he have made it there? He was a water shaper, so it was possible that he used a shaping of water to reach the sea before crashing into it, but if that were the case, where had he gone?

To find him, Tan would have to speak to the udilm. The last time he'd attempted it, he'd nearly drowned. He prayed it would not take a similar experience to reach them this time.

I will return, Tan said to Asboel.

Then he leapt to the air on a shaping of wind and shot himself into the water.

CHAPTER 23

To Water

COLD WATER MET HIM, sucking the breath from his lungs. The last time he'd been immersed in water like this, he'd nearly been transformed into one of the lisincend. He had called to the udilm, but they hadn't answered. The nymid—always the nymid—had answered him, saving and restoring him.

Now he *needed* to reach the udilm. How had he managed the connection before? It was more than simply calling to water, more than letting it wash over him. It had taken a near drowning before.

Tan let the rest of his breath leave his lungs and sank toward the bottom of the sea.

Black water swirled around him, cold and heavy, pressing on him. Flashes of color streaked at the edge of vision. Pain filled him. Much longer and he would die.

Udilm, he called. *Answer He Who is Tan!*

Speaking with water required him to send in great rolling waves. Udilm was different than the nymid. The sea was vast and unforgiving, the power of the waves crashing constantly overhead.

The udilm's answer came slowly, but it came. *You should not have come.*

You would choose the bond? You would choose Par-shon over Doma?

There is no choice to those captured.

Water swirled around him and the blackness faded slightly, leaving the outline of a face. Tan stared at it, feeling a surge of anger. *There is always choice. You can choose another bond as you once did. There is one with me who once had bonded udilm.*

The great water elemental shook, the water becoming agitated. *Many have been lost.*

More will be lost if we fail, Tan said. *This is why I come.*

You have come for the Child.

Tan hesitated. His feet touched the rocky bottom of the sea. He was distantly aware of the cold and the darkness around him, but it was vague. Instead, he focused on the udilm, needing to reach them, needing their help. Not only might they know where to find Vel, they might know where to find Elle.

You know of the Child? Have the udilm bonded her?

She was not meant for the sea.

The where is she?

You must ask the others.

Others. What other elemental would Elle have found? The nymid would have told him if she had bonded to them. And udilm had restored her. Why wouldn't udilm have bonded her?

What of Velthan? He used his full name, though water would have a different way of calling him. Vel had once been bonded to udilm, but Par-shon had severed the bond, had stolen it when they captured him.

Udilm once knew him, but he is gone. He abandoned water.

Not abandoned. Had it separated from him. Stolen.

The udilm swirled around him, massive and powerful. Tan sensed irritation and anger, but it matched what surged through him.

The others will be sent from these lands. That is why I have come. That is why the Mother allows me to speak to you. You will help, Tan demanded. *You will protect these shores once more.* Anger at what Parshon did, how they used the elementals, gave his words power.

You would command the udilm?

Tan considered his answer carefully. Commanding the udilm was different than simply asking them for help. When he'd transformed, he had asked for help restoring him, but they had refused. They felt he had sacrificed too much. But now was not the time for gentle choices. Now was the time for strength and action.

I would command, Tan decided.

The udilm swirled around him, pressing on him with the weight of the entire sea. Tan stood there, shaping earth and air to hold himself in place, pulling fire through him to keep from the frigid change in the water. Udilm continued, surging over him with wave after wave of massive power. Tan still remained.

Enough!

He added a shaping of spirit. Water subsided, the waves easing.

You will help, Tan said. *Find the Child. Find Velthan. Restore him if you can. Protect the shores. Resist the bond. I will do all I can to assist you.*

The sea calmed as udilm no longer attempted to pound over him. There was no sense of agreement, but he would take the silence.

Tan shaped water and tested the draw of the elemental power. Pulling on the udilm, he shot himself free on a streak of shaping.

Chaos greeted him.

The ground bulged over Asboel, holding him in place. Sashari lay stunned on the ground. Cianna attempted to hold back a dozen shapers, but he sensed her growing weary.

Tan roared. He freed Asboel with a snap of earth augmented by his sword. The draasin snarled, lashing his tail through the shapers, knocking four down, and then he pounced, crushing them beneath him.

The others reacted, shifting their attention to Tan, hanging on a wave. Tan pulled on the udilm, commanding the elemental to sweep over the shapers. As the wave crashed down on them, he lifted Cianna to the air on a shaping of wind, directing Honl to keep her safe.

Water pounded, wave after wave, and then finally receded, leaving only the draasin.

Tan lowered Cianna, who ran to Sashari. The draasin blinked slowly and attempted to stand. Her hind legs trembled and gave out. As they did, Tan noticed that one wing had been damaged during the attack.

What was this? What happened here?

They waited until you were gone. Then they attacked.

Should I not have gone?

You did what was needed. Sashari knows the risk. Asboel lowered his head to meet Tan's eyes. *If we are lost, you will protect the hatchlings.*

It will not come to that, Tan said.

Only the Mother can say with certainty. This is a hunt greater than any we have ever taken together. You are powerful, Maelen, but they are many.

Tan went over to Sashari and laid a hand on her side. *I will protect the hatchlings like they were my own bond.*

He sent it with spirit and fire, directing it toward Asboel and Sashari. Both of the draasin roared, and flames leapt into the air from their mouths.

No longer did the attack have the same easy feel. They were down one draasin and one shaper when they had so few to start with. And he would have to leave Cianna here to keep watch over Sashari.

You will keep them safe, Tan commanded to the udilm

He wasn't certain whether the water would answer, but then the waves crashed with increasing force along the shore. They would be safe for now.

Tan crafted a shaping of earth, drawing strength from the sword, and wrapped it around Sashari and Cianna. He didn't know how long it would hold, but it would give them another layer of protection.

"Find a place to hide. Sashari will need to heal," Tan said to Cianna as he shaped.

"You cannot do this by yourself," she said to him again. "Even you have limits."

Tan knew what some of them were. Incendin had tested them. Par-shon had already exceeded them. Now they would see the extent of his anger.

"For the elementals, I have to try."

He leapt onto Asboel's back. *We will hunt, you and I.*

The draasin roared his approval.

They started toward Falsheim. If there were as many shapers as it appeared, he would need to push the Par-shon shapers away from Doma and sweep them toward Incendin. The attacks they had faced already had been increasingly powerful, but there would be more. Tan had no idea how many Par-shon shapers had crossed the sea, but their numbers were limited only by their capacity to capture and bind elementals.

Fire burns brightly along those walls, Asboel said.

Would Par-shon allow him to get so close again or would they be ready for him this time? Would he even be able to do what he thought needed to get done?

This close, Tan sensed the effect of the fire burning. It pressed against him in an angry attempt to push him away. Not only Tan, but the draasin as well. Something about the fire prevented Asboel from flying too closely. He flicked his tail, his frustration prominent through the bond as they struggled to reach the city.

Could it be that the shaping wasn't meant to call the draasin as he'd thought, but to push them away?

Tan studied Falsheim through the draasin sight. The line of fire burning along the top of the wall shimmered a bright red. Flashes of lighter color moved within the fire, either shapers, or more surprisingly, he wondered if it might not be elementals. There was no sign of any Domans.

No, Tan!

The voice exploded in his head. The voice he'd been trying to reach for days. Elle's voice. *Elle?*

She'd been silenced. No response came, nothing that would tell him where she might be, but she had to be close. There was no way she would have reached him otherwise.

From above, the blue-painted slate roofs appeared like nothing more than an extension of the sea. There was even an undulating pattern much like swells of waves. Nothing moved within. Any of the people who had once been there were gone.

Falsheim was large, though not as large as Ethea. The massive walls circling it looked built to defend against the sea, to keep it from crashing on surges against those who lived behind its walls. Doma would not have abandoned her city.

But where would they be?

Can you see anything? Tan asked.

Asboel snuffed a streamer of flame as he circled, unable to get too close to the city. *There is nothing.*

Tan shaped spirit, mixing it with each of the elements, tying them together as he eased his shaping. He expected to find something—anything. Instead, it was empty.

Or was it?

Could their earth shapers really be so powerful?

Tan sent a shaping of lightning crashing into the top of the wall. It fizzled into nothing. No shapers were revealed. Nothing.

Another shaping had the same result.

Tan sat back on Asboel, frustration surging through him. He had heard Elle. She was alive. But where?

Udilm! Where is the Child of Water?

Tan sent it out as a booming question that slammed into the water. A massive swell came as an answer, sending spray shooting toward the sky, shaped at them.

Udilm answered, but did not answer him.

Tan suddenly understood: A shaper controlled the water elementals around Falsheim.

Could water obscure as well as earth? Wind had once helped turn Zephra into Sarah, hiding his mother from him, so why could it not?

It meant Falsheim was likely far more dangerous than he realized. And it meant that there might not be anything he could do to rescue Elle, or to help the trapped elementals.

I don't know if I'm strong enough to do this, Tan admitted.

And even if he managed to pull Par-shon shapers away toward Incendin, would there be anything that Incendin could do to defeat them? What of when they reached the kingdoms? There was even more elemental power there, especially Ethea, the place of convergence. How long would it take for Par-shon to trap them as well?

As Tan considered turning back, he heard Elle's voice again.

Tan! There was panic in it before it again cut off.

He had to help her. Tan didn't know if it would even work. If the draasin couldn't reach the city, what made him think that *he* could?

Asboel...I need to reach her. Can you watch over me? he asked.

You would use me like some sort of spyglass?

Attack when you can. I will draw the others. Keep me safe.

Asboel breathed out a finger of angry fire. *I will watch,* Asboel agreed.

Tan took a deep breath, calling the free elementals to him, and then jumped from Asboel's back into Falsheim.

CHAPTER 24

Within Falsheim

TAN USED A SHAPING OF SPIRIT, wrapping it around himself to shield himself from the Par-shon shaping as he descended. As he did, he held onto Asboel through the bond, afraid to release the connection. He streaked through the clouds, dropping toward Falsheim faster than he'd ever moved. There was a sense of resistance from the shaping around Falsheim, and then he passed through. As he sensed the ground, he shifted the shaping, pushing wind and earth together.

A soft fog covered the city, sweeping in from the sea. It hadn't been there before and didn't appear shaped, leaving Tan to wonder what had happened. A soft chuckling from Asboel in the back of his mind made him think that the draasin helped.

He was attacked as soon as he landed.

Fire and wind came at him, shaped directly in front of him. Tan felt resistance when he tried to shape, but he had known this resistance before. It was the same as he'd experienced in Par-shon, using runes branded on the walls. As he had then, he shaped spirit, augmenting what he could control, and pressed through.

Tan didn't need to see the shaper. Using his warrior sword, he caught the shaping and deflected it down. Then he blasted forward, spirit and fire drawn from Asboel. The shaper fell. A flash of light came as the elemental was released.

Another attack, this from behind him. Tan spun, catching the shaping and returning it upon the shaper. There came another flash of light.

Assist me.

Tan sent the request to earth, fire, wind, and water. He didn't know which of the elements he'd freed, but they could be summoned. They could fight against those who would bond them. The elementals were the reason that he didn't fight alone. They could help. They *must* help.

Two shapers, one to each side. Tan sent a spirit shaping at both. It struck with more force than he'd intended. One of the shapers fell. Tan made his way through the thickening fog and found her. She was small and young, dressed in dark brown breeches and the flared jacket of Par-shon. The bonds glowed upon her exposed skin, one for wind and earth. Using spirit, Tan freed them.

Assist me, he sent again.

He found the other shaper he had attacked. An older man lay on the ground, face smeared with ash and dirt. Runes for fire and earth, elemental opposites, were branded onto his cheeks. Tan used spirit to free these bonds.

Assist me, he said.

A series of shapings drew him. Tan jumped on the wind, augmenting it with fire, unwilling to use his elemental bond to Honl here until he knew whether Honl could be separated from him. He landed in the midst of the shapers, readying his attack.

The sensation of power pressing down around him increased. This was different than before. They were not attacking him the same way as the others had, not sending elemental power at him. Instead, it swirled around him, the shaping itself forming a rune around him.

Tan tried a shaping for spirit, drawing on Asboel as he attempted fire.

His shaping faltered and failed.

He tried again, this time reaching for each of the elements, mixing it with spirit. Again, the shaping failed.

The power surrounding him increased. There came a tearing sense, a painful ripping within his mind. With a growing terror, Tan understood what they attempted.

He had thought he needed to be in Par-shon for them to separate him from his bonds. He was wrong. They had drawn him here to attack, thinking to outnumber him. That must be the reason for their shapers spread throughout Doma. They intended to weaken him before he could reach Falsheim.

He focused on the sword, using spirit first, knowing it was the one element they could not use, and tried binding it to a combined shaping of the other elementals. Spirit built, drawing through the sword, straining against the shaping that threatened to overwhelm him. Spirit was pushed back against him.

Tan sagged. It had taken all of the strength he could manage to attempt that last shaping. He had grown so accustomed to the elemental powers aiding his shaping, to drawing on them for strength, that he had forgotten what it was like when he had to rely solely on his own stores of power. Now that he needed them, now that he was cut off from the elementals, he did not have the strength needed to escape.

A frustrated scream came from him, echoing through Falsheim. He would not fall, not in a city that was not his home, not so far from Amia and with Asboel so tantalizingly close.

He dragged on another shaping, straining through the sword, reaching for fire. If he could reach fire, if he could draw on Asboel, he might be able to break the pattern of shapers surrounding him enough that he could escape from the shaped rune and free him to reach the elemental powers.

Fire built within him. It came slowly, but it came. Tan added it to the sword, drawing through it, praying to the Great Mother that the runes would augment the shaping enough.

There, like a flicker of power, he sensed Asboel.

Asboel!

He couldn't know if his sending worked. It had taken all of the strength remaining to him to reach for the draasin. Tan sagged to the ground.

The shaping continued around him. He sensed power building. The pain tearing through his mind increased, leaving him weakened, barely able to stand. This must have been how Asboel felt when Parshon attacked him.

A gust of wind blew through the fog.

Tan saw his attackers. He stood on a cobbled street. Squat stone buildings rose up all around him. On each slate rooftop, there was a shaper, no longer attempting to obscure themselves. Each focused on him.

Tan swallowed and raised his sword.

The blowing wind caught the sword. Tan thought he might be too weak to hold it in the air, but the wind itself held it there. A flicker of light from the fading sun caught it before Tan realized that it wasn't light, but fire. The fog that had been in the air coalesced and dripped along the sword. The earth rumbled beneath him.

Power returned, flowing into the sword. He felt it surge with elemental strength, strength that was freely given. He stood, drawing upon it with renewed vigor. Saa and nymid surged through him. Earth elemental power that he had no name for rumbled through him. The sword exploded with light.

Tan pointed at the nearest shaper. He bound the shaping together, not drawing from him, but the elementals themselves, drawn *to* him, and added his shaping of spirit to it. The shaping exploded from him, striking the two nearest him.

The light struck them, and the elementals bound to the shapers exploded away from them.

Assist me, Tan called.

More elemental power swirled toward his sword. He focused on two other shapers, the light-infused shaping streaking from his blade and crashing into them. The bonds shattered.

The shaped rune around him failed.

The shapers changed their focus. Now they attacked Tan. Elemental power struck him, buffeting against him, the sword, everything. He stood rooted in place, reaching through the earth on a shaping as he strained to sense where other shapers might be hiding.

The city held dozens. Too many to search and hunt out one by one.

Tan called on the elementals. Power swirled around him, fed by unnamed elemental power answering his call. He pressed out through the sword, through the elementals he sensed, and turned them against the shapers within the city.

Power exploded outward. Whatever shaping had surrounded the city failed with a thunderous *crack* and a flash of flame that faded into nothing.

But not all the elementals were freed. Seven shapers took to the air.

They faced Tan, circling him in a tight pattern and a shaping of air and fire. Smoke trailed from them, cloying and thick. Tan felt their shaping build, drawing away the power he'd gained from the elementals. One of the shapers stood at the head of the others, bald and with dark, piercing eyes. He wore the same leathers that Tan had seen in Par-shon. Bonded elemental runes glowed across him, more than Tan could count. Not the Utu Tonah, but one with nearly his ability.

Tan shifted his shaping to him, but that power was deflected. The man raised his arm and smiled as he withdrew a sword covered with glowing runes. A warrior sword.

The shaper attacked, sending a shaping more powerful than anything Tan had ever experienced before toward him. Tan ducked behind the sword, clutching it in front of him, holding the blade out and praying that it would catch the shaping.

As he did, he begged of the elementals again.

Assist me.

Power burned through him. Tan held his arm out, trying to maintain the shaping as the Par-shon bonded circled over him.

A loud roar echoed overhead.

Tan opened his eyes to see Asboel streaking toward him. The draasin flew with his jaw wide and open, fire and steam shooting from his mouth. The Par-shon bonded scattered, fearful of the draasin. The flames struck everything around Tan, scattering harmlessly around him.

The heavily bonded shaper lingered a moment before he scattered with the others, disappearing and leaving Tan shaking among the broken remnants of the city.

Asboel landed in a clearing within the city. His great golden eyes searched around him, checking for another attack, but everything Tan sensed told him that the Par-shon shapers were gone. A few remained, but those were shapers whose connection to their bond had been broken. The flames along the city wall sputtered and eventually faded.

You have hunted well, Maelen.

Two fallen Par-shon shapers lay unmoving, one with his back twisted at an awful angle, the other with her head bent impossibly. He did not feel as if he'd hunted well.

Par-shon had planned this, whatever *this* was. *Did they think to capture me?*

They are tightly bound to the elementals. It is possible that they could have held you.

The only reason he could think that Par-shon would trap him was to separate him from Asboel, but why would they risk it here?

This shaping intended to separate us.

Asboel sniffed, steam streaming from his nostrils. *They would have you hunt alone. They could bind you then.*

But why? And why had this shaping reminded him of the one he'd found in Incendin? What was the purpose of the shaping?

He stepped into the street. Asboel's lazy fog still lingered. It drifted slowly back toward the sea, receding like the tide. Had udilm helped here? Tan didn't think so. Whatever elemental power of water he'd used had come from the mist itself, different than udilm, different even than the nymid, and more like the mist he saw swirling around Asboel when they flew.

Tan focused on spirit and earth, drawing power from Asboel and his proximity, and shaped. *Elle!*

He pressed out with the sending, using more than a simple sensing of spirit. There came the sense of resistance, and then it faded.

Tan!

He heard her joy. *Where are you?*

As he asked, he felt a steady rumbling, as if the city itself would collapse. Then it cleared.

Beneath the city.

Tan frowned. How could anyone be beneath the city? *Where?*

Come to water.

Tan glanced at Asboel. The draasin seemed to have heard, too, because he flicked his tail. Tan took to the air with a quick summons to Honl and floated above the city. Asboel launched after him with a great flapping of wings, hovering and keeping a close eye on Tan.

Reaching the water took him past the walls and out to the rocky shore. He lowered himself, looking for where Elle might be. Water crashed along the shore. The sense of udilm was in the water, and Tan was aware of something almost like relief.

The great elemental had been freed from whatever bonds held it. There would be others of the udilm trapped, their bonds forced upon them, but for now, water could serve Doma again.

Protect these shores, Tan asked.

He didn't expect a response. The udilm had been angry at the fact that he had dared demand service from them. But the waves slowed, the angry splashing eased, and a peaceful sliding of waves pressed around him.

From within the walls and from above, the city seemed to have an even and flat course. But from the water, he saw how it was built above the rock, the buildings nestling atop massive stone pillars that plunged into the sea bed. Shadows moved between the rocks. Tan didn't need earth sensing to know that was where he would find Elle.

When she came to him on a sliver of water, sliding across the rock as if sailing atop the waves, his jaw nearly dropped in surprise. Elle had changed.

She had always been short and smaller than him, especially in the baggy clothes she had taken to wearing while in Ethea and studying at the university, but in the time he'd been away, she had filled out some and grown about three inches, and now the thin white dress she wore actually fit her. Her brown hair had grown long and she wore it down across her shoulders. Eyes that had once matched her hair now were lighter, almost misty colored. She would be a lovely woman someday.

An older boy stood next to her, eyes narrowed at Tan, angling himself protectively toward Elle. Tan smiled at him, but it only made the boy more defensive.

"It *is* you!" Elle said. She threw her arms around Tan and hugged him.

He hugged her back, more shocked than anything, and stunned to silence. When he collected himself, he pushed her back and stared at her. "Elle? What happened here? How are you alive?"

"I didn't think you'd come. I've been trying to reach you for the last few weeks, but there's been no way to get through to you safely. Those shapers have blocked me somehow."

"I don't understand. How were you alive under the city?"

The boy opened his mouth as if to object. Elle whispered to him, and the boy clamped his mouth shut. Tan almost laughed, wondering what she'd said. He had been subjected to her moods before. Though he had not known her long, he felt he had known her well.

"Falsheim is built on a shelf. Not many know that."

"What do you mean? What kind of a shelf?"

Elle nodded to him. "Come. I'll show you."

The boy shook his head and stepped in front of Tan. "Elle, we don't know anything about him." A shaping built from him, weak, but water responded, sliding around Tan's ankles.

He waved the shaping away with a quick draw on the elementals of water. The boy stepped back.

"Ley, you need to relax. This is the shaper I was telling you about. If he's here, it means he's brought shapers from the kingdoms to help. How else do you think they managed to scare away those others?"

Ley's eyes narrowed to slits. "We don't know they're gone, Elle. They been gone before and come back. If they're gone, then they'll return with more, just like the last time—"

"The last time, we didn't have the kingdoms' shapers." She turned to Tan. "Who came with you? Which Masters are here to help?" She glanced at Ley. "He's friends with Theondar! Likely the warrior is somewhere here, too."

What had they been through that she would come to expect the kingdoms to save them? How long had Par-shon been here? And how had they managed to stay hidden?

Above him, Asboel snorted fire.

Tan nodded toward the sky. Ley looked up, his eyes widening as he took in the draasin.

Elle let out a relieved sight. "You brought your draasin," she said, working her jaw up and down. "I warned you. That's what they're after."

"I know what they're after. They're from across the sea, from Par-shon. They try to separate shapers from their bonded elementals, using those bonds to form their own. They nearly separated me again," he said. "And they have learned to trap elementals, force them to bond."

Elle tipped her head as if listening to the steady sliding of the waves against the shore. Her lips moved silently. Tan realized she was speaking to one of the elementals.

As Tan stood in the sea, he felt them around him. Not only udilm, but the nymid mingled, sliding from the narrow stream and joining the sea. The nymid flowed back out of the sea, but for that brief time, the two elementals were joined. Then there was another elemental, the one he'd sensed on the mist but never known well enough to put a name to. As the waves caught the rock, the misty spray splashed up, catching Tan. There was power in the mist, different than anything he had ever known. It was this elemental that had blown in like a fog over the city when he attacked the Par-shon bonded.

That wasn't you, Tan sent to Asboel.

You think I would use water? Smoke would have served better.

Tan laughed and the boy shot him a glare.

"What elemental have you bonded?" Tan asked Elle. "It wasn't the udilm, was it?"

The corners of her eyes were pinched and drawn. "At first I thought it was because they didn't want me. I was stranded, Tan. The village that found me took me in, but they did not treat me like Doma should treat one of their own." The boy's face went ashen and Tan knew that he had been one of the villagers. "When the lisincend came, they thought I was wrong. Who had ever heard of a winged lisincend? But I'd seen the draasin, even if I barely remembered it." Her brow wrinkled as she worked to make out Asboel soaring overhead.

Tan considered calling him down, but it would only scare her and the boy. And Asboel wasn't simply flying to avoid Elle; he watched for the shapers' return.

"You saw one of the twisted lisincend?" Tan asked.

Elle started walking, waving Tan onward with her toward the rocks beneath the city. Tan realized that with enough water, the rocks would be completely covered. Perhaps the udilm had served the city better than he'd realized.

"They attacked Falsheim. Or they *seemed* to attack Falsheim, but it wasn't the city they attacked at all. They came after the others. At first, the lisincend was enough to scare them away. The city was scarred. Many had died, and those who remained went below to hide behind the storm walls. When the others returned, the city was mostly empty."

She led him beneath an archway in the rock. Green mold grew along the black rocks, clinging to them, and water dripped softly onto his head as he ducked under the overhang. Once through, it was completely dark. Tan considered a shaping of fire, but decided against it. This was Elle's home.

"What is this place?" he asked.

Elle chuckled. "When Falsheim was first built, they did so on top of these rocks." When she turned back to him, her skin had a faint green sheen to it, much like Tan saw from the nymid. "Doma had many shapers then, not like today. Now, all of her shapers are stolen by Incendin." She spat the last. "I didn't know about this place when I first came, but water led me here, led us to safety."

She stepped to the side. Spread out below was a massive series of tunnels. It reminded him of what was beneath the palace, down to the runes marked above the tunnel entrance. Tan paused and stretched out with a shaping of earth and spirit. Deep within the tunnels were thousands of people.

Doma lived.

"You saved them," Tan said.

"It wasn't me, the people knew—"

"No," Tan said to her. Here he thought he would have to come to Doma and rescue the people, but that wasn't needed at all. He might have pushed Par-shon out of the city, but Elle had already saved her people. "You hid them." Tan smiled, thinking of the Elle he had known when they were both in Ethea. She had changed nearly as much as he had. "You found water and you saved your people."

"Not me. They survived by knowing that we would reach help. I told them I could reach you like I reached water. This place makes it difficult and I hadn't dared go out, but when I felt the shaping around me, I knew the kingdoms had finally sent their shapers." Elle met his eyes, hope swelling there. "Where are the others, Tan?"

"There aren't any others, Elle. The draasin. Me. There was help, but we ran into trouble near the border and they were stranded."

"It was *you*?"

He nodded.

"How... how is it you scared them away?"

He didn't fully understand what he'd done. The elementals had helped. Maybe freeing them from the forced bond had really been all that was needed. The elementals had given him strength when it seemed like everything was lost.

"I don't know. They're gone. That's all that's important."

"That's what I tried warning you."

"What do you mean?"

"We got the city to safety. Most have stayed here, but a few we've rescued from above. They have overheard the shapers. They were readying for an attack, but they needed something they did not have. A bond they didn't have."

Tan nodded. "I know they were. That's why I'm here. Par-shon has been fighting with Incendin for decades. They've managed to keep them off their shores, I think by using the lisincend and the shapers they've stolen from Doma, but now Par-shon has come for the draasin—"

"I don't think it's the draasin. I don't know what they waited for, but it wasn't that."

Par-shon had been gaining elemental power here, forcing the bonds, but then they had waited, staying within Doma, not moving away from the city and attacking Incendin any more than he'd seen.

What had they been waiting for? From what Elle said, it was not for him.

The Utu Tonah wanted the draasin bond, but what had Tan missed? What else would he need to ensure it? And now two of the draasin were bonded. The hatchlings were safe, protected beneath Ethea. Only Enya remained free.

Why then, would Par-shon push fire away?

CHAPTER 25

Spirit Claimed

AS HE RODE ATOP ASBOEL, Tan considered what he actually knew. Sashari and Cianna would make their way to Falsheim where Elle would welcome and protect them while Sashari healed. Par-shon had invaded Doma to pull elementals and their power from the lands, enough to change the complexion of the land. Other Par-shon shapers might still be out there. Certainly the heavily bonded shaper remained. There had to be a reason for it. They had expected him in Doma, but they hadn't attacked in the kingdoms, almost as if they'd intentionally drawn him away.

A chilling thought came to him, one that he hadn't considered before. Par-shon shapers had managed to hide in Doma and in Incendin without notice. They could obscure themselves using shapings of earth, bound to the elementals. But if they could obscure themselves in Incendin and Doma, what prevented the same from happening elsewhere? Could they have already reached the kingdoms? Could they have used a similar shaping in the kingdoms? In Chenir?

Tan! Amia surged suddenly through their connection, urgent and agitated. *The People are under attack. There's only so much—*

And then she fell silent.

Tan roared, leaping from Asboel's back and pulling lightning and thunder toward him in a shaping. *Asboel, meet me in the kingdoms.*

Hunt well, Maelen.

The shaping swept him toward Ethea, faster than a thought.

Tan landed near the circle of wagons forming the Aeta caravan. Some were tipped. Screams filled the air. Fire burned, pressing on him much as it had in Doma, attempting to force him away. Shapings had flung chunks of earth, scattering them all around. Wind gusted around him. Elemental power raged.

Amia? Tan sent to her in a panic.

Here! Help us, Tan, she pleaded.

Tan raised his sword, calling the free elementals.

There was a sense of hesitation, then power filled the sword much like it had in Doma. The blade blazed with a bright white light so powerful that he nearly had to close his eyes against it. He lifted to the air on a shaping and stretched out with earth, sensing the attack. Powered as he was by the elementals, he sensed the shapers around him. There were nearly a dozen, possibly more hidden by the earth.

He pressed out and away from him using a mixture of elemental power. Tan felt the elementals surging around him, not only ara and ashi, but saa and hints of the nymid. There was an earth elemental he didn't know, but he felt it the same.

Power surged, colliding with the Par-shon shapers.

The elementals bound to the Par-shon shapers were strong, more than strong enough to resist what Tan could draw. His shaping pressed back to him and, like it had in Doma, power began to spiral around him, the shaping itself becoming the rune to separate him from his elementals.

It would not happen again. Not here, not in the kingdoms, and not with Amia nearby and in danger. He would do everything he could to stop Par-shon. And this time, he did not have to do it alone. With Amia, he was never really alone.

Amia.

He whispered her name through the shaping. She pushed through their bond, adding to his shaping, assuming control. The shaping built with strength and control, power cultivated with all the time she had spent learning from the First Mother. The shaping that built was one that only the First Mother of the Aeta could craft.

Then she released it, sending it out in a wide circle.

The Par-shon bonded had no chance, not against a shaping drawn from the combined strength of Tan and Amia. It overwhelmed them. Light exploded from a dozen places and over a dozen bonds were shattered.

But not all. There was one, too powerful for even Amia. Through the connection, Tan recognized the heavily bonded shaper he had seen in Doma. Not the Utu Tonah, but nearly as powerful. Bonded elemental energy raged around him. Tan fought, drawing as much as he could from the free elementals, pulling from Amia, resuming control of the shaping. There was another flash of white light, and then the resistance simply disappeared.

Tan sagged to his knees. Strength slowly seeped back into him, borrowed from the elementals.

Amia?

She crawled from beneath the nearest wagon. The ends of her golden hair were singed. Tan ran to her, stumbling as he did. She caught him, taking his face between her hands and kissing him.

"I thought I lost you. I couldn't sense—"

Tan kissed her again. "Doma. There were too many shapers. They obscured themselves from me. I hadn't expected so many. When I realized what they were doing..." He trailed off, knowing that Par-shon shapers could be anywhere. "What was this? Why would they attack here?"

Amia turned to the wagons, touching her hair and smoothing the burned edges down. Her breath came out raggedly. "The archivists. They wanted the archivists," she said. "I tried to save them. Regardless of what they've done, they are of the People. I did what I could..."

Tan surveyed the remains of the wagons, searching for the archivists, and understanding now why the archivists had returned. Had they known? Had the archivists learned of what Par-shon planned for them...or were they a part of it? "Where are they now?"

Amia took his hand and they started around the wagon nearest them. It was toppled, fires smoldering over it. Tan shaped the fires out, smothering them with wind until the wood no longer burned. Inside the circle, he found the Aeta already working to clean up the remains of their caravans. Many of the wagons had been destroyed, fire leaving them charred and broken. The ground within the circle heaved. Tan pulled on the elementals of earth around him, easing it flat.

One of the Aeta—one of the Mothers Tan had rescued—glanced at him before turning back to direct the clean up.

Amia stopped at a wagon on the far side of the clearing. This one was not tipped like many of the others, but the top third of it had splintered away, almost as if grabbed by some massive shaping, leaving a gap in the wood.

"They were in here?" Tan asked. He barely needed to use earth sensing to know that the wagon was empty.

"They were. We had not decided what we would do with them," she answered.

"Did you find out why they risked returning?"

"Not directly, but I sensed fear in them. They would not speak of it."

Fear. Then maybe they *hadn't* been a part of Par-shon's plan.

Asboel circled high overhead like a massive eagle. "Was spirit still held from them?" Tan asked.

"I couldn't remove that shaping alone," she said. "What you did… well, it was more than simply spirit binding them."

Tan rubbed a hand across his head, trying to understand what had happened. When he shaped the archivists, he had used each of the elementals, not simply spirit. It kept them more fully obstructed. Without the help of shapers able to reach the other elements, they would remain trapped.

But why would Par-shon want the archivists? It had to do with spirit shaping, but Tan doubted they intended to use the archivists the same way that Incendin had used them. Unless it was to ensure their runes couldn't be overpowered by someone shaping spirit. Someone like him.

But why attack Doma at all?

"Go to Ethea," Tan said to Amia. "Roine will protect the People. Tell him that he'll need shapers to protect the city. Par-shon will hesitate to attack Ethea. The city is too well protected with shapers. Ferran will need to help now that he's able to hear golud. Warn them that Par-shon can hide themselves." Tan pulled her close. "Keep the tunnels safe," he whispered. "Don't let them learn of the hatchlings."

"What do you intend?" Amia asked.

"Only something stupid," Tan said. Could he really think to be going after the archivists? After all that they'd done, would he really rescue them?

For some reason, the idea of saving the archivists was harder than working with Incendin. That he could understand, but the archivists… they were more like Par-shon, wanting nothing but power. But to stop Par-shon, he needed to keep the archivists safe.

Amia hugged him for a moment, pulling him into a tight embrace.

"Spirit shaping was the only advantage we had," Tan explained. "If that's gone, then I'm not sure what to do."

"Be safe," she said. "And come back to me."

"I will do everything that I can to return," he said.

Amia touched his face, letting her fingers linger a moment. Then she turned away from him toward a trio of waiting Mothers, all needing her.

Tan shaped himself to Asboel. The draasin remained high overhead, keeping mostly out of sight. Tan landed atop his back and slumped between his spikes.

We must find the archivists, Tan said. *We must find why Par-shon would want them. How could spirit be used with the elementals?*

Asboel breathed out an angry blast of fire. *They have Enya, Maelen.*

Tan tensed, gripping the spikes on Asboel's back. *Are you certain?*

The connection to the fire bond fails. I cannot sense her.

Where was she last?

Asboel snorted in his frustration. *She hunted and receded from the bond. I do not know.*

Spirit shaping could hide her from you?

Possibly.

Can it force a bond that I could not simply sever?

Spirit is the reason our bond has changed.

We will find her, Asboel, Tan said.

Asboel's wide circles now took them over Incendin. Tan reached out with earth sensing, pressing out with earth and spirit, reaching across Incendin, striving to find where Par-shon might have gone. The landscape below them changed, the ground turning harder and more barren. The visible plants were more stunted and twisted. Tan sensed the bleakness beneath him, a sense of emptiness.

Yet there was life. Distantly, a city pressed on his earth sensing. It was different than the one he'd helped before. This was smaller, no more than a village, and nestled along the border. People moved within, but he couldn't tell anything more than that. He sensed another city farther along the border, lying along a shallow river. Tan had been mistaken thinking that Incendin had been completely arid. Many of their cities existed along the sea and along the streams leading away from the mountains.

Frustration seeped through him. He still saw nothing, sensed nothing that would explain where Par-shon might have gone. Asboel shared his frustration, and flew with increasing agitation.

Every so often, Tan sensed the pressure of fire. Shapings much like the one in Doma, and the one in Incendin, pushed against him. *Do you sense it?*

I sense it, Maelen.

Is that how they trapped her? Did they force her where they wanted her to go?

Asboel snorted a streamer of flame from his nostril. *It should not work.*

Perhaps not on you. You're protected by the bond. As is Sashari. But Enya…

Asboel swooped higher into the air, circling. The vantage gave Tan a new perspective as he looked through Asboel's eyes. Incendin flowed into the Gholund Mountains, which then dropped down into the kingdoms. From here, he could even see how Incendin slowly drifted into what would be Nara to the north, and to Doma in the east. Chenir would be far to the north and east, with the kingdoms off to the west.

Can you follow fire? Tan asked.

Not this shaping. It does not burn through the bond. It is masked.

Tan recognized the frustration that Asboel felt. They would have to find her another way.

Circling as they did, Tan thought of the ancient maps he'd stared at in the archived books. Over time, the kingdoms had drawn Vatten from the sea, using shapings that had been long lost. Rens had once covered what was now Nara and Incendin, but Rens hadn't been as dry as either was today. Doma had been larger, once a wider stretch of land, but water and time had worn it away. The Gholund Mountains had once been near the center of it all, separating each nation from the other with a natural boundary. With all the changes, it was no longer the center of the land.

Images of the maps floated through Tan's mind as he struggled to make sense of it. There was something important that he was only grasping at, something that he could almost reach. Staring at the mountains wouldn't give him the answers. Maybe there were no answers to be had.

Except, when he thought about it, the mountains weren't the center of the land any longer. With as much as had been claimed from the sea, Ethea essentially marked the center, made more prominent with as much as Doma had shrunk, if the maps were true. Ethea, a place of convergence. There had been another place of convergence, though that had been within the mountains…

Such places were not marked on maps, but did they need to be? Knowing the elementals, they would understand how the place of convergence was found. They would understand the power found in such places.

Where would Par-shon have gone if they wanted to draw elementals, force spirit bonds upon them? Where could Par-shon hide so that Tan couldn't find them? Where could they have taken Enya so that none would reach her?

Tan could think of only one answer: the same place the ancient scholars once thought to hide an ancient artifact of power.

Chapter 26

The Last Bond

THE MOTHER WOULD NOT ALLOW her place to be used, Asboel said when Tan told him.

The ancient shapers once used it to hide the artifact.

The draasin snorted in frustration but followed Tan's direction. Tan had considered a traveling shaping, but for this, he wanted Asboel with him. And Tan wasn't certain he could find the place of convergence on his own. Such places were protected. Without the elementals, he might not ever find it.

They flew quickly. Mist sprayed him as they streaked through the air. Tan felt the presence of other elementals and drew strength from them.

Tall pine trees cleared as they approached the broad swath of blue water of the lake at the center of the valley. The broken remains of the mountain stood at the end of the valley. As Asboel circled, searching for signs of Par-shon. Part of him didn't really expect to find anything.

He used a shaping, but all it did was crash to the shores and wash away.

Can you detect anything through the fire bond? he asked.

Asboel breathed a streak of fire around the valley, but nothing appeared.

Was he wrong? If he was, had Par-shon gone? Was Enya?

He didn't think that was likely. They had claimed the archivists for a reason. This was the logical place to bring them.

Maybe he could search another way, using the elemental connection that he shared. They would know this place better than anything.

Nymid!

He sent the calling with as much strength as he could draw. Once, it would have been difficult to reach for the nymid even from the shore, but now he sat atop Asboel and reached for them, much as he reached for Asboel through the bond.

There was no answer at first. Then, distantly, he sensed a stirring. The nymid was there, faint and struggling to reach him. Tan grasped at the connection.

He Who is Tan. They have come. They will harness the nymid. They will harness all the elementals, even the Youngest.

That meant Enya *was* here. *Where?* he asked.

Water surged briefly from the lake in a massive wave. As it did, dozens of figures became visible. Enya was suspended near the water, a masked shaping preventing her from moving. One shaper stood near her head, his bonds glowing all over his body. Tan didn't need to see him clearly to know that it was the one bonded nearly as much as the Utu Tonah.

Asboel roared, shooting flames violently.

We will save her, Asboel, Tan sent.

Then the nymid failed, and everything disappeared.

There were too many of the Par-shon shapers for him to take on by himself. If he had any doubt that they had used Doma to draw him away, he no longer did. With all the shapers here, Tan would not have succeeded in freeing Doma.

More than anything, he needed to stop Par-shon from forcing the bond with Enya.

But why did they wait? Why hadn't they already forced it?

There could only be one reason: they waited for the Utu Tonah to come and claim the bond himself.

There would be more than the thirty or more Par-shon bonded to face, more than the terrifying shaper who rivaled the power of the Utu Tonah. They would be facing the threat of someone bonded to more elementals than Tan even had names for. A shaper whose power would far outstrip anything he could summon.

The shaping created by Par-shon was incredible. There was a pulling sense to it, a writhing quality…and he detected spirit mixed within. Tan could not see the archivists, but he sensed the effect they had on the shaping. It called to the elementals, drawing them here toward the place of convergence with more intensity than he'd ever sensed.

They used spirit not only to trap Enya, but they intended to trap the elementals of these lands as well.

Tan couldn't wait for the Utu Tonah to appear. If it took him attacking alone, he would do what he needed to save Enya. If that was the sacrifice the Great Mother required of him, he would make it.

First, he would call for help.

Tan drew on all the elemental power he could. Asboel. Honl. The nymid. Earth elementals surging in the mountain near him, not golud but one nearly as strong. He wrapped his sense of the elementals together, shaping through them, and added spirit.

He touched the sword sheathed at his side. It would provide focus, if not power, much like the artifact had once provided focus. A part of him wished he had the artifact, but there was no time.

Shapings raged through him. Spirit bubbled through him, forcing awareness on him, depths of spirit greater than any he'd ever possessed, short of standing in the silvery pool of liquid spirit.

Tan drew upon Amia's knowledge of shaping, twisted and bound it toward his will. The shaping came slowly, dragged *through* the bond he shared with her, but distantly he sensed as she allowed it, provided it willingly.

Assist me!

The request thundered from him toward all the elemental powers he could reach.

The shaping swept down through the lake, touching on the nymid trapped within, surging through the mountains, calling to the earth elementals, whistling along the trees as it called to the wind, and demanding heat from fire. The shaping came from him with more force than anything he had ever worked, nearly rivaling the power he had known when holding the artifact.

The power of the shaping swept away the concealment the Par-shon shapers maintained.

Tan took a breath, drawing in as much power as he could, and unsheathed his sword. It was time to do everything that he could to stop Par-shon.

Hunt well, Asboel.

Hunt well, Maelen.

Then Tan jumped.

Lightning streaked from him as he shot from the sky. Tan twisted with his shaping, spinning in the air, drawing on the elemental power around him. It flooded toward him, filling both him and the sword.

Tan shaped through the sword. There would only be time to stop Par-shon. There would not be time to sever the bonds.

The shaping split, directed at the shapers he could see. Three fell quickly into the water. Tan spun, shaping again, and again he managed to reach three of the Par-shon shapers.

Asboel attacked. Fire raged from his mouth, streaming toward the lake. The shapers were ready for it and pushed against the draasin. Unlike before, the shapers did not attack Asboel, choosing to hold him back. The attacks that came were directed at Tan.

Power built around him the same way it had in Doma, swirling faster than he could react and forming a shaped rune. The bonded shaper controlled it as he hovered high overhead.

Tan pulled on the elemental power, drawing through Asboel, through Honl swirling around him, through the elementals around him as he resisted the shaped rune.

And failed.

Tan shaped again, again straining against the rune shaped around him. The power coming from it intensified. Much longer and he wouldn't be able to overcome it.

The rune held.

Asboel raged, roaring loudly. Tan suspected Asboel tried to reach him but failed.

He focused on what he *could* do. Power still filled him, filled the sword, from the elementals drawn to him. If he could use that power, he might be able to disable enough of the shapers to give him a chance getting free.

Wind pushed him down, cold and buzzing painfully in his ears. *Honl!*

The wind elemental did not respond.

His feet touched cool water that wrapped around his legs, attempting to pull him under.

Nymid!

There was no answer.

The shaping of the rune swirled around him, now oppressive.

Water pulled on him with real force. Tan kicked at it, shaping it away, but doing so wasted the remaining power he had access to.

He sent a streak of white shaped light toward the nearest Par-shon. He fell, but it was not enough. Tan aimed at the shaper who controlled the rune, but missed. Water dragged him down, wind pressing hard.

Tan screamed.

As he did, the air exploded around him. Fire streaked from Asboel. Wind whistled, pulling him *up*. A hand reached toward him and he grabbed it, freeing him from the water.

Cora stood on a shaping of water and air. "You summoned. I've never felt anything like it," she said breathlessly.

He looked to see Zephra battling a pair of Par-shon shapers. Theondar appeared with a streak of lightning and thunder. The ground rumbled, and Ferran leapt from the rocks in the distance.

How?

He would ask questions later. They were outnumbered, but the elementals had brought help. "They're shaping a rune around me," Tan said more calmly than he felt. "If you can free me from it, I can help. We need to hurry before the Utu Tonah arrives."

Cora leapt to the air. Par-shon shapers chased her, but she was a warrior shaper, trained by Lacertin. She knocked two shapers to the water with a flicker of wind and fire. Another shaper fell as she fought.

Tan had little strength remaining. He used what he had and pressed it at the nearest shaper. She collapsed to the ground. Another shaping he attempted failed.

The shaper still worked on Tan overhead, shaping with more intensity than he had while in Doma. There, Tan had managed to draw on the elementals to save himself. This time, the rune built with more power than he could resist.

He sagged again, his feet touching the water. Bonded nymid reached for him and pulled on him, dragging him into the lake. Tan resisted, pushing against it with a shaping of water and fire, knowing that if these bonded nymid managed to get him under, even with his connection to the nymid, he would drown.

Energy drained from him, the last of his reserves depleted. The elementals could not respond. Tan saw Theondar surrounded by four shapers, each essentially a warrior. His mother was pressed back against the rock, wind aiding her but quickly failing. Cora managed to stay in the air, but each attack she attempted was deflected. Asboel fought, but they kept him held harmlessly at bay.

Par-shon would win.

Water reached his neck, only his head remaining above the water, and then he was dragged beneath the surface.

Green swirled around him. The last time he'd been in this lake, the nymid had saved him from the lisincend. Now, the nymid would be the reason he died.

Help me, Tan cried out to the nymid. They were the first elemental he had ever reached, even before Asboel. *Help He Who is Tan.*

He continued to sink. The last of his breath left him.

Darkness came over him. He would fall, but at least this way he would not have to see his friends fall.

Lights flashed at the edge of his vision, the coming of his death.

He Who is Tan.

The voice came softly, but it was there. Tan reached for it.

Nymid. Help me. Help me save the others.

You would save Fire?

I would save all, Tan said. *The Mother demands it of me.*

Nymid swirled closer, the tint of green racing around him. Faces appeared, swirling nearby. One that looked familiar, the face of the nymid who had first helped him when he'd nearly died. *Nymid will help He Who is Tan.*

Light surged. Awareness of all the nymid flooded into Tan. They were different than the draasin, different than ashi. The nymid were vast and powerful, but interconnected in a way that the other elementals were not. They were more than an individual. They were nymid.

The forced bonds used by Par-shon would never grasp the significance.

Tan pulled on the nymid, wrapping them around him. The nymid armor, once so powerful, the only way that he'd survived the lisincend, surrounded him. Bonds forced upon the nymid failed Tan's bond to the nymid cemented.

Power and strength flooded back into him.

He surged to the surface of the water with the nymid's help. When freed, he let water roll over the shapers around Enya. Tan focused on the heavily bonded shaper overhead, drawing the elementals to him and breaking their forced bonds as they obeyed Tan's call.

The rune faltered.

More power filled him. Asboel and Honl returned. Amia, a distant worried sense, was there. The sense of the other elementals was different than before. It was not simply understanding that they were there, but awareness of where.

Other shaping surged all around the lake. Tan saw shapers he didn't recognize attacking Par-shon. There were other kingdoms' shapers there as well, a dozen in all. And Elle, somehow here.

The place of convergence welcomed them. Par-shon was pressed back. The heavily bonded shaper disappeared in a flash of white light, escaping once more.

Spirit shaping continued, but Tan could not determine the source. Where were the archivists?

The elementals around the place of convergence remained unsettled. Tan had no better word for it. Whatever Par-shon intended was not over. Enya remained captured, held near the edge of the lake.

He needed to free her, get to her before—

Asboel roared.

Power descended from the sky. There was no other way for him to describe it. The elemental power he sensed cowered away from it. The figure practically glowed.

The Utu Tonah. And he came for Enya.

He will force a bond onto her. That is why he sought the archivists! Tan sent to Asboel.

Asboel roared, flames shooting from his nostrils toward the Utu Tonah, who knocked them away, as if they were nothing more than a wisp of smoke.

Tan would have to stop him, only he didn't know how. If he did nothing, the elementals would fail. Enya would suffer. The kingdoms would fall.

Amia, he sent through the connection as he streaked toward the Utu Tonah.

She pushed through their bond, helping as he attacked with spirit, striking at the bonds covering him. The Utu Tonah only smiled at him, deflecting each attack with a shaping. Not a shaping of elemental power, but of his own.

He was not only bonded, but he could shape without the elementals.

Even with Amia's help, it would not be enough.

Tan needed the help of others. "Theondar!" he shouted. "Cora!"

The shapers flew to him, joining him as they faced the Utu Tonah, hovering in the air over the lake.

"You are more powerful than I imagined," the Utu Tonah said, focusing on Tan. "You were to have been captured by now to keep you from this, but perhaps it is best that falls to me."

Tan shaped spirit and bound it to the other elements and sent this at the Utu Tonah. Theondar and Cora joined, attacking with combined shapings.

Somehow, the Utu Tonah simply caught the shapings, as if he drew them into himself.

Power exploded from him, sending Theondar and Cora spiraling away.

Tan caught the shaping with the warrior sword and twisted it toward the ground. "This is my home. These elementals belong to this land."

The Utu Tonah smiled. "You think they are yours?"

"Not mine. The elementals belong to no one. They cannot be forced to bond."

"You know so little of your land. Once, men like you harnessed your elementals no differently than what I would do, only they have forgotten. I have not."

He sent a series of shapings at Tan, who caught this set with his sword, too. Tan tried to shape again, but it wasn't enough. The Utu Tonah caught each one.

Distantly, he saw more Par-shon shapers appear and surround Enya. They were each heavily bonded, more than enough to hold her while the Utu Tonah forced the bond onto her. Each held one of the archivists.

Tan broke away from the Utu Tonah, striking at the Par-shon shapers around Enya. They worked together to push shaped waves of power over Enya, spirit mixing within each one, each one weakening her. Their shapings mixed with those forced from the archivists, rolling spirit over the draasin.

Tan couldn't reach her in time. Another did.

Cora hovered over Enya, facing the Par-shon shapers by herself. She bound each of the elements together and the shaping surged away from her, hitting the Par-shon shapers, splitting their shaping. But it wasn't enough.

Their shaping reached a crescendo.

Cora must have sensed it. She dove in front of the shaping, catching it. Her eyes flashed up to Tan as she did.

"No!" he shouted.

Calling lightning and fire, borrowing from the draasin and saa and possibly other elementals of fire he had no name for, he struck each of the shapers at once. It pressed them into the water where the nymid pulled them down.

The archivists dropped to the water as well. A shaping held them in place.

Tan didn't have time to try to understand. He reached for Cora, who struggled to hover in the air, but he didn't reach her in time. She fell, landing atop Enya in a heap.

The draasin's eyes snapped open.

Above him, the Utu Tonah built a shaping. Tan recognized it as the same as that which the Par-shon shapers had used when trying to separate him from his bonds. The shaping began to swirl around the draasin, pulling spirit dragged from the archivists with it.

And then light surged, bright and blinding.

Tan's breath caught. The Utu Tonah had his bond.

Asboel, you must go. He has the bond, Tan said. *Hide with the others. I will do what I can.*

Asboel breathed streaks of fire, aiming it toward the shapers near the water. Darkness circled overhead as Sashari arrived, somehow healed. It was too late, though. The Utu Tonah had what he sought.

Cora sat atop the draasin. Enya turned her. In that moment, Tan expected Enya to attack the Incendin warrior.

No attack came.

Could it be? Had the Utu Tonah *not* been the one to form the bond?

Enya roared. Fire surged from her, steam rising from her wings and her body. Her massive tail swung around her, catching two Parshon shapers coming toward her. Then she took to the air, Cora still atop, now riding her.

Tan streaked toward Asboel on a shaping, landing atop the draasin. Sashari flew next to him, and Enya joined on the other side. All draasin stared at the Utu Tonah. The draasin bellowed as one, fire pouring from them.

Theondar and Zephra appeared. Three shapers that Tan didn't recognize rose on the other side. It took a moment to realize that they were the Incendin shapers he and Amia had freed. Elle swirled atop the water, waves crescendoing around her.

The Utu Tonah fixed Tan with a dark expression, easily blocking the shapings attacking him, and then, with a flash of lightning, he disappeared.

EPILOGUE

TAN SAT ON THE SHORELINE next to Roine. It was the same shore where he had first learned that he had the ability to shape, not only sense, the same shore where he had first reached Asboel, and the same shore where he had nearly lost Amia. Too many memories had happened on this shore.

Now Asboel lounged near him, Sashari and Enya sitting together. Cora and Cianna spoke to each other in hushed tones near the massive draasin, the excited way they kept looking to the draasin making it clear that they exchanged information about their bond. Zephra and Elle sat at the edge of the water, Elle with her toes swirling patterns while she reconnected with her cousin.

So many had died. Par-shon shapers had fallen by the dozens. The archivists were destroyed by whatever shaping the Utu Tonah had used on them. And shapers of the kingdoms had fallen, left lifeless on the shores of the lake. For a place where the elementals convened, a place where so much good should exist, all it had known was death.

"I sensed your shaping," Roine said, dragging Tan's focus away from the line of fallen shapers. "It was a summons, but I've never known anything like it."

Tan felt exhausted, but it was a physical fatigue. The elemental powers had restored him, giving him strength that he wouldn't have otherwise. Now that he'd bonded the nymid—truly bonded to them, not simply known how to speak to them—he had a vague sense of all the elemental powers around him. What would he be able to sense if he were ever to bonded to earth?

"Did Amia reach the city?" he asked. He was too tired to reach through their bond to know.

"She did. I welcomed the Aeta behind the walls of the city."

Tan nodded. They would be safe there. The Aeta might not want to be a part of the kingdoms, but they had suffered too much to continue to wander. At least Amia would see them to safety.

"Par-shon came for the archivists," Tan said. "That's why they wanted to control the Aeta. They wanted safety. They must have known what was coming for them."

"They could simply have been running from Incendin," Roine said. Tan shot him a heated look and Roine raised his hands. "Zephra might be right—"

"Zephra was wrong," she said, turning to face him. "And Tannen was right."

Tan watched his mother, waiting for her to say something else.

"Par-shon hides from us," Tan said. "I didn't really understand until I was in Doma. But they can be everywhere. They had reached the kingdoms before we even knew. We will need more than shapers to keep ourselves safe. We will all need to work with the elementals."

In the distance, Ferran stood atop the rocks, somehow holding himself above the ground, reminding Tan of how the Par-shon earth shapers managed to travel. If Ferran could bond to the elementals, others would need to learn.

But it wasn't only the kingdoms, was it? The elementals were found throughout the lands. In Doma, where Elle had bonded a water elemental Tan hadn't known existed, to Incendin, where Cora had now bonded Enya. Could these other shapers learn to bond?

"I would never have believed I would fight alongside Incendin shapers," Roine said.

"And Doman," Elle spoke up.

Roine sighed. "And Doman."

Cora and Cianna had made their way over. "They chose to answer the summons," Cora said. "There might be others, but it will take time."

"Even the lisincend?" Roine asked, his voice harder than it needed to be.

"Someday, you will learn just how much you would sacrifice to keep your kingdoms safe," Cora said. "You might come to understand why our brightest shapers risk the torment that is the transformation." She forced a smile at the three Incendin shapers where they sat to the side, staring at the draasin.

Tan had already learned what the kingdoms would do to keep safe. Althem had demonstrated it all too well. And before him, the ancient shapers had once done the same. "We can't repeat the mistakes of the past," Tan whispered. "We must be stronger. Better. We're part of the same land. All of us must work together to prevent what Par-shon intends."

Roine stared at the Incendin shapers, his face unreadable. Zephra watched Tan the same way she'd once appraised the kitchen staff in the manor house. Slowly the hard expression on her face eased and she closed her eyes, nodding to herself. Elle sat and looked from Roine to

Tan to Cora, as if unable to fully comprehend.

"Besides, now Incendin has a shaper who's bonded one of the draasin," he said.

Cora smiled.

Cianna barked out a laugh. "But we have two!"

Roine managed the faintest of smiles. Tan suspected he worried about how he would keep the kingdoms safe, especially now that he knew about Par-shon and their ability to conceal their presence. Tan didn't have the heart to tell him that it was no longer about keeping only the kingdoms safe. They would need to keep everyone safe. They *had* to work together, or they would fail.

And he was beginning to suspect they would have to bring the fight across the sea. They needed to defeat the Utu Tonah, sever his bonds so that he could not attack again.

For now, he would rest. He was exhausted. All he wanted was to lie and listen to the soft breeze through the trees, to the water lapping at the shore where the nymid swirled, connected through each of the streams and lakes all around him, to the steady rumble beneath the earth…

Tan, Amia sent, interrupting him.

He focused on the connection, on the urgency in the way she spoke.

You must return. Bring Asboel.

Tan looked over to the draasin. He was injured, though not as badly as the last time Par-shon had attacked him. *What is it?*

Amia paused. When she spoke again, her voice was pained. *The hatchlings, Tan. They are gone.*

As tired as he might be, he stood and went to Asboel. *Come, Asboel. We must hunt.*

DK HOLMBERG is a full time writer living in rural Minnesota with his wife, two kids, two dogs, two cats, and thankfully no other animals. Somehow he manages to find time for writing.

To see other books and read more, please go to www.dkholmberg.com

Follow me on twitter: @dkholmberg

Word-of-mouth is crucial for any author to succeed and how books are discovered. If you enjoyed the book, please consider leaving a review online at your favorite bookseller or Goodreads, even if it's only a line or two; it would make all the difference and would be very much appreciated.

Others Available by DK Holmberg

The Cloud Warrior Saga

Chased by Fire
Bound by Fire
Changed by Fire
Fortress of Fire
Forged in Fire
Serpent of Fire
Servant of Fire

The Dark Ability

The Dark Ability
The Heartstone Blade
The Tower of Venass

The Painter Mage

Shifted Agony
Arcane Mark
Painter for Hire
Stolen Compass

The Lost Garden

Keeper of the Forest
The Desolate Bond
Keeper of Light

Made in the USA
Middletown, DE
15 January 2021

31796899R00172